17 Minutes on Sunday

Two drivers battle to reach the top of a dangerous sport

Rich Gilberg

illustrations by Todd Buschur

Printed in the United States of America
Published by Braughler Books LLC., Springboro, Ohio

First printing, 2019

ISBN: 978-1-970063-26-4 soft cover
ISBN: 978-1-970063-27-1 ebook

Library of Congress Control Number: 2019911498

Ordering information: Special discounts are available on quantity purchases by bookstores, corporations, associations, and others. For details, contact the publisher at:

  sales@braughlerbooks.com
  or at 937-58-BOOKS

For questions or comments about this book, please write to:

  info@braughlerbooks.com

Braughler™
Books
braughlerbooks.com

Dedication

I dedicate this book to Beverly, who supported
the project from the beginning.

Credits

I would like to thank many people who have informed much of this book. Many have shared their knowledge of and experiences in auto racing. I owe much gratitude to Mike, Phil, and the late "Mutt" Anderson; Tom Bigelow, Donald Davidson, Larry Dickson, Bill Holder, Lynn Paxton, Buzz Rose, Johnny Rutherford, Jim Simon, Rosemary and Steve Stapp, Mike Thompson, Bruce Walkup, and Brent Whited.

Others provided invaluable assistance: Dr. Mark Hess shared his medical knowledge, Elaine Rosier and Meredith Matheny provided insights into horsemanship, Ed Eidemiller, Peg Thoma and Robert Gilberg critiqued the manuscript, Dave Kramer shared his collection of New Bremen Speedway photos, Karen Moeller provided valuable insight, and Jane Ann Vest helped prepare the manuscript.

Illustrations are by my good friend, Todd Buschur.

I also thank Joe Freeman, Ralph Hibbard, Marcus Plonus, Mike Whitney, Dick Wallen, and Exceptional Equestrians for rights to use photographs.

There are many others who have contributed to this fictional portrayal and may have been inadvertently omitted.

Preface

When I was young, my parents began to attend AAA (American Automobile Association) and, later, USAC (United States Automobile Club) sprint car races in the Midwest. I was fortunate that they had the patience to take a restless seven-year-old boy along to the speedways at Winchester and Salem in Indiana; Dayton and Rossburg (Eldora Speedway) and my hometown race track, New Bremen, Ohio. My first race was at the Winchester Speedway in 1954, and I can never forget the echoing sounds of Offenhauser engines in those old stands, the cars shining in the sun in the pits, and the pungent aroma of burning castor oil. We followed the drivers and cars every weekend that we could. The heroes of my youth were not football, baseball, or basketball players, but the drivers who took incredible risks for relatively little financial reward. Some were successful in the "big time" of Indianapolis, and I saw many of them before they reached that level. But many paid with their health and, at times, their lives. I think that I understood the risk from a tender age. I witnessed the worst of this sport at my first race at Winchester.

In my ignorance or lack of understanding, I thought that these men raced cars for a living, full time—that was their job, right? Yes, it was true of a few, but many, if not most, worked regular jobs. Some worked in factories, shops, farms—forty-hour laborers. The whole range of American labor.

And many, if not most, had families. They had wives and children and all the events, stresses, and rewards that those relationships entail. Many of these men were working a full week, trying to go to a little league game, a movie, a swim meet, a piano recital, or, in other words, the typical life of many.

One incident opened my eyes to this. I was at the Dayton Speedway, in probably 1965. A driver was walking toward his car, helmet in hand, preparing to qualify. His wife came running, shouting, "Tom, the boy was playing on the trailer! He slipped and cut his head open!" Here is this man preparing to drive a dangerous vehicle with very few safety features at one hundred miles per hour, and his son has been hurt. It suddenly dawned on me: these men have that part of their lives, too.

So, I have tried to include that as part of this story. Their experiences were like most others, but on weekends they drove very dangerous cars. What do you call such men? I would call them genuine super-heroes.

Chapter 1

Tom Lawton sat at his desk in the Pine Street Service station. It was just a little after nine o'clock, closing time on a Saturday night. His "office" was a chair at an old oak desk, both second-hand from the school that was torn down years ago. When sitting there, he was below the level of the oak and glass display case between his desk and any customer, the case that had the candy, gum, cigarettes, matches, and air fresheners. The chair was so low and the case so high that he was nearly hidden from the sight of anyone coming in.

Tom had checked the pumps and written the day's consumption in the company log book. He took the cash out of the register, counted it, filled out his bank deposit slip, and put it in the bank bag. He walked into the service bay, shut off the air compressor, put a few tools away and walked outside to look around. He put a lock on the kerosene tank and locked the restroom.

It was a small, old brick station with just two pumps, regular and "high test." It had been painted white a few years ago, but the bricks were grimy. It had the look of a 30's era gas station with an actual peaked roof still over the pumps. Very few stations still had that convenience by the 1960's. There was one door at the front. The display case, with an old NCR cash register, was to the left as you entered and behind that case was where Tom sat. There was a single window right beside Tom's desk where he could see the pumps. A black rubber hose stretched across the drive-up to the pumps. When a car ran over it, a bell rang to announce a customer at the pumps. It was that time when attendants pumped gas for customers

A service bay with hydraulic lift had been added about five years ago on the left side (west) of the office. It had a glass overhead door and the sides of the cement-block bay had large windows that provided plenty of light for the work that Tom could do. He was a basic mechanic: oil changes, grease jobs, tune-up work (points and plugs), tire repair or replacement, belt replacement, etc. If a driver had serious engine or transmission trouble, they went out to Wally's on the other side of town. He was prepared for the big jobs.

If one walked fourteen feet past Tom's desk, he would enter the old service bay. It was perhaps five feet wider and longer than a car. Here was a six-feet deep pit that Tom used to service cars before the new bay had been added. This was now the car wash bay. It was always dark and damp. There was a rack where the chamois were hung to dry. Tom had once gone to the dump and salvaged an old hand cranked ringer from a washing machine. It was mounted on the back wall. This was where James worked—here and at the pumps, gassing up cars of the two thousand or so mostly blue-collar people who lived in town. There were two restrooms: the men's inside the station; the women's was entered from the outside, a convenience to afford a bit more modesty.

Both were cleaned once a month, whether they needed it or not, as Tom joked. The whole building was hardly more than 30 by 40 feet.

Tom went outside to walk around the building one more time before leaving to go home. *Damn! Look at that hose! If you tell a kid once or fifty times…!* James, his high school

employee, would hear it all again Monday, "Every hose has a natural wrap!" Half of the compressor hose was lying on the gravel and the rest looked like spaghetti hanging on the hook. It was not the newest station in town, but Tom tried to keep it reasonably neat and clean. He wheeled the oil display rack into the space between the lift ramps, hit the button to run the overhead door down, and left a few notes for James on the desk. He was a good kid, but still a kid, and had to be reminded of things all the time.

James should be OK on Sunday by himself. It was late April, and the weather forecast called for a cool, cloudy day and that would keep traffic down. It was still too early for boating, skiing, and swimming at the nearby lake. And Sunday drives are best on sunny days. James couldn't really do much on a car so his attention wouldn't be distracted by customers with car trouble. Just sell gas, candy, and cigarettes. Tom turned off most of the lights except for a few nightlights, looked around once more and closed the front door.

He put the keys where James knew he would find them in the morning: up under the roof overhang above the kerosene tank, on a ledge and out of sight. He got in his ten-year-old car and went to the bank night deposit. Then he started the drive home.

It was short drive and Tom was not in a great hurry. He and Janet lived in an old two-story farm house on the south side of town. He had bought it fifteen years ago when the farmer who owned it built a new house on his two hundred-acre farm. Ed Ward sold it with about five acres of land and a barn and kept the rest of the land to farm.

The little town was quiet now, not that it was ever much else than quiet. There were just a few boys, perhaps 15 years old, not able to drive yet and still riding bikes, hanging around the one bridge over the river (a word that really needs quotation marks—more of a creek) downtown. They waved and tried to hide their cigarettes from Tom. He knew their dads and might rat them out. Any older kid had a date and was probably at a movie, or the Shangrila—a dance hall in the next town. That's about all there was to do.

He was stopped at a red light, a red light for nothing, in this sleepy town. He actually thought about running it, but then thought, *Probably the night cop hangin' around with his lights off* (just two in this town, day cop and night cop). Howard, the night cop, an ex-classmate, would turn on his siren and lights, stop him, and give him some crap before letting him go with just a nod and a grin. Tom went through the bank drive-up and made his deposit.

He drove past Bennie's, the only tavern in town. A red neon sign was right to the point—"Bennie's Beer Food." Clever advertising! Well, two out of three ain't bad. There were about a dozen cars parked on the street nearby, and Tom knew who the owners were just by looking at the cars: Austin

Healy sports car means rich kid Carl, flame-painted '55 Chevy means basketball star Butch, old Studebaker means…Then his thoughts wandered and he began to think about Sunday.

Tom Lawton was not a big man, about 5 feet 8 inches tall, and was a little pudgy, weighing perhaps 180 pounds. His hair was thin to the point of sparse and receding. There was really none to comb. It was cut short and in the style of his youth when he wore a crewcut. It was still cut that way, but one could count the number of hairs standing straight up, perhaps a half inch long, in the low teens per square inch. His complexion was pale, and did not assure an observer of rugged, good health. He wore a cap all day and when he took it off, his face showed the "farmer tan." There was a clear line, mid forehead where the tan stopped. Above that, his head was pasty white. His arms were tanned only from the elbow to the hands. The rest—upper arms, chest, stomach—all neglected by any sunlight.

Tom was a man who worked hard, but hot days especially sapped his energy. It was an issue that did not seem to require, at least for him, much medical attention. He thought he was healthy enough and seemed to know where his limit was. But on some hot days in August he didn't look so well by the end of the day. "I'll just take more vitamins," was his answer.

The drive home was on auto-pilot as he thought about Chuck's car and Sunday's race. It was at one of his favorite tracks, the flat half-mile dirt track at the Vigo County Fairgrounds. He had never won a race on that track, but he enjoyed racing there. Even when his dad took him to races there when he was young, the name of the place, the talent that always seemed to show up, the spectacle of the first few laps of practice; it all was overwhelming to a young boy. And tomorrow he would be driving on that track. In a good car, for a change. Chuck Williams had had his current car for about three years, and kept making it better, bit by bit. Chuck was a smart, thoughtful man who attended to details, asked lots of questions of other mechanics, and took his time trying to make the car faster. He believed in incremental, not revolutionary, change. Slowly, over the past two years "did not finish" performances became "next-to-last," then a tenth place, then a sixth place, until last year, his car won a race. Then early this season, Chuck hired his new hot shot, and things really began to change.

Tom was nearly home and it was time to come back to the present. Tomorrow he'd be a race car driver, but today he was still a husband, father, and gas pump jockey.

He drove up the gravel lane, parked the car outside, stepped up on the porch, and sat down in the swing beside his wife, Janet.

"Gassed up and ready to go?" she asked.

"Yeah, you going along?" Tom asked.

"Not this time. I told you that this afternoon. Think Tina could use some company. She misses us during the day. You work, I work and…."

"Right. She's in school all day, and goes to the rehab clinic once in a while, but she does need you," Tom said.

"And something, I don't know what, happened at school today. Mr. Carlson brought her home. He said it was not really a huge deal…it was at the track meet and he saw what happened. He thought maybe he could help her calm down. Said he'd talk to you Monday at the station. She's up in her room, reading, I suppose."

They both sighed the sigh that means resignation and frustration at the same time.

Tom put his arm around her. "I'll miss you tomorrow. So nice to see your face there. Always good to see your smile when I'm not in the car. Not many smiles in the crowd."

Janet laid her head on his shoulder. "Yes, I know, and you know, too, it's usually better for me to be there. Just staying home all day or night and…well, every phone call…I just… you know."

"Yeah, but you know I drive as much with my head as my foot. I'll be OK, always have been," Tom said.

"How did this whole thing come about? I thought you didn't have a car tomorrow? Were just going to go there and see if anyone needed a driver?"

"Chuck called early. His young Arizona hot-shot broke his arm Friday night in a midget race, so the seat is open. Maybe not for me for the rest of the season, but it is open tomorrow at least. You know Chuck, and that car is one of the best. Just one good race could turn into two and…who knows? Or it may help open another good ride."

They had gotten married young. Tom had no desire to go beyond high school. His dad had no education beyond that and did not encourage Tom or his brother Walter to do much more. Just get a job. The money you lose not working for four years of college…You will never make that up. That was the story around this town and Tom had no answer for it. And then the fires of young love distracted any thoughts of academic work.

Tom worked at the Pine Street Station when he was in school. Jim Deeters, the owner, had often told Tom that he should get out of town, go to school, join the army, just get out of this place for a while. But none of that seemed to make an impression. Then there was his girlfriend, Janet. He saw a life with her could be all that he needed. But Janet became pregnant and plans seemed to make themselves. Soon after the baby was born, Jim Deeters died and Tom's dad said, "Buy that station, son. What else you gonna do? I'll co-sign a loan."

· · · · · ·

Chuck Williams and his wife "Ernie," Ernestine, lived in the country near Muncie, Indiana. He had a large two-bayed, cinder-block garage painted white. Out front were gas pumps. At the rear was another service bay, dedicated to his race car. The whole area around the shop was graveled. There were two cars parked at the side and near the front marked "For Sale" and behind them an otherwise empty field with a few junk cars and one old derelict school bus—slowly being dismantled for parts. All in all, the shop was neatly maintained. On the other side of the garage was Chuck and Ernie's house. The gravel went right up to their lawn and blended it all into "garage-house-car lot." Not a thing of beauty, but just suitable for their life: a 50's ranch house with two bedrooms (one was Ernie's sewing room), kitchen, living room and one bathroom. The basement was like a second living room with TV and comfortable couches and chairs, but really more reflected Chuck. There were some trophies and lots of black and white photos of his race car, drivers, victory lane celebrations and all the souvenirs he picked up, first as a childhood fan and then in his years as a car owner. There was one special group photo and commendation from the time he served as a pit crew member on a winning Indianapolis "500" car.

Chuck drove a school bus. That was a steady, reliable income, but really just supplemented his garage work. Chuck had a contract with the local school district to maintain and repair the fleet of buses. He drove for a few hours in the morning, and Ernie took his afternoon route. But that bus maintenance contract was his meal ticket.

His nephew Donny worked for him full-time: pumped gas, repaired cars and buses, towed cars in, anything else that might come up. And there was one high school boy who worked a few hours during the week and could fill in weekends if they—Chuck, Ernie, Donny—were gone with the race car.

Children never happened for Chuck and Ernie. They went to a few doctors who really offered little hope or advice. This was in a time before fertility specialists and clinics and the many resources available today. But Ernie was friend to the many children who called her "Grandma." She was a cook at the school and beloved by the kids in the lunch line, unlike many of the "lunch ladies." After noon cleanup, she'd be ready to take that afternoon route. Kids from kindergarten to high school rode her bus and many, at one time or another, had received a tender verbal hug like, "Oh, sweetheart, tomorrow will be better—I'll see to it!" or a not-so-tender verbal slap up side the head like "Son, that better not happen again on my bus 'cause I know your uncle, your daddy, and I went to school with your grandpa and I'm not shy 'bout callin' any of 'em!"

Chuck got the call about his regular driver early Saturday morning. It was a young–sounding girl who seemed tired and scared at the same time. She said her name, but Chuck didn't quite catch it—Pammy, Tammy, Sammy? This kid, Billy Wallace, had tons of talent and testosterone, but like most young guns was not about to settle down soon. A broken arm would slow him down for what, four weeks? Usually six weeks for a broken arm, but he will want to race again in three weeks, if he has his way. By then Pammy-Tammy-Sammy will be long gone and there will be someone else.

Chuck spent the afternoon changing a few things on the car. Tom Lawton had driven for him once a few years ago and Chuck tried to accommodate the car more to what he thought Tom might like. He spent some time tinkering, looking at throttle linkage, and tightening bolts here and there. Chuck liked to take his time when he was getting a car ready the day before a race. Best to do that and not make any mistakes.

At four o'clock, Chuck went in to clean up and get ready

for dinner. A quiet Saturday night with Ernie, a good night of sleep, and that's a day.

But sleep did not come easily this night. His mind started going over things and he went through his mental checklist. He tossed around and tried his usual mental "slow down" tricks, but nothing worked. So, as he often did, Chuck poured some whiskey in a glass, added ice and a little soda, and went out to the garage. He sat in a folding lawn chair beside the car and just looked at it. The checklist became more concrete. He'd look at the car and think about details: *I changed that left rear tire, checked the throttle linkage, checked the seatbelt anchors.* This is what helped to settle his mind. Then he'd walk around the car and just touch the tires, the roll bar, the steering wheel. Then he'd get a clean rag with a little wax on it and wipe over the smooth, aluminum body. Everything else was dark and quiet outside, Ernie was sleeping in bed, and here he was all alone with the car, gleaming in the bright shop lights. It was quiet and Chuck's thoughts began to slow down. "Guess we're ready for Sunday."

* * * * *

About sixty-five miles away in a little town near Dayton, Ohio, Eddie Spencer sat watching TV and eating a take-out burger and fries meal. Eddie was in his mid-sixties, living alone in a 12 by 40 mobile home. His wife had died four years before and with her went half of the income. She had been a secretary in a local auto parts factory. Eddie was a warehouse manager, but scheduled his vacation time to work at the Speedway in Indianapolis during May. He served in any way he could—assigning garages to new teams, driving other officials around the track when needed, observing practice laps from a corner stand—just about anything to stay close to the sport and this big race. He had never done particularly well in his few "500" appearances during his driving days, but that all lived on in his memory, every day. The "500" and the races in which he had excelled, back in the 20's—he had loved it all and still did.

Eddie and his wife had two children who were now living in California and Arizona. Those two sons were busy with careers and families. A secretary and warehouse manager did not make a lot of money, but what they did earn had gone into paying for two college educations. They had mortgaged a house, but with his wife gone, Eddie had to sell the house and move into the mobile home. It fit the modest needs of an older widower.

Eddie Spencer had been a young, up-and-coming driver in the 1920's. He especially excelled on the huge "board tracks." Many of these speedways were built in the late teens and 20's. They were wickedly fast, banked (sometimes approaching forty-five degrees), and deadly, in light of the speeds (100 to 150 mph), they could generate. The cars of that era were not designed with driver safety in mind. Drivers did not wear seatbelts. A "helmet" was a newsboy hat turned backward or a leather aviator headcover. An accident in such a car at those speeds with that sort of driver "protection" seldom ended well. Drivers could drive some tracks without "lifting" the accelerator, speed was limited only by mechanical limitations and driver courage. Tires were a critical weakness. They were at their performance limits and often blew out unexpectedly at speed.

Crowds many times reached tens of thousands, and sometimes approached a hundred thousand, at the peak of popularity of these venues. But the tracks were at the mercy of the weather, and over time the board surfaces deteriorated and with the economy failing in the late 20's, owners did not have the money or desire to properly maintain the tracks. Towards the end of the "board track era," some tracks developed holes during a race and workers repaired them, mid-race, from underneath while cars continued to speed around. Splinters flew up from tires and became lethal weapons. At some of those races, young boys crawled under the track and popped their heads up through the holes to watch. Very disconcerting for a driver, to say the least!

It was on these tracks in the 1920's that Eddie "Speed" Spencer excelled. His car of choice was any racer built by Harry Miller, cars that were works of automotive art in this period. But Eddie started out as a "riding mechanic" with his uncle, Nelson Spencer. Riding mechanics were supposed to keep the driver informed of engine conditions (watch the gauges—oil pressure, water temperature, etc.), tire conditions (drivers could not see the right rear tire, so the mechanic had a wooden paddle that he would rub on that tire to check for blisters), pressurize the fuel tank with a hand pump, and look for competition coming up from behind. Some things that a driver could handle on his own. After a while, sanctioning bodies realized that the riding mechanic just increased the probability of injury or worse by one hundred percent. The riding mechanic became a thing of the past and the sleek cars had just one occupant.

When Eddie thought he'd had enough experience riding with Uncle Nelson, he asked for help getting started as a driver. Nelson was ready to oblige. The huge crowds, glamour, and the money that could be made at that time made it an attractive opportunity. It was a sport on a par with baseball at the time, much like football today. Movie stars attended the races. Politicians and beautiful women came to the board tracks dressed as if they were going to the theater. So, Nelson thought, *This kid seen the good and bad. He's no innocent, knows what he's getting into.* So, Uncle got him a ride in an old, worn out, but safe three-year old Duesenberg. It was a start.

Then Uncle Nelson was killed in an accident out in California, at one of those "glamorous" events that attracted many of the beautiful people of the day. The dark side of the sport began to take its toll on attendance. Gruesome accidents ruined a Sunday outing. And newspapers, eager to sell their product, often sensationalized the lurid details of the frequent tragedies as speeds increased. In spite of all that, Eddie pursued his own racing career and quickly became a young sensation.

Eddie paid his dues in the old Duesenberg converted from a two-man car. It was big and ungainly compared to the slim, sleek Millers. Eddie knew that some good races in that old "Duesey" might translate into a ride in one of the Miller projectiles. They were so slim that they made his old car look like a cow. A Miller was not much wider than a man's torso. The engine was a "straight eight," the narrow engine allowing a slim car body. The tires were skinny and tall. Air flow may not have been a great consideration then, but by default the cars sliced the air like a knife.

Eddie started his career driving the board tracks. He had not driven on county fair dirt tracks so he did not have the instinct of a short track driver. A dirt track driver learns that a controlled slide is the fastest way around most dirt tracks. This requires a lot of steering wheel work, steering right to maintain car control, twitching the wheel left and right around the turn. That kind of sudden action was unnecessary, and downright deadly, at 100 miles per hour on a board surface. Slight, smooth wheel movements were called for, just as they are today on big, fast asphalt ovals. Eddie sat at Uncle Nelson's side and saw that he most often turned the steering wheel just ever so little, letting the high banks of the turn almost steer the car through the turn. He learned that the tires had to be carefully watched for wear. In a one-hundred-mile race there might be seven or eight tire changes. The other factor was engine reliability. Engines may have been capable of great speed, but for how long? So, Eddie learned that pacing your tires and engine were important. In those days a driver could not run "flat out" for a hundred miles. Drive a planned race and watch the competition. To finish first, first you have to finish. Those were the lessons he learned.

Eddie's TV was tuned to the news, which was reporting the daily catalog of shootings, stabbings, robberies, and assorted stories. After the weather, the sports reporter went through the latest news in the world of "stick and ball" sports and ended with, "And don't forget, Race Fans, we're just a few days away from May 1, and you all know what that means. Skip Johnson will be in Indy for opening day, covering all the events leading up to the big race! Count on News Center 5 for all your 500 news!"

Eddie looked up from his burger and saw just seconds of video clips from some old races. He recognized a few cars in the short film and thought, *That blue number 4. Jerry Accorso used to work on that car.* Jerry used to race with Eddie, and it took him back years and years to their driving days. He could see Jerry sitting in a Duesenberg racer. He could remember sitting in his car on tracks like the magnificent Beverly Hills track, or the incredibly fast Culver City speedway, waiting for the race to start. He was dressed in gleaming white "coveralls," his uniform with team name stitched in front. His goggles were perched on top of his white cloth helmet. There was a steady hum from the huge crowd just yards away in the stands. Once in a while a child—always a boy—made his way close to the fence and stood there just staring. Sometimes a faint whiff of perfume was carried on the air, conjuring images of a lovely young lady; or the pungent smell of cigars might disrupt that reverie.

There was the steady patter of an announcer, yammering on about the day's events like a carnival barker. He remembered his mechanic and crew quietly standing around the car, or fussing with last minute checks. Looking down at the track, he could see wood splinters all over the surface, oil stains soaked into the wood from leaky engines, split boards that could turn into holes big enough to cause a challenge, to put it mildly. Then a lovely young lady might ride by in an open car, Miss What? Miss Some City 1926? No matter, she would just distract his thoughts momentarily, and cause him to wonder why he was sitting in this car. A driver a few rows up, might fire up his engine and the heavy/sweet smell of castor oil would drift across the track.

Eddie suddenly became aware of ketchup running through his fingers and onto his shirt. "Wake up, old man!" he said out loud, to himself. The local news was over and must have been for, how long-five minutes? Walter Cronkite was in full serious mode about the Russians or the Chinese, or maybe… Cubans…? Always problems out there, but Eddie had few concerns about that part of life. He had always been about cars—fast cars—and race tracks.

For some reason success on the race track came easily for Eddie. But it was a narrow kind of success. Eddie's particular talent revealed itself on those big board tracks that sprang up around the country in the 1920's. Those speedways were a reflection of the era. The Twenties were a time of change in so many ways. Economically, some parts of society benefited from the changes wrought by good times. There was money to be made in new and exciting ways. The automobile industry grew as more average Americans made an automobile a part of their daily lives. Motor racing grew with the booming economy. The board tracks were often built near population centers, and rail lines or interurban lines provided transportation to

growing numbers of fans. The tracks had large grandstands which gave fans a mostly unobstructed view of the cars and entire track. Fans did not have to choose which section of the track from which to watch, as one did at a road race. There it was all on view. Unlike the county fair dirt tracks, dust was not a problem to obscure the action or leave the crowd dirty at the end of the day.

And Eddie took to these tracks as if he were born to drive them. He seldom drove county fair dirt track races. He found the dirt and imprecision of the driving style, sliding through the turns with abandon, not to his liking. On the brick surface at Indianapolis, and even more so on the board tracks, a driver dealt with a more consistent surface, one without the ruts and deep holes that appeared after just a few laps of dirt track racing. Indianapolis and its brick surface were a challenge just as were board tracks, but usually one knew what to expect on lap twenty, thirty, forty, and so forth. A driver did not have to deal with dust so thick he couldn't see more than twenty feet in front. Oddly, Eddie was more comfortable driving 130 miles per hour on a board track than 80 or 90 on a dirt track. His results were in accord with his comfort level. He learned quickly and finish places advanced to fifths, thirds, seconds, and then a string of wins that seemingly made him an overnight sensation, just as some actors suddenly burst to fame in the movie industry. Magazines and newspapers printed stories about these new stars.

Racers, actors, and athletes were among the heroes of new industries in a new, vibrant America. This was the exciting world that Eddie seemed to have waiting for him in the late 1920's.

But now, Eddie was living in this mobile home on the outskirts of Dayton, Ohio, miles and years away from Beverly Hills, Culver City, Miami, and many other vanished wooden speed bowls. His career was cut short by an accident not of his making. At Culver City he was driving a front-wheel drive Miller, holding to his usual plan of a steady, fast pace. He could drive "foot-to-the-floor" when necessary, but his success came from using his head, too. On lap 125 he was passed by two cars making a dash for the finish of the 150-lap race. The two cars tangled in the first turn, perhaps fifty feet in front of him. One car, a purple and yellow car, literally launched itself through the wooden guard rail, hovered for what seemed minutes, then disappeared beyond the track. The other car began to barrel roll, arcing down to the inside of the track and ejecting the driver onto the wooden surface. Boards and debris were everywhere it seemed, and unavoidable. It was those broken guardrail boards that ended Eddie's career. He woke up in the hospital that night with one good arm, and a stump where his left arm had been. His legs were still there, but the left would never be the same.

* * * * *

Billy Wallace was from a town outside Phoenix. He was twenty-three years old, skinny and short, just 5-6 with lots of "small man syndrome" to deal with, whether he realized it or not. He probably did not. Insight was not a strong suit with him, in so many ways. He ran on intuition most of the time, and usually it suited him quite well, on the race track at least. Calculation and logic were unnecessary, as far as he was concerned. Just go with what feels right. That worked well on a dirt track and for much of what he encountered in life.

Billy's dad was a mechanic's helper, or "stooge" in racing parlance. He didn't have the skills to maintain or build a car by himself, but he followed directions well, and knew his way around a race car and the tasks that needed to be done on race day. He traveled weekends to help on his best friend's modified stock car at Southwest dirt tracks. Occasionally they raced in southern California, but most often stayed within a 50 to 60-mile radius of their home in Arizona. Billy tagged along with his dad, who was happy to take him along and show him the spectacle of auto racing. Maybe his dad secretly hoped that Billy would want to do what seemed natural, get involved in the sport that was a part of many weekends. Helping in the pits until he was chased out by the officials and then hanging around the fence right behind the pits gave Billy an education that few young boys got. Tire selection, fuel mixture, "corner" weight, track moisture, "cushion" and all the vocabulary of racing became part of his life from the time he was eight or nine years old. When other boys would have been learning about "hitting the cut-off man" or "blitzing linebackers," racing became young Billy's world, a dangerous world of men probably best not suited to a young boy. But that was the world he grew up in.

And this world also introduced him to the worst side of the sport. Billy could remember the first time he ran to the scene of an accident, all the quiet men surrounding the upside-down, steaming, leaking car, the driver on the gurney, blood oozing from his ears, ambulance with its hatch open. A ring of men, arms outstretched, holding back on-lookers. A lot for a nine-year-old boy to take in. But what he learned was this: wrecks happen, get used to it, and don't run the next time if you don't want to see it.

The world of most eight or nine-year-old boys is baseball games, history and spelling tests, playground scuffles, favorite TV shows, comic books, and so on. That was not the normal that Billy grew up in. After school, Billy hung around the gas station where his dad worked, fixing cars and pumping gas. That was where the race car owner/mechanic stored the car during the week. Mom wasn't in the picture anymore. She split up with dad years ago, departing with a tow-motor driver, and happily giving up custody. Billy hung out at the station until about six or seven o'clock, then went home to fix something for his dad and him for dinner. Fried bologna, spaghetti with a jar of meat sauce, macaroni and cheese, a bag of chips, beer for Dad, Coke for him; that was home-cookin' in the Wallace house. Not bad, not good, just cookin'.

Billy cleaned up the kitchen after dinner and did his homework in about fifteen minutes, seventeen if it was difficult, then settled in with Dad for the evening. *I Love Lucy, Perry Mason, Gunsmoke*: that was the usual evening entertainment until Billy dropped off to sleep on the couch. Sometimes he slept the night there, in his clothes if Dad fell asleep in his chair. If not, dad would shake him awake, "Hey, get to bed, Billy."

There were times when his dad was busy with somebody's car problem, and the station owner was gone chasing down parts, then Billy would sneak into the back room where the race car was. He would take a quick look out the garage door, and if Dad was busy, he'd jump in the car. It was big for him, but what a feeling. The seat seemed to hold him by the hips. He'd put his hands on the wheel and move it a few degrees left, right, and watch the front wheels wiggle. He was too

short to reach the accelerator pedal, but he'd take hold of the
gear lever without moving it. That would be a sure sign that
he had been up to no good. In his mind's eye, he could see a
brown dirt turn rising up to meet his front wheels, flick right,
then left. If he came back to his senses soon enough, he'd jump
out before he got caught. If not, Dad would yell at him with
something like, "Not a place for boys, Billy! Get out!" or "If
Walt ever catches you in there, you're dead meat, boy!" A few
verbal hazards that were worth the pleasure.

And then when he was about twelve or thirteen years old,
he noticed older guys at the station would drop into a low and
secretive murmur when a particularly pretty girl stopped for
gas. He began to understand that there was that world, too.
Probably before he really should have. And then one day at a
race track, standing on top of a truck to better see the race, he
glanced down at a girl lying in a reclining lounge chair. She
was sunning herself in a bathing suit. She was probably about
twice his age, mid-twenties. She didn't give a hoot about race
cars. She was so beautiful and shapely, and for a while Billy
didn't give a hoot about race cars either. So…that was his
introduction to girls. Cars and girls were to become Billy's
world, and they seemed to mesh quite well, at least for Billy's
purposes.

Chapter 2

Tom arrived at the Vigo County fairgrounds at about eleven o'clock in the morning. This was better known as Terre Haute Speedway, a half-mile, flat dirt track in western Indiana. He parked his car, checked in at the race officials' booth, and walked through the track gate and across the wet track (water truck had done its job), carrying his helmet bag. It looked as if twenty-seven or twenty-eight cars were already unloaded and backed into their pit areas. A few hundred people were in the stands and some old country song was drifting over the grounds. The officials wandered from car to car, going over some last few details, asking about who was in the car today, and just making idle chit-chat with mechanics. The track announcer made his rounds of the cars and drivers, gathering some interesting stories—media people call it "color" now—to add to his afternoon commentary for the fans.

There was the smell of hamburgers, hot dogs, and popcorn in the concession stand, and the unmistakable smell of heavy gear oil in the air, a sure sign that someone was changing rear end gears. A number of these cars were coming from the mile fairgrounds race on Saturday in Missouri, and this flat, half mile track required a lower rear-end gear.

Tom could see some drivers milling about, talking and joking. Some were always that way, loose and ready to joke and fire off a quick line, verbal jousting; perhaps trying to get a little under some driver's skin, or young guys trying to cover up a case of butterflies. Then there were the serious ones, some old, some not so old. They walked around their car with the mechanic, looking at each tire, sometimes asking a question, sometimes not saying anything, smoking cigarettes. One driver sat on a wheel near the fence, putting on what he called "driving shoes," engineer's boots with the heels cut off. He was chatting with his wife, who sat on a lawn chair on the other side of the fence—no wives in the pits. Then Tom saw Chuck wave at him. Chuck always tried to arrive early enough to get his favorite pit location: center of the pit area, close to the concession stand and restroom facility.

Tom walked up to Chuck, shook hands, and said, "Well, this should be a good day. Not too sunny. Lots of good guys, good cars…."

Chuck cut him off, "And maybe at least one driver who thinks once in a while…"

"Billy's got some learning to do, but…."

"Yeah, but I wish he'd learn a little faster, damn fool! Maybe he should learn on some other guys time. You know what he did Friday night?" Then Tom proceeded to go through the story as he understood it from the owner of the midget car (a smaller version of Chuck's car) that Billy drove for last Friday night when he broke his arm.

· · · · ·

Thirty minutes later, Tom was suited up and prepared to get in the car. Chuck's car was always clean and ready to go. The car was painted a gleaming red and the number, 11, was in gold. Striping and trim were in the same gold. The magnesium wheels were painted gold. The seat was trimmed in brown leather. This was a quality car, and Tom knew he was a lucky man today, as did several envious drivers. He pulled

on his open-face Bell helmet and tightened the chin straps. He stepped into the cockpit, sat, and tightened his shoulder harness and lap belt. Chuck stood to his left, grabbed the roll bar, and he and his nephew Donny pushed the car to the inside of the track and motioned for a push truck to pull up behind the car. Tom thought of this as a bit of good fortune that seemed to come out of nowhere. He'd had a good season two years ago, strong top five finishes in a number of races and one win driving a good car for an appreciative and respectful owner. But that owner died, and last year Tom spent much of the last season hopping from car to car. A new crop of young drivers came into the sport, and that new talent seemed to suck up all the good cars, and Tom looked like yesterday's news. Old and reliable, but not a young gun. But young Billy Wallace's bad luck, or bad judgment, could have given Tom a new chance. That's the way of the world, right?

"Tom, we ain't worked together for a while, but I know what you can do. Car should be ready to go, just let the oil warm up some. Try it out and we'll go from there," said Chuck. "I'll send Donny to watch and listen over in turn two. It's kinda cool now and that always makes me wonder about the fuel injector pill, maybe change that to run a bit richer?

Just have to listen to it." A push-truck (pick-up truck with a heavy wooden plank for a bumper, recruited locally) gently nudged the rear bar as it pulled up behind.

A few other cars were slowly circling the track, mostly just idling.

"Ok, Boss!" Tom slipped his goggles up from around his neck, reached down between his legs and pushed the gear lever down (one gear, no shifting, no clutch), put on the two-wheel brake locks (rear only), and switched on the fuel. He let the truck push him eight or ten feet and then switched off the brakes, allowing the rear wheels to turn over the engine. He flipped on the ignition switch. The engine first sounded like an air pump, puffing out air as they moved down the straight-a-way, but then it caught, sputtered once and then fired. It threw Tom back in the seat with a blunt force, like being kicked by some huge animal. It did not idle well. It was an engine that was tuned to run wide open, so the car bucked and lurched over the track. Only when he got on the gas did it seem to even out, run smoothly. The red car had an old small block 283 cu. in. V-8 Chevy engine from a wrecked '59 station wagon. Chuck had the cylinders bored to increase displacement to about 302. It had a Hilborn fuel injection system and magneto ignition. This "stock-block" engine was rapidly replacing the Offenhausers which had dominated most of the top-notch racing circuits for many years. Its appearance was not as pleasing as an Offy, but it was brutally successful. An Offenhauser engine was cast in gleaming metal alloy. The Chevy V-8 was just painted cast iron. The dissimilarities were many, and old fans did not appreciate the intrusion of Detroit "iron." The Offenhauser engine had a long and treasured lineage, unlike these passenger car engines. But racers use what wins.

This dirt track was fresh and Tom could feel the ridges and small bumps left by the grading equipment used by the track crew to prepare the surface. Sitting high in this open car, he was exposed to the wind, rocks and dirt clods, and much more in the event of an accident.

A few more cars came out on the track. As he circulated slowly, he could see about a dozen or so cars would be in this "hot lap" session. Tom made sure that he had plenty of room between him and any other cars.

Don't get too close to anyone now. Tom thought about what could happen: somebody driving over his head, or too close, an untested racing surface, any number of things could spoil what should be a good day.

After a few laps, Tom's eagerness and patience wore thin, and to send a message to the starter, he'd gas the engine when he was under the flagman's perch, above the outside guardrail in the middle of the front straight-a-way. On the next lap, he waited until he got into turn one, and got on the gas hard for a split second, enough to make the back of the car slide out to the right, and fling dirt over the guardrail.

Damn! This could be a good day. Track is good and tacky right now and this car feels good, he thought. Another lap, and the flagman, began to circle his yellow flag in the air, indicating that the green flag was about to wave. That meant about eight or nine laps of wide-open practice, time meant to let drivers get a feel for the track and their cars.

Next time around, the green flag was out, and Tom put his foot down. The car immediately leapt forward, a brutal sensation that very few men have experienced. Instantly, there was the first turn, a surprisingly short arc that led to the backstretch. Tom stayed on the gas as long as he felt comfortable on this first lap and let the rear end of the car drift out to the right behind him, his right rear tire digging into the damp clay. A split second later, his foot was down again, and his rear wheels were clawing at the track, launching clods out of the track. He steered the wheels to the right and held the sliding car partly sideways. He noticed the left front wheel slightly skimming above the track surface. Then seconds later he was on the backstretch, where the car straightened out and headed into turn three (really there are just two turns the south turn and the north turn, but tradition was still to identify four turns). Same approach as before: let the back end slide out, and then hold it there. Steer to the right and stay on the power. Steer with the right foot, he learned long ago, and it became second nature to him. Stay on the power and you can hold that slide, get off and the car straightens out, slows down, and so does your speed. A skilled driver can drive a dirt track like this—partly sideways—faster, if he can maintain the slide. Unless the track dries out and turns to something like pavement.

After about ten laps, the fifteen cars, following much the same path, began to wear a groove in the dirt. Above this groove, the dirt from the tires would accumulate and form what drivers called the "cushion." Below the cushion, the tires had scrubbed the track smooth. Above it, to the right, was soft dirt. A ridge marked the line between those two areas. There was an area of moisture right there that provided traction for the churning right rear tires. That was the fast way around a turn, as long as it lasted. But as more cars used that route, it began to wear away and steadily moved higher on the track, closer to the outside guardrail. Guessing how long it would last was a talent that could lead to a checkered flag. Guessing wrong meant…second or worse.

It didn't take Tom long to realize that this could be a very good day. Each lap, he got a little faster. The car felt solid through the turns: let the rear slip out to the right a little, steer into the slide, and hammer the gas. This car was so unlike some of the cars he had driven, cars whose behavior could not be predicted.

The starter waved the red flag, meaning this session was over. All the cars slowed and entered the pits, except for one driver who took an extra lap. Tom pulled up on the gear lever, backed off the accelerator pedal, and the engine immediately slowed. He coasted toward his pit, punching the throttle to let the engine rev up then idle down, and as he drove over the dusty pit area, little puffs of dust rose up behind the exhaust pipes at the back of the car each time he punched the throttle. When he pulled into his pit, he cut the engine off quickly so Chuck could get a good spark plug "read."

Chuck grinned, said, "Not bad, Tom, not bad at all. I had you around twenty-four, twenty-four and a half. Should put you in the first or second heat race, no worse."

"Car feels good. Solid."

"What d'ya think? Any changes? I looked at my book. Well, Ernie looked at the book. This is the way I had it set up last year when we were here, except for that rear end gear. I put in a 5.35 this time," said Chuck.

Donny began to check over the car, looking at tires and checking air pressures. He opened the engine cover and looked for oil leaks, checked the radiator and hoses for leaks, bounced up and down on the rear of the car, checking the suspension.

"You wanna keep that right rear tire that way, Chuck? Donny asked.

"Yeah, leave it. That's a good tire. If we change anything at all, we'll put a little more air in it, just before the feature," Chuck answered. Then he turned away and went to work, checking fuel level, giving the wheel wing nuts a thump with his brass hammer, and looked over the engine. A man of few words.

Tom said, "I appreciate the vote of confidence, Boss."

"That's why you're here, Tom," Chuck said.

Tom wandered over to the fence where Ernie sat in her

lawn chair, writing notes in "the book," Chuck's constantly updated log of each race, driver, weather and track conditions, lap times, changes to the car, results. It was Chuck's bible, going back several years. He said he'd be lost without it, but in truth he probably had it all in his head anyway. Ernie also bought a program at each race on which she wrote cars, drivers, qualification times, race line-ups, and results.

"Nice job, Tom. You looked real good," Ernie observed.

"Easy job in that car," Tom said.

"Where's Janet? Comin' later?

"Nah, staying home today with Tina."

"Well, that daughter of yours is a gem, Tom," Ernie remarked. That was enough to send his mind back home where Janet and Tina were now. Tina was fifteen and in the throes of adolescence. Stress piled on top of her other challenges was not what she needed. He and Janet could not see a clear future for their only child. And here he was miles away.

"Hey, Mister...Mister! Can I have your autograph?" On the other side of the fence was a boy, maybe ten years old, and a girl about Tina's age, he noticed. Probably a sister. Tom smiled, signed the boy's program, and said thanks to the boy. As the boy and girl walked off, Tom was sure he heard the boy say something like, "Don't know, but there was a name on his uniform, so had to be a driver."

Tom wandered over to the concession stand and got a hot dog and a Coke. He chatted with another driver, a young man who won two races last year and seemed to have a promising future. They talked about the track, conditions, the competition, and eventually got to the season ahead and next year. C.J., (Carl Jones, Junior), was one of the young "phenoms" and was expected to keep climbing the ladder of opportunity. Many saw a good car for him at Indianapolis soon and, with luck, an eventual "500" win in his future. Tom could not help comparing himself to C.J. This kid had so much in front of him.

They exchanged "good lucks" and walked off, C.J. turning to another driver and Tom back to his car to take his two laps on the electronic timer.

Time trials went well and they didn't. Three laps—one to warm up, then two on the timer. Tom's first timed lap was about what Chuck expected, 24.6. And as expected, that would be good enough for second heat, third at worst. But Tom was a bit too aggressive on his second lap, lost control in the first turn and spun. So, his heat assignment would stand on that one good lap, not bad, but could've been better.

When the pick-up truck retrieved him and pushed him back to the pits, Chuck looked okay with it, but a little less than supremely confident. "Like I said, second heat. Can't fault a racer for tryin' to go fast. Good thing you went third today. Goin' out last on this track is always bad. Those last guys won't have much track left to work with. Could've been us! But it's not…so…we're good!"

As it worked out, Tom had twelfth fastest time. That put him in the second heat race. The sanctioning body, in order to "package the show" for the fans, scrambled the heat race line-ups to provide a more exciting race. The first heat, the "fast heat," today would have the fastest seven cars, but the line-ups would be "inverted" with the fastest cars starting in back. The first four finishers earned their starting order back to get into the feature race. The cars that finished fifth through seventh, were forced to race in the second heat, thereby getting another chance to finish in the top four and transfer to the feature race. This system was meant to encourage more aggressive driving, more passing, and a better show for the fans. If the fastest car started in first place, that driver would probably just run away with the eight-lap heat race, right? Boring. There were times, though, due to mishaps, mechanical issues, poor driving, or any number of variables, that a driver was forced to race in all the heat races and the semi-feature and still not finish well enough to earn a spot in the feature race.

Tom's performance in time trials meant he would start in fifth place, inside position of row three in the second heat race. There were seven cars in each of the heat races. He only had to pass one car to get into the feature race. He had eight laps to do that, or around three minutes, give or take. The guys in front of him were slower, so easy chore, right? Well, they would get a lead right away and have the advantage of track position in the groove. They wouldn't just let you pass, so it was not such an easy job. As it worked out, Tom got a good start and the driver in front of him, third place starter, didn't and Tom slipped under him and past as they entered the first turn. Tom held fourth place for two laps when C.J. in the blue number 2, had a big, steamy exit from the race. This was not necessarily the end of his day. It could be a minor issue, such as a loose water hose. With luck, C.J. could fight his way into the feature race with a good finish in the remaining heats or semi-feature after his car was repaired. Rather humbling for this young gun. Tom ended up in third place, ensuring himself a good starting position in the thirty-lap feature race. He could have contested second place, but there were just two laps left when C.J. dropped out, and advancing one more place would not greatly affect his starting position in the final race. *Play it safe, Tommy*, he thought to himself.

Tom pulled the car out of gear on the backstretch after the checkered flag and coasted into his pit. With the engine shut off, there were other, seldom heard, sounds: the tires were rock hard and the coarse treads made a sound all their own, the ruts and holes in the track shook the sheet metal body panels, even the suspension parts and brakes squeaked. Then there was the crowd. He could hear a few fans applauding the winner or their favorites. It looked as if there were several thousand people in the stands. The track announcer, giving the results and next race line-up, filled in the dead air with his chatter.

Chuck and Donny were standing in the pit as the car quietly coasted in. Chuck said, "Third place gets us in the feature, Tom. The money race! That'll do." He turned and went to work. There were two more heat races and a semi-feature before the car had to be ready to go. Chuck wanted to get some of the prep work done right away, except for tire selection and any weight adjustments to the chassis. He had to add fuel, open the hood and look for oil and water leaks, quickly dust off any visible frame parts and look for cracks, look at front spindles. The next three preliminary races would take about thirty minutes and the track could change a lot before the feature race, so the last two jobs—tires and weight—were best handled just after that next-to-last race.

During the heat races, Chuck would usually ask his driver to walk around parts of the track with him and talk about conditions and what, if anything, to do to the car. They could see if the track was drying out and predict how long the "cushion" would last . If the track dried out and got hard, it was more like pavement. If they started the race with a soft tire, thinking that there would be a good cushion and enough moisture in the track to afford traction, and the track turned dry and hard, that soft tire would likely overheat and fail. At a new track, Chuck tried to get a good look at the dirt itself. Sometimes he'd take a handful and see if there was sand in it—a sure indicator of a track that would probably get dry. He'd look at the car after the first warm-up session. Did dirt stick to the bars of the nose guard or rear push bar? If so, the track might be tacky and provide good traction. If the dirt slid off, the track may dry out and turn hard and slick.

A mechanic could address that hard, slick track in a number of ways. He could put a hard compound tire on the right rear. And he could "jack" more weight into the left rear.

Weight "jacking" was discovered years ago by drivers and mechanics. Perhaps, it occurred to a creative mechanic that he could do what drivers, even passenger car drivers, often do when going around a turn. They lean into the turn, using body weight to counter the natural force that seems to throw them to the opposite side of the car. Leaning helps to put some weight back on to the "inside," left side, of the car, giving the tires on that side traction that centrifugal force reduces. Or perhaps some driver, looking at a car from the front, saw that it leaned toward the inside of the track, tried it out and found that it handled better. But however it started, mechanics learned that more weight on the left side made a car faster, usually.

Mechanics found that the weight on a car with a transverse front spring ("buggy" spring) could actually be shifted by driving a steel wedge between the spring leaves on the right side of the front spring. This had the effect of shifting the car's weight to the right front tire and left rear, balancing rear wheel traction more evenly as the car drove through a turn. The more weight "jacked" into the right front and left rear, the lighter the left front corner of the car, so at times in a turn the left front tire was hanging in the air, often three or four inches off the track. Sometimes the resulting weight bias on the right front tire caused it to wear excessively, especially on pavement. Later the steel wedges were replaced by bolts on the front spring shackle that could be tightened to achieve the same effect. In the 1960's, torsion bars and sometimes coil springs replaced leaf springs, allowing better chassis tuning,

Trying to guess correctly how the track might change could easily affect one's finishing position. A driver who thought that the track would hold enough moisture and cushion might find that condition was worn away in twenty-five laps. Others, who set the car up for a dry and hard track, might find that those conditions developed only in the last five to ten laps. So, what are you going to do? How long will the track stay the way it looks right now, before the race starts? Are you going to set up for the track as it looks now and hope it lasts, or are you going to set up for what you think it's going to be in the last ten laps? Sun, wind, moisture in the track, what others will do: all factors to consider. These are the things that Chuck liked to talk about with his drivers. There was his "bible," there was his experience, and there was his driver and his particular style to consider. Chuck and Tom, mostly Chuck really, because Tom deferred to Chuck's experience, decided not to touch the weight. Chuck considered the weather. An overcast day like this with little sun meant the track might not get too dry. They let a little air out of the left rear and did not touch the right rear, deciding against a harder tire. They would gamble that the track would not dry out. The big decisions were made.

"Well, Tommy, let's get ready to race!" Chuck smiled, smacked Tom on the back, and they headed back to their pit.

Tom stopped at the infield restroom. When he stepped out, zipping up, a young fan entered for his turn. *Hope the boy isn't too disillusioned*, he mused.

Tom walked through the pit fence gate, passed a few driver friends, exchanged "Good Lucks," with them, and hurried to his car. The last race before the thirty-lap feature was just winding up, so they would have about twenty minutes before push-off. Tom took some cardboard from his helmet bag. It was salvaged from old shipping boxes from the station. He had cut them up into pieces six or seven inches square. He proceeded to wrap these around his arms and then wind electrical tape around them. A crude but effective way to ward off rocks launched from churning tires. He wiped his goggles clean and slipped them around his neck and let them hang on his chest. Hinged on his white helmet was a clear face shield. He would start the race with his goggles on and the visor down. When the visor got mud-spattered, he could slip it up, and his goggles would serve for the rest of the race.

Chuck and Donny had just finished fueling the car and giving it a quick final check. The track announcer was asking all cars to be pushed out and lined up on the track for introductions. Tom was not the type of driver who relished this part of the show. A few drivers loved it, but Tom just saw himself as a gas station owner who sometimes raced cars—nobody special. The announcer started at the back of the field, saying, "Now folks, get ready to write this down in your programs! Starting on the outside of row nine, in car number five, the Woesterman Builders Special, from Bowling Green, Kentucky: Johnny Bayman!" The driver would step up to his car, wave, and proceed to strap on his helmet and get in his car.

The public address man worked his way towards the front, each driver taking his turn, the cheering getting more enthusiastic with each introduction. Then he came to Tom. "And now, folks, a guy from just over the state line in Barton, Ohio. Starting on the outside of row four in that beautiful red number 11, the Chuck's Garage Special: Tom Lawton!" Tom was standing beside the car with his hand on the roll bar. He turned and waved to the crowd. There was the applause that always surprised him. When it died down, Tom could hear the beer vendors working through the crowd, "Ice cold beer here! Get your beer right here!" He could hear some loud guy, drunk, bragging about something. The smell of burgers drifted down from the stands. There were some young boys standing at the fence taking pictures of him. That surprised him, too, each time. *Boys, I'm just a gas station jockey, really*, he thought to himself, even as he smiled to the boys and waved. "Good luck, Tom!" a boy's small voice squeaked under the barking of the announcer. That kind of stuff never failed to amaze Tom. He winked at the boy. His thoughts flashed back to his own family, momentarily. *Better focus, bud*, he thought.

Then all the preliminaries were finished, Tom was strapped in the car, helmet on, and white shop rag wrapped around his mouth and nose to filter out dust. The push-truck was bumping the rear push bar, and Chuck just nudged Tom's left shoulder and nodded. Tom nodded back. Time to race.

Car after car was push-started by the trucks. The first eight or nine cars began to slowly circle the track as those trucks went back for their next push start. It took about seven or eight minutes to get all eighteen cars going, and another two laps for all the drivers to settle into their proper row. There were nine rows of two, and most of these drivers were experienced. There were two former series champions and at least four others who were Indianapolis drivers. Mostly guys you could trust, but there were a few Tom would approach on the track with caution. The kind who would "accidentally" bump you out of the way. One thing to do that in an old jalopy with roll cages and a roof, but much different in these cars with just a spindly roll bar behind the seat.

Eighteen racing engines, even at pace-lap speed of fifty or sixty miles an hour, make quite a racket. Being in the middle of it all is another thing though. And it may all look smooth to the fans, but in the car the sensation is different: cars lurch forward and then just as suddenly lag. Racing engines do not run smoothly at low speeds, so each driver struggles to maintain a proper pace with an engine that wants to open up and go. Keeping the engine from "loading up" with fuel is important so it doesn't sputter when the driver nails the gas.

The cars were close, perhaps the row behind was four or five feet away. The car in front was the same distance, or less, away. And drivers were to maintain formation going from fifty miles an hour to about eighty at the starting line.

The starter signaled one more pace lap and then the next time, as they left the fourth turn, the green flag would fly. This assumed that each kept his proper order, in which case the lights in the turns would flash to green and the race was on. If someone "jumped the gun," there would be another pace lap or two and they'd try again. This time, all went well and all eighteen cars shot ahead to the first turn.

Tom was lucky to be starting on the outside of a row. As he entered the turn, he was already high on the track and lined up to race the groove and settle his right rear wheel against the cushion. At the start he was not at full speed, but positioned well to move up. Tom's "row-mate" had disappeared behind him, reducing the chance of being bumped on his left. He was just four or five feet behind the car in front of him, taking the same line through the turn. The driver who started on the pole was already about to exit turn two and head down the backstretch. The dust wasn't bad, but a few pebbles and dirt rattled off his visor, thrown up from the cars running down low on the track. Tom could see the white car that started outside row two was running hard, and sliding wildly. When they entered turn three, Tom figured he was in seventh place. Ahead of him, Tom saw the white car nearly spin in turn four. That caused a chain reaction as the next two cars checked up, and steered toward the inside of the track. Tom saw the white car recover and steer high on the track near the guardrail and drive through the loose dirt. The fifth and sixth place cars were low on the corner, and there was a great expanse of good track open. Tom steered between and past the three slowing cars into fourth place. Not bad-eighth to fourth in one lap!

Now it was time to settle in for the rest of the race, get a rhythm going and hope for the best. One thing he knew for sure, there was no way he would catch the leader. That was clear after two laps. He was out of sight. Sometimes Tom could catch another car in his peripheral vision. If the car was a color that stood out, and there was not much dust, Tom could get a glimpse of a car on the backstretch when he, Tom, was in turn one. Not today. That yellow car was long gone so if he saw him again it would be him lapping, or pulling out with a problem.

Tom found his rhythm and the next dozen laps went by quickly, but smoothly. In just a minute and ten or fifteen seconds, he would complete three laps. The laps became a blur of speed: short straight followed by a turn, straight followed by a turn, straight followed by a turn, repeat, repeat.

Chuck stood out a few feet from his pit where he knew Tom could see him. He'd stretch his arms wide to indicate that a car was far behind, or hold up both hands, fingers spread wide to indicate the number of laps remaining, and other rudimentary signals. Hands clapped together meant that someone was moving up to pass.

After about twenty laps, the groove and cushion had steadily progressed up the track surface, getting ever closer to the guardrail. Many of the cars were running the same route, high on the track, and they were wearing it away. That was only natural, unfortunately, with so many following the same route. The leader was nowhere to be seen, but second and third were within striking distance. Tom pushed harder and saw the gap between him and those two cars shrink. The car responded well to a more aggressive approach, especially in turn one, which seemed to hold a little more moisture up high. Tom could hammer the gas split seconds after slightly lifting and then throw the car into a slide. He noticed that second and third were coming back to him. The third-place car moved into second and Tom quickly caught up to, dove under and passed that car in turn three. A nasty looking rut had opened up in turn three and Tom had to just drive through it and hang on. So, that's third place. Not bad at all. Five laps to go. Eighth to third. Not bad at all. Keep that rhythm and focus for these last few laps. Amazing how thirty laps, thirteen minutes or so can wear out arms, until they begin to ache and burn. That's the kind of thing that makes a driver hope for a yellow flag, just to relax.

Then Tom began to sense that something had changed. The car seemed to run fine, but there was a chattering from the rear of the car, the right rear tire seemed to be thumping, out of balance. That probably meant that the tire was throwing chunks of tread from overheating. Maybe they guessed wrong on the softer tire. He would have to nurse it along for the last few laps, back off and hope to get to the checkered flag. But then on the backstretch, he heard a car coming up on him. A driver can't sneak up on another car, even with all his own engine noise, a car coming from behind is unmistakable. Tom thought it was the leading, yellow car, lapping him. Chuck was standing closer to the track, giving him frantic signals, clapping his hands together. *So, what, I can't compete with that car today!* he thought.

On the next to last lap, he found out who it was. It was the guy who started beside him, running low on the track, passing him on the inside. Well, they guessed better. They set up for a drying-out track, and Chuck and Tom figured the other way. That's the way the race ended, with Tom in fourth place. *Not bad. Made some money. Showed Chuck and some other guys that I can do this.*

When Tom pulled into his pit, the yellow car was parked on the front stretch surrounded by fans. The announcer was ready to interview the driver and introduce the trophy presenter, a pretty young girl. Tom coasted into the pits and shut off the engine. Chuck, Donny, and Ernie all gathered around the car, smiling and congratulating Tom. Then it was time for a cold beer from Ernie's cooler, a few minutes to let down, take off his helmet, and wipe his face with a cold, wet rag. Then get ready for the fans. Being gracious came easy to Tom. He learned it being a business owner, dealing with the public. But it often took some extra effort after a race. He was hot, tired, sweaty, and his arms and shoulders ached from thirty laps of wheel twisting. Fans had little understanding that drivers had to make a mental transition, a transition from ten minutes of intense, high speed madness, to the world of, well, everyone else. But he stood there for a good half hour or so (the sanctioning body's rule–do not load up for thirty minutes after the race, meet the fans!) and signed programs for kids and posed for a few photos. *Gotta wonder what they do with those programs and pictures, but probably doesn't matter. If it means something to them, it's worth it,* he thought. One fan asked Tom about a slow car that would not give way when being lapped, as drivers are supposed to do, and suggested that Tom should give him a lecture. Tom said, "Oh, I don't think so. He'll learn."

After the crowd thinned out and Chuck and Donny had loaded the car and equipment on the trailer, Tom went into the restroom to change out of his dirty, one-piece uniform. A fan who was well on his way to a Monday hangover slurred something like, "Hey, uh, Wally…nice job today. You gave that blue car a ride out there. Uh, g' luck next week at…uh… oh, hell, wherever, g' luck." Then it was time to wrap up with Chuck and see if there might be an offer for the next race.

Tom walked up to Chuck, helmet bag in hand, "Thanks for the drive today. Great car!"

"Well, here you are, Tom. Forty percent of winnings, just like always. Three hundred and twenty-five."

"I appreciate the ride today, Chuck. Money's good, but just this opportunity means a lot." Tom left it at that, hoping there would be a "See you next week," but there was none forthcoming.

Chuck just said, "We had a good day, Tom, a good day. We'll talk, Tom. Call you later."

And that's where it all ended. What that meant, Tom didn't know. He walked to his car and drove home in silence. No radio. Just the sound of the spring wind rushing past his open windows. Just the sound of the car: tires whining, engine humming, the bump-bump of the concrete road every twenty feet or so. And his thoughts returned home to Janet, Tina, and Monday morning at the station.

*   *   *   *   *

A few hours later he turned up the gravel road to home, parked the car, picked up his helmet bag, and wad of cash, and walked in the front door. "Well, racer-man, how'd you do today? Glad that telephone didn't ring. Well, it did…twice. Once when James called to ask about, I don't even remember! Something about prices for wiper blades, I think. That was at about three o'clock and I just thought to myself, 'Second or third heat race. What happened?' But it was just that fool kid and his questions. And then another time he called, around four, and I figured that was in the middle of the feature race…But… there you stand so…OK."

"Well, Hon, this was a fair payday. Fourth place got me three hundred and twenty-five. Not too bad for seventeen minutes work on a Sunday. And you know what I always say. I drive as much with my head as…"

"That doesn't always make it any easier for me," Janet cut him off.

Things got quiet for a while. Tom figured that this was not the time to talk about the decent payday he had. He went to the fridge and got out a Seven-Up, two glasses, and ice.

"Night cap?"

"Sure."

"Bourbon?"

"No, well…no, no, too late," Janet said.

Tom split the soda and got some chips from the cupboard. "What'd Tina do today?"

"She slept in, read for a while this morning. After lunch, I talked her into taking a little walk with me, out back to the barn to look at her horse," Janet recited slowly, deliberately as if introducing something more.

• • • • •

Tina had mild cerebral palsy that was diagnosed soon after she was born. It affected her right leg only. Her mind was good, unaffected by the illness, and she was a cute girl; not a prom queen/cheerleader beauty, but a pretty girl with brown eyes and hair. Though much less than when younger, she still spent time in a clinic, attending to issues of muscle strength and control. She attended the local public school where she earned average grades. Young people are often cruel, unknowingly or knowingly. The effect is often the same on the person who is the object of comment. It was an incident of this kind that had occurred on Friday at a track meet. It turned ugly and Mr. Carlson, the track coach, had seen it.

Nature had dealt Tina a challenge that few of her peers could fully comprehend. She was fifteen now, dealing with all the issues of adolescence, compounding the rigors of her daily life. Janet understood all these things and tried, as best she could, to help her only child grow into a woman. Janet worked flexible hours at the farm store. Her boss accommodated her hours spent at the clinic with Tina. But she could only look at her income now and in the foreseeable future, Tom's income at the station, now and in that same future, and it was all too much to ponder. What kind of future could Tina have? What kind of life, career, could she aspire to?

And then there was the big issue that hung over all this: Tom wanted to drive race cars. Not just cars-stock cars, for instance—but sprint cars, probably the most dangerous kind of auto racing imaginable. And he was fairly good at it. Tom thought, with good reason, that with just the right combination, a string of successes might lead him to Indianapolis and the pot of gold there. His age was working against him, though.

The mortality rate in sprint car racing was a fearsome statistic. Each sanctioning body in the country (and there were many, of varying levels of quality) often lost two or three drivers a season. Then there were the injuries that were not fatal. What would she do if Tom was out of the picture, or at the very least, unable to work. How then would she provide a future for this girl? She and Tom had been through this many times, and he always ended his part of the argument with variations of "It's what I do." And Janet accepted that argument and realized that she would have to deal with whatever happened. Leaving Tom would not gain her any financial security.

It was true. It's what he did. He had shown promise in jalopy racing, even when he was in his late teens. Once he was at a local dirt track trying out an old Ford coupe. Another driver just happened to tow his sprint car to the track, late on a Thursday afternoon, for a practice session. He watched Tom from outside the track and then drove into the pits when Tom took a break. The driver had a first-class car and had the air of experience and confidence. He said, "Nice car, son. Mind if I try it out?" Tom's reply took him by surprise, "Sure, if you let me drive yours." It was a fair trade, but more important, what the other driver said put ideas in his head that would not go away. After the "car trading," the driver said, "Son, you could do quite well at this stuff." Tom could not let that encouragement go.

. . . . .

"Tom, I wish you could spend more time with Tina, for her and me."

Tom squirmed a little, expecting that this conversation was going a familiar way. But Janet just wanted to talk about Friday's incident. He relaxed and just listened. He was a pretty good listener, for a man, and soon found himself agreeing that just a walk or drive with Tina could mean a lot. "You know, James could take over at six in the afternoon sometimes. I could take her out for burgers at the Dari Queen," Tom offered, hoping he would actually follow through…wanting to follow through. They chatted idly, tiredly, amiably, for another twenty minutes until they were both ready for sleep before starting another week in a few hours.

. . . . .

Monday morning and Tom was at the station at six, opening up. A few men always stopped on their way to work—local factories, small town shops, businesses, grocery stores—to get gas or cigarettes. Some just stopped to say hi and chat about nothing in particular, just because they were old friends. Some had read the morning paper sports section and noticed that Tom had had a good day on Sunday and wanted to just give Tom an honest "Good job!" And there was often one wise guy, usually the same one, with a sneering "Too bad you didn't win."

Tom would take it as best he could. He knew that things travel fast in a small town, and an angry outburst might show up as smaller receipts. Something he could not afford. So grin and say, "Yeah, but there's always another day to try." Then as the wise guy drove off he could ventilate to himself.

High school track coach Jay Carlson stopped at the station at seven, on his way to school. "Tom! Nice job over at Terre Haute yesterday! Good qualifying time and a great…fourth place, was it?" He had done his homework and read the morning sports.

Tom was flattered. An educated man looking up little details like qualifying times? "Thanks, that means a lot."

"Well, I can relate, a little. Dad used to say he wanted us to know about more than books and basketball and Bibles, so he took us to see lots of stuff. Went to the "500" a couple of times."

"Didn't know that, interesting. Say, I understand there was an issue with Tina Friday."

"Yeah. You think we could go downtown tonight after you close? Get a sandwich, pizza, or coffee and pie, or whatever? Just talk a little?"

"That's a great idea. I'd like that. I close at eight tonight and…"

"How bout I swing by and pick up you then?" offered Carlson.

· · · · ·

Tom and Jay Carlson sat at Bennie's and had pie and coffee. Jay was no teetotaler, but he was new in this small town and figured that the coach drinking beer on a Monday night might be a bit risky. They small-talked for a while and then Jay got to the incident Friday at school. Seems that it was not intentional, just ill-considered. An off-hand comment about something at a track meet. Tina worked as a track stat and was within hearing range when some kid made a comment about a sprinter who ran like he "was lame." It was that sort of situation. It was awkward, cruel, but not intentional, and Tina's reaction was emotional but understandable.

Jay said, "Mrs. Bolton, our counselor, chats with Tina as often as she can. Doesn't want to make a big, obvious deal of it, but she tries to catch her in the hall, between classes, you know. Asks how things are going and...."

Tom interrupted, "You know, and my wife and I talk about this all the time, Tina is a regular girl, with added challenges obviously, but some day much of that will fade away. She'll find a niche, some job, a career. Someday, I believe, some guy will see her for the wonderful person she is. We all know someone who has overcome...um...what? Polio for instance, other kinds of illnesses. It leaves them with difficulties, but many go on, stronger, in some ways."

"You're right, Tom. Tina has an obvious challenge, but that might give her insights that may serve her well in the future. When all this high school stuff is over."

"I really appreciate what you've done, Mr. Carlson. Just taking notice of that incident last week and spending time to talk about it here tonight. You are a busy man and..."

"Hey, just wanted to explain."

"Well, what you have done means a lot." Tom picked up the check, smiled and said, "You ought to come to a race someday. I'll get you a pit pass! See it from the inside!"

"That would be a great treat, Tom. Name the day!"

* * * * *

There was no sprint race scheduled the following weekend. There was a race scheduled for the Indianapolis cars out east, so the sanctioning body did not want to conflict with that race. Some of the same drivers that Tom competed against drove at that level, too. On Tuesday, nine days after the Terre Haute race, Chuck called in the afternoon when Tom was at the station.

"Tom, I got a race car with no driver in it."

"Well, now that's too bad. Whatever can we do?" Tom

knew what was coming and could hardly keep from shouting.
"One little catch, an extra small chore. You up for another
job, besides driving my car at Winchester on Sunday?" teased
Chuck.

"Couldn't be that bad, do ya think?" asked Tom.

"Well you just decide how bad. I'd like for you to pick up
Billy 'Knucklehead' Wallace and take him along. Maybe you
can slip a little common sense into that hard head of his."

"You drive a hard bargain, but that car is worth it. Tell
him I'll pick him up around eight o'clock, without his latest
sweetheart taggin' along."

Chapter 3

It was about sixty miles from Tom's home to Winchester, Indiana. Stopping in Pendleton, where Billy was staying for the summer racing season with his aunt and uncle, would not take much extra time, that is if Billy was there and not in some motel with his latest admirer.

But Billy made it easy and was at his uncle's house, where he was supposed to be. He flung open the front screen door, let it slam behind him, and yelled over his shoulder, "See ya later!" He trotted to Tom's truck, big brassy smile on his face, stuck his hand through the open truck window to shake with Tom, and said, "Tim Lawton, I'm Billy Wallace! Read about you in Speed Sport News but don't think we ever raced, did we?" Billy opened the car door and slid into the passenger seat, awkwardly accommodating the cast on his left arm.

"Well, late last season when you first came out here, I was at that race at Terre Haute in September and…"

"You were there? Didn't know that. I damn near whupped Chuck's guy in that race, you know. If I hadn't got caught behind that…what's his name…guy in Thompson's car…uh… old guy? Anyway, I was lappin' those backmarkers and gainin' on first place until that guy messed me up! So, 'kissed my sister', second place, when I should have won and kissed the trophy girl! But, Chuck liked what I did in that one-race deal, almost beatin' his guy, and that's what got me his car this season. That is a nice little race car, Tim, I wanna tell you. Another three weeks and I'll be ready to go. Young guys heal fast, ya know."

"Don't want to rush it, Billy," offered Tom.

"Can't keep doin' nothin' like this for much longer, Tim. I see the papers and read about what's goin' on and it's just drivin' me nuts!"

"I'm *Tom* Lawton, not Tim Lawton."

"Oh, crap! Sorry 'bout that. Say Tom, how you like that red number eleven? Some sweet ride, huh?"

"You're right about that, Billy. That car will go where you want to put it, do what you want it to do," offered Tom.

"Just like a good date, right? Hah!"

"Don't know if I can relate that car to a girl. You probably can, Billy. Much better than me," Tom smiled and glanced at Chuck's "wonder boy."

Billy Wallace was not a big man, slight of build and stature, but if he was short on some attributes, he more than made up in other ways. Confidence had served him well in the past in most situations, be they school playground, football field, classroom, dance floor, the gas station where his Dad worked, you name it, and Billy had found that just the self-assurance of being right was the best way to start any transaction. So, a broken arm would not slow him down. Doctors could say what they liked, but Billy was sure he could prove them wrong.

"I'm giving this arm another two weeks and I'm back in the car, Tom."

"Better re-think that, Billy. If you don't let it heal…"

"I know. I heard that from the doctor and nurses…plenty! I got things to do, you know!"

"Yeah, but you got to let it fix itself. You know the story

of Ruttman and his broken arm and how that stretched out a couple of years when it was not properly healed," Tom cautioned. "Rutt had a great career that could have been so much better, legendary, you know, a Foyt of the fifties. Another Bryan"

"I know, I know, but…Chuck gave me the patience lecture." Billy grew quieter and stared out his window as they drove through a few sleepy Indiana towns.

"Yeah, well. Guess we're looking at this thing from two different perspectives, and ages. I never had many opportunities at your age, so I guess I just think a little waiting now can pay off later. You know, old guy perspective."

They drove on for another ten minutes, through another "pumpkin corners" cross-roads village. Moms and Dads and little kids, all in "church clothes," were going to Sunday services. A lady was in her back-yard garden, stretching string out to make neat rows for planting her garden. On the outskirts of town, a farmer was plowing with his old John Deere tractor, the engine seemed to "pop" in such a way that you could count each engine rotation. The smell of freshly turned soil hung in the country air.

Tom broke the silence, "You don't want to screw up this deal in Chuck's car. He won't wait if he can't count on you in his car this summer," said Tom. "I'm just keeping him in the money till you get better. I know that, so I'm not messing with you, so I can drive it longer. My deal with him is just race-to-race till you can drive again. Don't hurry that arm cause…."

"I know!" Billy shot out.

Tom continued, "I don't know exactly what happened in that midget race, I heard something about you tryin' to go *between* two cars. But just think to yourself a little, 'Maybe if I just wait an opportunity will present itself.' Don't force things to happen all the time."

"Yeah, I know." Billy seemed to let down a little, almost agreeing, but not quite.

Subject covered? Maybe as much as possible. Tom tried to move into other territory. They talked about Chuck's car and the way he liked to set it up. Billy said that he was in the stands at Terre Haute for that last race and thought the car sounded like it bogged down coming off the corners. Tom said he had mentioned it to Chuck, and he said that he may have been off a little on rear-end gear selection. He'd look at the "bible," make a note of it, and next race at Terre Haute in August, perhaps try a lower gear in hot laps.

By the time they got to Winchester it was about ten o'clock. Tom parked the truck as close to the track as he could, gathered up his gear, and headed to the restroom to change. Coming out, he caught up with Billy.

"Billy, you gonna help out some today? Hey, Janet packed some lunch. Homemade potato salad and more. Ernie probably brought some stuff, too. Can't beat her fried chicken. They always set up about in the center behind the fence. Tina, came along today. She's my daughter."

"Oh, yeah?"

She's fifteen, for god's sake, Billy! Quit yer hustling!"

"Oops, sorry, Ti…uh Tom."

· · · · ·

Janet and Tina had decided to make it a family outing, packing a picnic lunch, cooler, and lawn chairs. They left home with the family sedan a few hours after Tom. Mom and daughter time, perhaps, if Janet didn't work too hard at it.

"How'd things go this week, at school?"

"OK, you know, it's school," sighed Tina.

"Better than last…," Janet carefully began to inquire, but she did not get far.

"Mom!"

The car got quiet and they both retreated to neutral corners. Janet stared straight ahead at the road and Tina stared out the side window, neither saying anything. The radio was playing some popular song so Tina turned it up louder. That was the way the next fifteen minutes went by, quiet and tense. Finally, Janet decided to try another topic.

"You going to take your horse to the fair this year, Sweetie?"

"Probably, I'm registered, don't you remember? But I gotta get ready somehow, I hope."

So that seemed to help. A change of topic and the "cooling off" period made the in-car environment more tolerable for the rest of the drive. Mother and daughter were able to talk about Tina's horse, which she dearly loved to talk about, and they naturally ventured into side issues: another girl and her horse, the rapidly ending school year, the track team (touch-and-go for a short time), summer jobs, some friends, some non-friends.

"You know, Mom, I just don't get it with Dad and this racing stuff. Long as I can remember, it's not been easy for him. But he won't quit."

"I know, it's a world that I was never part of till I met him and he started talking about his old jalopy stock car. It never failed to fire him up. Why? I don't know. Then he had some success and that just encouraged him. Then some people said he could move up, get into that 'bigger pond', if you know what I mean."

"Do you believe that? That he can really 'move up', like you said? He just seems frustrated and...well not angry, not unhappy, just seems to want something else often...." Tina trailed off.

"I know. But you know, he does have some skill. Chuck Williams wouldn't ask him to drive his car if Dad wasn't capable. You ought to talk to him yourself about it. Now that might give him a shock, you bringin' that up. Who knows what he might tell you?"

"Oh, sure…that will be quite a conversation with Mister Communications. I can hear it all now,' Yes, no, maybe, don't know, we'll see, yep, kinda.'"

They both laughed about that, just as they arrived at Winchester Speedway in eastern Indiana. By some measures, Winchester was the oldest track dedicated to auto racing in the country. It started as a flat half-mile dirt track, but over the years the owner banked the dirt turns up high. Then the high banked dirt turns were oiled to keep down dust and pack the surface. After the war, the track was paved with asphalt. The result was a fast and dangerous high banked track, but not a smooth track. It did not have a proper foundation under the asphalt. That combined with Indiana winters resulted in a bumpy surface. The guardrail at the top of the turns was improved over time. But it was so fragile in the early days that cars sometimes broke through at speed and plummeted twenty feet to an often fatal landing. There was a pedestrian bridge at the south end of the front straightaway. An old, rickety wooden grandstand stretched the length of that front stretch. The back of the stands was enclosed with wooden lattice. The roar of racing engines was magnified by that enclosure and the roof over the stands. This was a not a track for the faint of heart, fans or drivers. There was a passage right in the center of the stands that race cars on trailers were pulled through to the pit area. Over the top of that gap was painted "Through This Portal Pass the World's Fastest Racing Cars." This was not a place always associated with laughter.

Janet parked the car and gathered all the picnic parapher-nalia: cooler, blanket, picnic basket, bag of necessities (sun tan lotion, rain gear, crossword puzzle, pens, sunhats), camera, and folding lawn chairs. When Tina got out of the car, she quickly noticed several teen boys nearby. This was a problem. Tina was cute and attractive to boys, but her limp was an issue. In the past, boys have suddenly turned away when they have seen her walk. Tina had learned not to make eye contact. It was a way to avoid the change in a boy's expression when he first saw her walk.

Janet loaded as much as she could onto a little two-wheeled cart that Tom had made, and she and Tina carried the rest. It was about 11:30 and they had just enough time to get to a good spot behind Chuck's pit, where Ernie was probably already set up. Time to say "Good luck" to Tom and catch up on all the gossip that Ernie had to dish out.

Billy Wallace walked through that "portal" in the stands, through the dark of the covered grandstand, and out into the sunlit front straightaway. There were twenty-eight or twenty-nine cars lined up in the pits, all in various positions: diagonal, back to the stands, nose to the stand, one car parallel to the track taking up two spaces, a few on the front stretch with oil heaters plugged in. There were probably two or three men tending to each car. Add another six or seven officials, thirty-some drivers, photographers and media, and assorted kids who had to be shooed out. That made a crowd of maybe a hundred people. That didn't count the fans inside the track on the other side of the fence and in the partly filled stands. It was all quiet now, just sort of a low undertone with the occasional sound of hammers tightening wheel nuts, wrenches clinking, and a relaxed chatter among acquaintances. Billy had already talked to Chuck and anything that was said was behind them now. Both were ready to move on to the next race when Billy could get back in number eleven. Chuck knew he couldn't fault a driver for wanting to compete and win.

"Well, if it ain't the "One Armed Bandit" hisself!" joked Chuck. It was all good-natured kidding and Billy took it as such. Each man knew that the other was valuable for his immediate success.

Billy grinned, "Grease monkey, keep my car pretty and keep it fast. I'll make it first, soon!" With that behind them, they settled into small talk. A few drivers stopped at Chuck's pit, near the center of the pit area, in front of the concession stand. Most just wished Billy well, and tried joking about the accident. Some inquired about how long he would be out, searching to see if his car was open. Then Billy heard a female voice call his name.

"Come on over here, Billy Wallace! We got lunch and a place to park that cute little tush of yours for a while." It was Ernestine "Ernie" Williams, Chuck's wife, "bible" keeper, picnic cook, and sometime driver psychologist. Her face and arms showed that she had spent too much time in the sun at race tracks. The rest of her showed that she had probably consumed too much of her own fried chicken, infield picnic food, and beer. Her hair was a brown-gray, tight-curled frizz. She was short and pudgy, and a roll showed under her shirt. Not a beauty, but she didn't care. She knew who she was, liked herself, and was liked by most all she met. "Come on, Billy! Over here! Now, I know we ain't talked but once, and my grouchy old man's not happy 'bout some things that happened, but that don't mean we can't get along!"

How can any young guy not like someone who's just like his favorite aunt? "Ernie, I'll be damned...." Billy suddenly noticed Tina and Janet sitting with Ernie and tried to recover. I...I...mean darned...scuse me ladies. Ernie, you didn't tell me there would be ladies and beautiful young girls here today!"

"Why, yes, all of us here are beautiful young ladies," joked Ernie.

"Why sure. You may not be young, but you are still beautiful." Billy could not help himself. It was his way, always schmoozing. After Ernie introduced him to Janet and Tina Lawton, Billy sat in a lawn chair beside Tina and helped himself to a drumstick and a beer. He tried to small-talk high school stuff with Tina for a while. He was not too many years out of school, so he thought he could relate. He was smart, not in a bookish way, and his intelligence was obvious. And he was blessed with a natural charm that won many admirers of both genders. Tina's answers were occasional smiles and shy responses: yes, no, oh I guess, well. Billy just went on as Tina stared down at her folded hands. Ernie and Janet watched and were amused by Billy's transparent attempt to be a gentleman. Billy's default with women was usually hustling, but this girl was young and seemingly fragile, somehow. So it threw him off his game. Even Janet knew this was harmless banter, so her "mom defenses" were not activated.

Janet said, "Billy, how was your ride this morning with Tom? Did he say more than five words? Maybe three whole sentences? I've known that man for many years and I know he's not a talker. Good man, just not a talker."

"Mrs. Lawton, I don't know Tom very well yet, but we had a good drive and some talk. You haven't known me but a few minutes, but you might already see that I can kind of carry a conversation. It's what I do, not always well, but it's what I do," observed Billy.

"You may have put him at ease like that. But he is an easy man to get along with. He'll help you any way he can, I can promise. When it's time to get out of that car, he will. And he'll tell you anything about the car," offered Janet.

"I have no doubt, Mrs. Lawton, none at all," Billy assured her.

Just then Tom walked through the fence gate, stood behind Janet and Tina, and put a hand on their shoulders, caressing each. Ernie looked up from her salami sandwich and announced, "Well, lookee here. Here we have our driver!"

Tom smiled, said, "That's nice to hear."

Billy stood up, put down his beer and said, "You got any time at all, Tom? I'd like to chat about, what do those sports writers call this place, the 'hills'? These banked tracks are all new to me."

"I don't have much time right now, but let's wait till after hot laps and before qualifications. Chuck drew a late time trial run, so I'll have some time. And anyway, I saw a guy down in turn one I'd like you to meet. Ever hear of an old-timer named Eddie Spencer?" asked Tom.

Another oldie, thought Billy. But wisely said, "No, can't say that I have, but what the hel…heck? I do have the time, don't I? By the way, Tom, how does a guy like you end up with two sweethearts like these two Lawton girls here?"

"Luck, Billy, just plain old luck!" offered Tom.

· · · · ·

Tom stood beside Chuck's car quietly getting ready. He slipped his goggles over his head, letting them hang around his neck, pulled on his helmet, and stepped one leg at a time into the car while Donny held the belts. Tom settled into the seat, squirmed a little to get comfortable and tightened his helmet strap. "Anything I should know, Chuck?"

"This is our first pavement race so we'll have to see about that rear-end gear. I hope it's not too low. I don't want to wind that engine too tight and blow it. And when you come in, make sure you don't kill the motor way out there on the backstretch. Keep the revs up, out of gear of course, but keep punchin' it as you coast in, then shut off when you get back in here. I wanna get a clean read on the plugs. And keep an eye on that right front, Tom. I stiffened that corner with a half wrap on that spring. I hope that's enough. Let me know. And, of course, I turned down that right shackle bolt, put some more weight on that left rear."

"OK, boss. Think I can remember all that?" joked Tom and pulled up his goggles.

With Chuck on the left side of the roll bar, and Donny on the right, the two men pushed the red car up to the edge of the track and motioned for a push-truck. There was the usual nudge and roar of the truck, the rasping of the slick tires on the pavement, the chuff-chuff-chuff of the engine turning over, and then the "mule-kick" of the engine when Tom switched on the ignition. A few sputters, and Tom drove under the pedestrian bridge and low into turn one, the cold engine chugging a little till it evened out. Another car, a yellow number seven, that had started three or four minutes earlier passed Tom higher on the banking, probably going around fifty miles an hour. Tom sped up and fell in behind that car, not close, but about twenty feet behind. He knew the driver fairly well ("Smitty was what they called him) and had seen him win a feature race here early last year. Rex Smith, or Smitty, had won the Terre Haute race a few weeks ago. He was a good driver with a reputation for being super aggressive, but Tom thought perhaps he could learn a little just by staying close for a few laps. Down the back stretch the engine evened out and the car gained speed, going around fifty or sixty as they entered turn three, through turn four and down the front stretch. After just two laps, the starter gave the sign to get ready for the green flag.

Tom allowed the car in front to get a little lead, came out of turn four and saw the green flag. The car leapt forward, slammed him back into the seat and within seconds, the turn one banking rose up to meet him. Tom remembered the first time he raced here and how that banked turn looked like a wall. It was still an impressive sight, but not as intimidating as that first time. He was not quite up to racing speed as he steered for the middle of the track, through the turns and onto the back stretch where speeds approach one hundred and twenty miles per hour. This time, he drove higher on the track, perhaps two-thirds to three-fourths of the way up the track, as he entered turn three, the centrifugal force pushing him down into the seat and tugging his head to the right. It might look like a smooth ride to the fans, but this is a bumpy old track. It has sections that were patched and smoothed out as much as possible, but it is a bumpy ride, especially with higher speeds. And that speed and bumpiness turns into chatter that blurs one's vision. The surface never failed to make Tom think about his dad singing an old Spike Jones line when they drove over bumpy country roads: "It doesn't ride like a Cadillac. I wonder who designed it!" But Tom will be considerably over those speeds today.

Most cars tended to drift high between turns three and four and often give the impression of heading for a collision with the wall. Tom was accustomed to this now and knew not to get way out of the throttle. Exiting the last turn, he could go full throttle down the front stretch, and approaching turn one, foot down on the power, foot on the brake, hard. Keep the engine speed up and slow the car with the brake. Get off the throttle too much and the car would just lurch with the sudden change in forces. Over time, Tom had learned that getting off the turn fast was perhaps more important than going in too hard, sliding, correcting, and losing momentum. Smooth was the key here, if the driver can do that on this bumpy bowl at a hundred miles an hour. Tom got about seven laps before the starter waved the flag to end this session. He noticed that the guy he had fallen in behind was a little closer. "That's a good sign," he thought as he pulled the car out of gear and coasted back to the pit, punching the throttle to keep the engine speed up, like Chuck told him.

Tom steered for his pit, braked to a stop, and cut the

engine. Chuck said, "I had about eighteen seventy or eighty. You think she's winding up too tight, peakin' out a little too early on the straights? You notice that right front tire? I was down in one, and I didn't see the sign I look for." Chuck had his "haze" theory: he believed that the right front tire should have a barely visible, smoky blue haze coming off the right front tire in the turns. That indicated to him just the right set up that he liked, one with a little "push." Lots of smoke meant that the front end was pushing too much. A sure way to wear out that tire. No smoke could mean the driver wasn't driving fast enough, or the back end was loose. Neither one a desirable situation.

Tom said, "You know, that gear seemed okay to me. Might try just a little more left rear weight, ya think"?

"Maybe. My stop watch showed you should get into the second heat, at least. How about we wait till after that? See how hot it gets. Track temperature is something to think about."

"You're the boss of the car, Chuck. Let's go with that plan."

Donny was at the rear of the car, seemingly trying to lift the car. Chuck walked back to the rear of the car. "Seem OK to you, Donny?"

"Think so. Try those rear wheels, weight feel okay to you, Tom?" asked Donny.

Tom dipped his knees, took hold of the left rear and lifted on it. Then did the same on the right. He did not intend to lift the car off the ground, but the resistance he felt would give him a rough idea of left to right weight distribution. "Feels fine to me, but there must be a better way to figure this, you know."

Tom told Chuck he'd be back in fifteen or twenty minutes. He went through the pit gate to Ernie and Janet's "camp" to grab a Coke and meet Billy for their chat. Tina said, "Dad, I don't know how you do that. I can't understand it."

"Hon, it's easier than it looks. Guess I'm just used to it. Course I don't know how you ride that nag of yours. How can you trust a ton of animal with a brain the size of a walnut? That make any sense to you?" Tom just chuckled at what he thought was a clever observation. Tina smiled and rolled her eyes. Billy was about to offer his thoughts but for once didn't say anything. "Come on, Billy, let's talk racin' on the dreaded 'Midwestern Hills'." They walked off towards turn one as the next hot lap session was just getting underway. A few cars were circulating and others were being push-started. It was easy to talk now. In a few minutes, when the cars were up to speed, communication would be next to impossible.

"Here are a few things I learned about this place. Now, don't overdo this, but you know you will steer just slightly to the left in the turn. You ain't gonna dirt-track this place, all twisting and man-handling. Just slightly, I said. You'll see. Those banks do a lot of the turnin' for you. Hit the brake just before the bridge, but stay on the gas. Use both pedals at the same time. You go into turn one too damn hard and you'll just be trying to recover the car when you should be getting back into it. It's more important to get off the corner hard than go in too hard. A good, steady, strong middle-of-the-turn sets you up for the back stretch. Feather back into the throttle and then hammer down as you exit turn two and stay on it down the backstretch. See that old billboard down there? That's my marker for three. Same thing. Feet on both pedals, brake and power at the same time. Get in smooth, not crazy fast, then pick it up as you exit, getting off the brake. Then down the front stretch, and do it all over again. You'll get a rhythm goin' after a while. Oh, yeah, forgot something. The car wants to drift up between three and four. Scared the hell out of me the first few times, but the guy I first drove for here, said be patient and the 'track will come back to you.' I swear to God, that's what he said. He drove here years ago. I didn't understand it, but he was right. I don't know what happens there, if the bank flattens out for a couple yards and then rises up, I don't know. And one more last thing until I think of another last thing. Don't get too high comin' out of four. That bank just dips away and if you're too close to the wall, it almost seems to pull you in."

Billy started, "I drove a paved semi-banked track out in Kansas once and found myself kind of tip-toeing around those corners and...." Just then the green flag came out and it was no use to try to talk. But this was a good place to stand and watch how to do it, or not do it.

After about three laps of green flag running, some guy in a red and yellow car lost control right in front of them. The car slid up to the guard rail, grazed it, and rebounded back on a line that took it to the inside apron of the track. The driver glanced back to see if other cars were close. Seeing that he was safely out of danger, he just sat with his hands on the wheel, staring straight ahead, waiting for a push truck.

"Well, Billy, that's gettin' in too hot," said Tom matter-of-factly. "Let's go over there. That's the guy I want you to meet." They walked a little off to the left where Eddie Spencer stood leaning on the fence. "Eddie, I want you to meet Billy Wallace. Billy-Eddie...Eddie-Billy."

"Pleased to meet you, son. Read about you in Speed Sport News. Tom here is keeping Chuck's car warm for you until you get that plaster off, huh?" asked Eddie.

"Yeah, that and he just gave me a lesson in driving these tracks. Must say, this is all new to me," said Billy.

"I never drove here. I drove back in the 20's, Duesenbergs and Millers. Really liked the board tracks. Not much of a dirt racer. Indianapolis a few times."

"You know, Mr. Spencer, I never heard of a board track till once in the school library I found they had a few racing books, way up high so I had to use one of them ladders with wheels. And that book had pictures of those tracks. Pretty spectacular. Banked even higher than this place, I bet," Billy said. "And you drove them?"

"I loved it! Downright loved it! What a ride that was! But them tracks were short-lived. The weather would get to them. Then the Depression got to them. But it was a big deal then. The press wrote us up and big-time politicians and even movie stars came to the races. By '29 or '30 it was mostly over. Over for me, too, as you can see. But what a life while it lasted!" said Eddie without a trace of regret or self-pity. More wistful than anything else.

"You know, Billy, I work at the Speedway in May. Come on over. I'll introduce you around. Got a lot of friends there. You can kind of get a feel for the place without having the pressure of the spotlight on you, like them rookies. Enjoy it as a spectator with the inside ticket this year, then next year…and I know you will be there next year…as a driver… it will be easier, kind of like goin' home." If Eddie had more to say it was soon drowned out by the resumption of green flag practice laps. After the flag fell for that session, Billy and Eddie shook hands, exchanged "glad to meet you's" and parted company.

Billy spoke first as he and Tom walked back to the camp. "Message for me there, Tom?"

"I don't know if it's a lesson, necessarily, Billy. Just wanted you to see a man with a lot of history. He ended up working in a factory. Now he's alone, living in a mobile home. He had a lot going for him at one time. Not a bad life now, but could have been a bigger life. That's the way life breaks sometimes, that's all."

About a half hour later, Tom was strapped into his car, sitting quiet and alone as Chuck and Donny were back by the fence, in an intense discussion about something. His helmet muffled the usual pit noises and PA chatter so Tom felt nicely isolated for a few minutes. He glanced off to his left and could see Tina, Janet, and Ernie standing by the fence. He waved and smiled. They must have been looking past him because there was no reaction. Then Tina poked Janet and they both waved. Tom looked straight ahead at the bridge. Some kids were being shooed off by the track helpers, losing their prime spectator spot. Nice, quiet time here, right now, isolated in his helmet. He glanced off to his right at the gloomy old stands. There was a family near the front row. Lady in a nice dress. A dress at the race track! *Don't see that much*, he thought. Antsy five-year-old boy, coloring or scribbling in a book. The dad had binoculars up to his face, scanning the infield, then leaned over and said something to the boy, who glanced up and went quickly back to his coloring. He looked back to his left and he could see Eddie and Billy standing near the turn one infield fence, and then a tap on his helmet brought him out of his daydream. "Wake up, Tommy! Loudmouth Larry on the squawk box said it's time to race!" It was Chuck. Donny just chuckled as they shoved the car to the apron of the track.

Tom had a good starting spot in the second heat. His time trial put him in third place, inside the second row. That was okay. But better would have been on the outside of that row. After the usual few laps to get lined up correctly, the field idled down the backstretch and began to accelerate in the fourth turn. The starter leaned out from his perch with the green flag furled and held behind the yellow flag. He looked for proper order, all lined up, four rows of two, no one getting out of line hoping for a way to slip past the car in front. When the pole position car was about a quarter of the way up the straight, the flagman waved the green flag and all eight engines instantly roared for just seconds. The sudden increase in volume abated just as suddenly as drivers backed off for the first turn. The second-place starter, a black car with gold numbers, shot into the lead. The pole position starter settled in behind him and Tom followed in third. First, second, and third all got in line and headed down the back stretch. As they entered turn three, Tom was bumped from behind and his car slipped up high on the bank momentarily. He recovered and maintained his position to finish lap one where he had started, in third place. "What the hell was that, or who?" he said actually, aloud, as if talking made a difference. He went through the line-up as he remembered it. Then he recalled that Smitty started inside row three, behind him.

He watched the second-place car in front of him trying to go under the leader as they entered the first turn. The driver carried too much momentum into the turn and the car slid up, nearly hitting the leader. He had to back off the power and did not get a good run into the back stretch. Tom saw an opportunity to gain a spot, but thought better to wait a lap or two and see what second place would do next. As they exited turn four, the second-place car lagged slightly. Either he decided to play it safe for a lap or two, or he had a problem of some sort.

Tom decided to pull to the inside and just show the nose of his car to that guy, let him know that he was there, make him think a little. As soon as Tom pulled even with his rear wheel, Smitty did the same to Tom, but on his right rear wheel. *So, that's the guy who hit me!* he thought.

As they entered the first turn, first, second, third, and fourth all fell back in line, with the leader stretching his advantage racing down the backstretch. The second-place car slipped high in turn three, Tom saw an opening, steered low on the track, and was now in second place. The leader was getting away from the pack. Tom in second now had to wonder about where Smitty was. Right behind him or still in fourth? Did he follow me through when I passed second place? He got his answer just after the white flag waved, one more lap to go. In turn one, Tom felt that punch in the rear again. Once might be accidental, the second time means it's on purpose. The first four cars all held their positions as they finished the heat race. As they slowed down going down the backstretch, Smitty sped by Tom and never looked, no "I'm sorry" gesture, no wave, no raised middle finger, no grin, no nothing.

"Lucky to hold on to second place, Tom," said Chuck when Tom pulled his helmet off.

"What the hell was that with Smitty?" asked Tom, throwing down his gloves on the seat.

"That's the way he is, Tom. You can't let him get away with that."

"This ain't jalopy racin' here! A guy could get killed doin' that crap! That's bound to happen once in a while, by accident, runnin' close. Those were not little taps!"

Chuck persisted, "Well you just can't let him do that. Give it back to him. Stick a wheel into him! That's the language he understands!"

"I can't do that," Tom said.

"Don't expect him to treat you any different then, Tom!"

Tom walked through the pits, toward the first turn, and under the walk-over bridge. A fan said, "Nice race, Tom. Go get 'em in the feature." Tom smiled, said thanks, and walked on. He stood by himself between the first two turns to watch the next heat race and cool off. *Chuck was probably right, there should be some response, but what? Talking to Smitty would be a waste of time. Threatening and punching is not my way. Say something to an official? Really that is their job. They should have seen it, once if not both times. He's probably done that before. Maybe just cool it and see what happens.*

"Hey mister, can I have an autograph?"

Tom looked around, expecting some young boy to be holding out a program, so it took just a few seconds to put voice and girl together. It was Tina standing near the fence. He smiled, waved, and walked over to her. "Why sure. What's a pretty girl like you doin' in a dump like this?" he joked. "So who do I make this out to?" Tom wrote something on the program.

Then their voices dropped into the confidential range to avoid fans from listening in. "When you got out of the car, I could tell you were mad, Dad. That guy hit you twice."

"Yeah, I counted both times. I had a better seat to see, or feel, it both times"

"Scared me!"

"Surprised me, and made me mad, but I might be over that now. Somebody kind of got my mind off that," Tom said and smiled. How's your mom doin' over there?

"She was ready to go yell at somebody, an official, or…oh I don't know. Ernie settled her down."

"Well, when you go back there, you tell her you talked to me, and that I'm alright, OK, Hon? Just say,' Mom, Dad always says he drives with…' and that's all you need to say. She'll finish it." Tom smiled and handed the program back to her. When she turned to walk away, a boy came up and asked if he could take Tom's picture. Tom stood up straight, smiled for the camera, and said, "Thanks, son. Enjoy your day." Tom walked back to the pit area just as the next heat race was getting pushed off.

The next two heat races went off without any major incidents, although C.J., driving a blue number five, gave himself a thrill in the fourth heat when he spun. He had been running in sixth place, struggling with an ill-handling car, when the car did a half spin between turns three and four. The two cars behind him were high on the banking and avoided contact. It meant that he would have to finish well in the semi-feature, a twelve lap "last chance" to get into the final race, the thirty-lap feature, the money race. Apparently C.J.'s mechanic tweaked something correctly because the car seemed more stable in that race and the team transferred to the feature, at least.

Chuck and Donny were working on a few last-minute chores while Tom was talking with a race official. "Well, Russ, you saw it, or if not you, one of the other guys, right? Once is accidental, twice isn't.

"I know, Tom. I talked to him about it last year once, and it seemed to settle him down for a few races. But there's only so much we can do...."

"Give him a fine! Simple enough, seems to me!" Tom started to walk to his car.

The official called after him, "You could give him some of his own medicine! We don't have to babysit you guys." Tom just walked away and didn't reply. Russ and Chuck could be right.

When Tom got to his pit the car had already been pushed out on the track. Most of the drivers were ready for intro-ductions, standing beside their cars. He turned back to the "family camp" and waved to Janet and Tina. He gathered up his helmet, goggles, gloves, and white face cloth and strode out to his car. He did not have a great starting spot, ninth place in a field of eighteen. A local racer, Buddy Burk, had surprised everyone with one blistering lap that put him on the pole. Carl Connors was in his usual car, the white number two, starting in second place. The driver starting there is positioned well. That is a natural line into turn one.

Tom was buried mid-pack, inside row five. Not so good.

He could get caught up in something not of his making. Smitty in the yellow number seven was behind him, outside row six. Interesting to say the least. Then C.J. was three rows behind Smitty, starting in eighteenth place. Now that gives a guy a long way to go. He'd be lucky to gain five or six places when the race was over.

Introductions over, drivers in their cars, push trucks ready, and Tom was just trying to get into his "racer zone." This was not a time to look at the crowd, the fans, even his family. Just focus for the next ten or eleven minutes of racing. When the green flag drops, barring any red or yellow flags, thirty laps at racing speed could take just ten minutes. Incredible to think about. And incredibly exhausting. The extreme mental focus, the expenditure of energy, and the centrifugal forces all combined to exhaust a driver in that short time. There are reasons that these races are short and those are just a few of those reasons.

After one false start and one lap to get re-set, the flagman waved the green flag. There was the usual quick rise in volume as eighteen engines accelerated at the same time, followed by the sudden fall in tempo as the leaders backed off as they entered turn one. The white car with Connors driving took the lead as Burk stayed low on the track and settled for second place. Tom fell back one place to tenth as the driver to his right was up in the racing groove, the natural advantage. After following that car through the first turn, Tom tried to drop low and get a good run down the backstretch, hoping to pass as they entered turn three. He didn't have enough speed, so he settled for holding his position to finish lap one. Tom tried the same move on lap two and found that he was closer to passing this time, but still could not get around. The field began to stretch out into single file, with many drivers trying the same maneuver: drop low coming out of turn two or four, then hope to power through on the straightaway. Local guy Burk showed his lack of experience racing closely and began to retreat to the rear.

After about five laps of this, Tom finally got around and was now back in ninth place, where he started. *Not going to set the world on fire this way,* Tom thought. Connors in the white number two was long gone. Tom knew that he'd be lucky to get sixth place. Even after just seven laps at this pace, Tom's uniform was already soaking and his arms began to ache as much from tension as exertion. *Too bad race cars don't have power steering, he thought.*

On lap nine, he could see one of the cars that started in the last row appear a straightaway ahead of him. That meant that Connors and the other front runners were already lapping the slower cars. Tom was into a rhythm now. Flat out down the front stretch, get on the brakes at the bridge, ease off brakes, then feather back into the throttle and flatfoot it down the back stretch. Watch for the billboard, brake, feather through three and four as you ride a little high. He ran lap after lap like this and Tom could see that he was steadily gaining on the eighth-place car. On lap twelve, the car that started directly in front of him in seventh suddenly pulled to the inside on the back stretch and slowed. *Good for me, up to eighth! Big deal, huh?*

The car felt solid, nothing seemed amiss. He noticed Chuck's "haze" on the right front tire. *Wonder how long I can smoke that tire?* Tom smelled some burgers from an infield grill. Then he caught himself drifting and thought, *Twelve laps? That's all you got? Can't be too satisfied with eighth place, Tom.* He re-focused and thought rhythm. As he crossed the start/finish line to complete lap fourteen, a yellow car showed its nose on his right. *Trying to pass on the outside in turn one? That's a risky move, but that would be just like Smitty.*

Tom held his ground, not giving up his groove in turn one, and the yellow car fell back. Then as they headed into the back stretch, Smitty tried the same thing, with the same result. Tom-eighth, Smitty-ninth.

Lap fifteen, on the back stretch, Smitty passed Tom after coming off turn two high then diving under Tom who was blocked when lapping a slower car. Smitty-eighth, Tom ninth.

Lap sixteen, and up ahead in turn one, the black car of Johnny Miller grazed the outside wall and the seventh-place car slammed into the rear of Miller. That car rode up the back of the black car, perched there for a moment, then rolled to the left and down to the track apron.

Tom usually tried to be aware of the track ahead. A driver can't do much about the things that happen ten feet in front of him, but with enough foresight he may avoid some unfortunate involvements. This time Tom saw something that didn't look right and it paid off. Smitty didn't see it or couldn't avoid it, and he slammed into the back of the black car. Tom steered to the left of the cars of Miller and Smitty, stuck together at the top of the banking. The other car was lying on its side at the bottom of the track. All the lights in the turns went red, and the field came to a stop on the front stretch. The track announcer cautioned the fans on the infield to stay away from the accident scene and let the emergency crews do their job.

Tom was grateful for a mid-race break, although this was not the best way to get it. Chuck came out with a cup of water and a rag as Tom took off his helmet and goggles. "So, what's that all about?"

Chuck said, "All I know is Miller slipped high, hit the fence and that new kid, Norton, got into him, then rolled a few times. Then Smitty slammed into Miller. Don't think it's bad, they said the kid was waving. But we come out ahead. Three cars out. We're up to sixth place now, Tommy. Car okay you think?"

"Car's good. We can't do anything about it, but you think that right front will be alright? We got, what fourteen, fifteen laps to go?"

"This break will let it cool off a little, maybe it won't blister. I think you'll be okay. Nobody's gonna touch Connors and them guys up front, but who knows, half a race to go yet so…." Chuck was interrupted by the announcer telling the drivers to get ready to restart.

After the usual few laps needed to get all cars push started and into proper order, the drivers were ready for the single file restart. There were fourteen laps to finish and any yellow flags, if there was a caution period, wouldn't count. On the restart, the fifth-place car stuttered when the driver, Burks, punched the throttle, and Tom made the best of his start and advanced to fifth place. That was the easiest gain he had all day. Laps seventeen through twenty reeled off quickly and uneventfully as Tom held himself in fifth place. Connors—the leader—and second and third places all pulled away quickly leaving only the fourth-place car close enough to catch.

But the rhythm Tom had developed before the wreck did not come back quickly. He seemed to be clumsy and had to think about what had all been so automatic and easy. The fourth-place car, another red car, was within striking distance but Tom's confidence level was not high. On lap twenty-two, Tom thought he'd try Smitty's tactic: show the car's nose on the outside of the straightaway, back off, repeat a number of times, then just when that driver thinks you're going to pass on the outside, slip under him. And Tom did just that on lap twenty-seven. So, fourth place again. That's where he ended the race—holding steady, not going backward, not bending any equipment. Maybe earn a few more points with Chuck.

The checkered flag was a welcome sight. Coasting down the back stretch, he relaxed and now could feel just how tired he was. His uniform was soaking, his arms and shoulders ached, and he felt like he couldn't hold his head up. He shut the engine off and just enjoyed the quiet. Tom rolled into the pit area and was welcomed by his crew. All he could do was smile. *Maybe I shouldn't be so happy with fourth place,* he thought to himself. *But I love this stuff! How lucky can a guy be? Is there anything as much fun as this? Well, I remember one driver said, 'It's the most fun you can have with your clothes on.'* Tom chuckled to himself, remembering that. Fun, yes, but his hands still shook for several minutes as he sipped a cold beer in the pits and signed souvenir programs for fans.

· · · · ·

Monday morning at the station, Tom had to deal with his usual post-race let-down. Pumping gas, changing tires, and all those mundane jobs didn't match up to a day like Sunday. He got to the station earlier than usual, about five o'clock, to allow himself time to look at any notes that James may have left for him, drink an extra cup of coffee or two, maybe even smoke a cigarette. He had quit years ago but still could snitch one here, alone. By the time he got home any traces on his breath would be gone or hidden so Janet wouldn't give him another lecture. "Those things will kill you!" she'd say. Well, there's other things that could do that, but that would be a poor defense.

He sat at his desk replaying the race, Billy, Smitty, Janet, Tina, and the whole day at Winchester. And once again, he didn't have any understanding with Chuck about the next race. It was at a track that was new to the sprint car circuit. It was at a little Ohio town called Rossburg. They called the track Eldora. *How did they come up with a name like that? Well, if you can have towns called Russia and Palestine and*

Potsdam and Versailles in Ohio, I guess you can call it what you like. Some of the minor league organizations had run sprint cars there, but this would be a first for the Indianapolis level fraternity. Tom had raced jalopies there and knew it would be a different experience for the 'Big Leagues," as they called the Indy set. But that was not until mid-June. The Indianapolis 500 was coming this week, the 30th was on Friday, and then the Indy boys would go to Milwaukee for the one hundred mile race the following weekend. So, there was a layoff for the sprint cars. There were some midget races during the lull, but Tom never enjoyed them or had much success. Better just tend to things here for a while. Run the station, be a husband and father. But Billy broke his arm three weeks ago. Add to that the next three weeks, and there you have the healing time for a broken arm. So, Billy gets back in Chuck's car, and Tom does what? Race midgets? Death traps in Tom's book: underpowered, twitchy, even less protection than a sprint car, if you can imagine that. But at least that is a way to stay connected to the owners and any new opportunity, so he might have to re-think his reservations.

A little before six, Tom was still sitting in the dark at his desk, drinking his second cup of coffee and stubbing out his cigarette. Nice and quiet. It wasn't like he needed this time to get ready for a day at the station. It was a little town with nowhere to go in a hurry.

"Might just as well turn on the lights and pumps and open the doors," he said out loud around six o'clock. The sun was just coming up, and a few friends went by, blowing their horns and waving. James would be in soon for a short time before school.

Tom checked the meters on the pumps and noted the numbers in his book. Then he put the bell hose out on the driveway and rolled out the oil can display. He ran up the overhead door and turned on the air compressor. *Ready for another big day here in Barton!*

The first customer was none other than the usual pain in the ass, Roger Hicks, the same guy who gave him a hard time after the Terre Haute race. "Well, Tom Terrific, the racing demon! Fourth place again, huh? Gonna win some day?"

"What can I do for you today, Roger? Fill up?" asked Tom, as evenly as possible.

"Oh, I'll fill up at Shell, other side of town. You know Hank don't you at that other station? Guess I'll fill up there. Just wanted to congratulate you on your, uh, what was that, fourth place finish yesterday?" Roger smiled and drove off, leaving Tom standing in the driveway. Roger was on his way to a local business where he drove a desk and added numbers all day.

James got to the station around six, plus ten minutes. That was his six o'clock. Tom couldn't fault him for being late. He didn't miss any big crush of business, so what's the difference. Tom was just glad to have a reliable kid around when he wanted to be elsewhere.

"So, how did things go yesterday? Problems?"

"Well, Mr. Lawton, I closed a little early. That okay?"

"What can I do about that? Re-open for fifteen minutes yesterday, or stay open fifteen minutes longer today?" Tom said, smiling. "That could possibly, just possibly, now mind you, be the difference of an extra fifty cents profit. Anyway, why'd you close early? Have homework? No, couldn't be that! School's almost over. A date?"

"Nah, neither of those, but I was hopin' to make a little progress with your second suggestion. See my older cousin wants to sell his car so he can buy a newer one, and…"

"You want to buy a money pit, don't ya, James?" laughed Tom.

"I just want some independence, Tom. My own wheels. So I don't have to borrow 'daddy's car' anymore. He always gives me a hard time every time I want to go somewhere."

"Lot of issues there, James. Insurance, maintenance, just for starters. And then there's that independence thing. That can be another issue, you know."

"You sound like my dad, Mr. Lawton."

"Just wanted to say that. Won't say it again, James. You're a smart kid."

Tom went back to his desk, sat down, took a sip of coffee, and started to read the special sports section about the big 500 coming up. He looked over the lineup and could see that he had raced with many of the drivers. He figured he was as good as most of them. They started about the same time as he had and maybe pursued their careers with a more single-minded devotion than he. He made compromises on his own terms. He did what he thought was right by his wife and daughter, thinking of his obligation to them first. And if he could reasonably fit into his life this desire to race cars, he did. But the cost of those compromises had slowed his advancement. And here he sat in a small town gas station while some of the men he had raced with were looking to start in the most prestigious race in the world. Men who would get paid thousands of dollars for finishing last. But, he had chosen this life.

Tom looked at the clock. James would be going to school soon, and Tom figured that if he was going to get the worst and dirtiest part of a muffler job done on Caroline Miller's car, he should get started soon. He drove her old Hudson up on the rack and raised it up. The noise of the air compressor right beside him drowned out the driveway bell when a car drove up to the pumps. James went out the door as Tom started to take the muffler off, shaking rust and carbon into his face.

James walked into the service bay and said, "Tom, the customer wants to talk to you."

"Can't you handle it? I'm a damn mess already."

"She said she wants to talk to you, Mr. Lawton."

Tom looked out and could see the Corvette of Suzy Hicks, Mrs. Roger Hicks. Tom walked out, wiping his hands on a shop rag.

"Why, Tommy, why don't you make that young boy do that dirty work for you?" He used to be Tommy in high school, but he had been just Tom for many years. That "Tommy" brought back many memories. Janet, Suzy, and a number of girls used to call him Tommy, but not anymore. He was just "Tom" now, even to Janet. But here was Suzy, a girl he dated around the same time as Janet, and she was calling him Tommy.

"Suzy, what can I do for you? Fill-up?"

"No, Tommy, I just wanted to congratulate you on your last couple races. You're doing well. I hope that continues. Roger reads the sports section every Monday for the race results, and he tells me all about it." Suzy was honest in her compliments, and her smile was candid and heartfelt. "That's all, Tommy, that's all I wanted to say. That and do be careful, please."

Tom was stunned. He stood there searching for a good answer, but all he could come up with was, "Thanks, Suzy. I'll remember that."

Then Suzy Hicks drove off, waving in the backward way that is easy to do in a convertible. And Tom stood there in the driveway watching and thinking about Suzy Harmon, now Suzy Hicks, a girl he dated in high school. They dated seriously for about a year, until a small argument became large enough, and they broke up. Sort of, that is. Tom started to go out with Janet Richardson, but found it hard to forget about Suzy. Their relationship revived for a few months, even while Tom was seeing Janet. But Janet became pregnant in the spring of their senior year and Tom did what he knew was right. It was not just a sense of duty because he truly did love Janet. But Tom was suddenly out of Suzy Harmon's life.

James left for school around seven thirty and Tom was on his own till James got out of school. Tom returned to the muffler job on the old Hudson, not a hard job but it stretched out to about noon with drivers stopping for gas. Then a cold cut sandwich and chips from home with a soda for lunch, and routine gas station work until five o'clock when James came in for three hours. Tom went home for dinner and went back for the last hour till closing at nine.

· · · · ·

Billy Wallace talked his girlfriend of the month, a twenty-two-year-old beauty named Betsy, into taking a few days off from her grocery store job to drive him to Indianapolis. Driving was too difficult with his cast, he said, as if she needed to be convinced that he really needed help. They found a motel not too far from the speedway in Indianapolis, paid for a room for two nights, and spent the rest of Monday by the motel pool.

After breakfast on Tuesday, Billy said, "Betsy, Hon, I'd like you to take me to the speedway this morning, okay?"

"What am I supposed to do? Go along? What's there for me to do? There ain't no race to watch!"

"Well, geez, I ain't no babysitter! You *could* put on your swimsuit and work on your tan by the pool! Read some magazines! I don't know. I want to talk to some drivers and owners, you know, work on connections," Billy grumbled. "Or how 'bout you go shopping someplace? They got shopping centers around here. Big fancy ones. Here's an extra fifty bucks. Be back at the main gate on Sixteenth Street around five o'clock, okay?"

"You better take me out for one helluva good dinner tonight,

Billy!" Betsy punctuated her anger by squealing the tires as she drove off in a cloud of dust and exhaust smoke. Billy grinned and waved as she drove off.

Billy walked up to the main gate at Georgetown Road and Sixteenth Street. It was locked, so he went to the little museum/office building nearby. He introduced himself to the first person he saw, a clerk at the souvenir desk. "Hi, ma'am, I'm Billy Wallace."

She stared at him momentarily and said, "And you are selling…?"

"I'm a race car driver!"

"Oh, I should have known. You do have a broken arm, I see. Now, Mr. Williams, what can I do for you?"

Billy's injured pride quickly showed. "That's Wallace, Billy Wallace. I'd like to go walk around the garages and talk to some guys, you know, friends, drivers."

"I wish I knew you, Mr. Wallace, have you driven here before?" the clerk inquired, coolly.

"Nah, I'm just getting started."

"Yes, I see that. She glanced at his cast. I'd like to help you, but…do you know anyone here?

"Sure! I know Roger Ward, the race winner!"

She was skeptical. "You know him personally? If he came in here, he'd recognize you?"

"Well…." Just then Eddie Spencer walked in. Billy said, "Mr. Spencer! Remember me?"

"Why, Billy Wallace! We chatted over at Winchester. What can I do for you, Billy? Glad to see you took my advice. Mrs. Culp, this is Billy…."

"We've met," she answered.

"Come on, Billy. Let's go over to Gasoline Alley. I want you to meet a few guys I know. Might help your reputation around here. Maybe we can find a mechanic who needs a little help on Friday during the race. What can you do?" Eddie acted like Billy was his favorite nephew.

"I know a little, but I drive better than I fix stuff," Billy ventured.

"Hell, I don't mean you're going to work on an engine. They might just need a guy to go get stuff. Be a 'go-fer'. Not glamorous, but at least you're here for the 'Greatest Spectacle in Racing' as they say." Eddie might be one of Billy's tickets to this place. The old racer and the young "hot shot" strolled through the gate and onto the speedway grounds. The empty grandstands rose up, it seemed to Billy, as high as a city building. How many years had they held fans cheering on the "500" drivers, just a few yards away? Empty and quiet for some three hundred or so days a year, but in a few days thousands of people will fill the stands for the great race. This was a big moment for a boy from Arizona. His first time to see this place. Billy hoped to one day be one of those thirty-three men, being cheered on by the thousands of people that fill those stands.

Eddie truly was just one of many tickets for Billy to the speedway. Eddie knew so many people here: drivers, car owners, mechanics, officials, administrators. There were so many introductions that Billy thought he'd never remember half of them. And, a good number of them knew of Billy Wallace! These few square miles were ground zero of American racing. The garages were used year-round by some teams. Many drivers lived in the Georgetown Road neighborhood, sharing small two-bedroom homes or mobile homes. They worked out of this little enclave for the racing season, trailering their cars to the Midwestern tracks, venturing to the East Coast, and at season's end to the West Coast for the year-end wrap-up events. They all read the "Bible" of auto racing: National Speed Sport News. That was their Sporting News, their Variety, of American racing. So, yes, they read about Billy Wallace. They read about his Southwest career. It should not be a surprise that this young man was on the mind of some.

By the end of Tuesday, Billy had that "go-fer" job for a team starting in eighth place in the big race on Friday. That meant Billy had to stay through clean-up duties for the team on Saturday morning. Thursday was "Carburetion Day," the last day before the race that teams are allowed to use the track. Billy thought, *Why go home Wednesday when they would need me on Thursday? This would not go well with Betsy. She would have to drive home alone Wednesday morning and she would not be happy. Should I tell her before dinner? She'd get mad and probably drive home right away. At least, I'd save some money on dinner. Or should I wait and tell her after dinner, kind of keep my promise to treat her to a good meal?*

Billy chose the latter option, and it didn't go well. Betsy left early Wednesday morning. She must have brushed her teeth and hit the road. Billy never heard her leave. He thought, *How do I get to the Speedway now? Selfish little twerp! But there are a lot more Betsys out there.*

* * * * *

Tom could have gone to Indianapolis with Chuck. Chuck was going to work as right front wheel man on a friend's car. He really should have gone. That was just another way to stay in contact with all the racing fraternity. It was always a good idea to stay connected. Who knows what a conversation might lead to? But Tom decided to stay home and spend some time with Janet and Tina. Janet had invited her sister and her family for a cookout. So, it was burgers, dogs, all the usual Midwest picnic food, and in the background "The Greatest Spectacle in Racing" on the radio. There were occasional comments and questions from in-laws and nieces and nephews, directed at Tom, about the race. He tried to answer as best he could, but there was only so much he could say, before he lost their attention. Some wondered if he was letting up on his dream, settling in for a nice family life and steady, safe career.

"You still want to keep driving, Tom? Want to be at Indy someday?" asked his brother-in-law, Jack Richardson.

Tom replied slowly, trying to be casual about his answer, "I just take one step at a time, Jack. Try to do a good job every race and hope that results will speak for themselves."

"Why aren't you at the track today?" asked Jack.

Tom didn't get a chance to answer. Tina said, "Daddy's taking me and my horse to some lady in a county down south, Preble County. What's that town, Daddy?"

"I gotta look it up again, Hon. I wanted to get an early start on Saturday, Jack, so I didn't want to fight traffic getting into the Speedway, then after the race drive three more hours to get home, and then work all day Saturday. I hired James for the whole day on Saturday so I'm free of that. Sunday's a down day on the sprint car schedule, so I got the weekend here at home."

Janet looked at her brother, thinking about any insinuation in his question. She had her doubts and worries, but still supported her husband's dreams. "Tom does try to balance his life, Jack. And he'll take care of us, I know. Some men get consumed by things, you know."

On the radio, the broadcasters were talking excitedly about an incident on the track involving one of Tom's fellow-drivers. The table talk quieted down as they all listened to the reports from the announcers. Tom picked up the name Smith. That would be the driver he knew as Smitty, the aggressive one who banged him around at Winchester. Not surprising that he would be involved in an incident, but this was at a considerably higher speed. Indianapolis straightaway speedways were near one hundred and eighty miles per hour as compared to, perhaps one hundred and twenty at a track like Winchester. Faster means riskier.

After about fifteen laps of caution flag running, the race resumed. The radio broadcasters said that early reports were that even though Smitty's car had turned over, he was lucky enough to walk to the ambulance. It was just another reminder to all at the picnic that this was a dangerous occupation.

The family's attention was drawn away and back to the race as conversation ebbed and flowed. A game of horseshoes began about the time the race ended. An older driver who specialized in just a few pavement races won the race. It was a popular victory. He had been racing many years and this seemed to be an appropriate closure for his career. Tom only knew him as fans knew him. He had never raced against the man, but was glad for his success. Soon after that, the party began to break up.

After clean up and some "porch" time, the time that Janet and Tom reserved for themselves, they retired to bed. Tina was on the phone in the dining room with someone when they went upstairs. About all they could make out was "Well, yeah" and some giggles and "Not really" and similar teen talk. It was just good to hear her talking to someone.

The last thing that Janet said before she rolled over to sleep was, "Tom, I know that maybe you would rather have been somewhere...."

She didn't get to finish. "Janet, I was here today because this is where I wanted to be. And tomorrow will be the same. That's where I want to be, where I should be. Perhaps it can't always work out like this, but this time it did."

"Well, it still means a lot."

· · · · ·

On Saturday morning, Tom hitched the horse trailer to his truck. A neighbor usually helped Tina get the horse in the trailer. Tom did not have a clue about horses, and Tina still could not always command cooperation from her horse. Today it went smoothly, so they soon started the drive south to a farm in Preble County. A Mrs. Anderson was going to help Tina prepare for 4-H shows.

The late May day was warm and Tom opened the windows for fresh air. Just a few cars around town had air conditioners, mostly owned by rich guys—bankers, business owners, doctors—and a truck was never even thought a proper vehicle for such a convenience. So, the drive was noisy and blustery, with gusts of humid air providing the only cooling.

"Daddy, you ever get scared in a race car?" asked Tina.

"Scared? Well, any guy who says he never gets scared is either a liar or a fool. But I can't say scared is the right word. Surprised is a better word. When I see a guy lose it in front of me, my first reaction is automatic. Look for a way out of the situation. So, scared, I don't think, not right then. Scared comes later when I have time to think about it. Not a good thing to do. Why?"

"I often wonder, 'How you do that?' I guess, from where we sit, it all looks so dangerous. It scares me."

"Hon, I drive as much with my head as my foot."

"I hear that all the time, Dad. Things happen that are beyond your control," Tina persisted with her concerned voice. "That's what I worry about!"

"Yeah, I know. All I can do is not get outside my own… oh…I don't know how to say it. It's like I have my own, uh, like I have a role in a play. If I learn my lines and all, I'm fine. If someone tries to get me to do something that's not my role, I've learned the hard way that bad things can happen."

Tina did not answer but just sat thinking.

"I can't tell you not to worry. But this sport is safer than it used to be. And I truly do believe that I could cash in much bigger someday. The fact that Chuck hired me to drive is a good sign. That makes an impression on other owners, too."

The truck was quiet for a long time and the warm air suddenly turned pungent.

"Eweeeee, skunk!" Tina said.

Tom shifted to another topic. "Hey, nice to hear you on the phone last night. Who was that?"

"Oh, just a kid from school," Tina answered and changed the subject. "Hey, do you know that guy who won the 500 last year?"

"Kinda. Met him once at Terre Haute, but he wasn't driving that day. He's in another class. He was like me trying to move up, 15 years ago. Now he's got it made, picks and chooses his races. And promoters pay him just to show up. Now they'll pay him even more. He'll probably retire soon. Could be me some day! "Tom sat up straight and flashed a grin at Tina to let her know that he was joking…kind of. She smiled back, letting him know she understood the joke.

Their conversation turned to the summer ahead, her horse, next school year, Janet, and small talk. Their route took them past pretty farms, neat little ranch houses close to the road, solid old two-story farmhouses with flowering bushes in bloom around porches, cows grazing in fields and farmers mowing hay. They passed through a few little towns, and finally after about an hour and a half, got to Gloria Anderson's boarding stable near Eaton.

They drove up a lane lined with white fences. In the fields were perhaps ten or twelve horses. Tina looked from side to side, smiling and taking it all in. She loved this. White fences, green grass, brown horses, black horses, a white horse, neat barns. In her imagination and dreams, she saw herself operating such a horse farm in her future. A lady, near Tom's age, but older, walked up to Tom's truck.

Gloria Anderson wore jeans and boots. Her face was

tanned, dried, and creased by hours in the sun. "Glad to meet you Mr. Lawton. We spoke on the phone a few weeks ago, I think. And I have really looked forward to helping out your young "horsey" girl. That was me about, oh well, we'll just say a few years ago!"

Tina looked surprised. She had been led to believe that this just came up a few days ago.

"Mrs. Anderson, this is Tina," Tom introduced them.

Tina said, "Glad to meet you, Mrs. Anderson. I'd like some help getting ready for shows."

"Honey, just call me Gloria, okay? I got started riding a little younger than you, but we had horses on Dad and Mom's farm. So, I just grew up with them, natural to me. What I know comes from years of working with these animals, trying to figure out what they're thinking, and then out-thinking them, or thinking a step or two ahead of them. A lot of this is communication, you probably know some of that already. Well, anyway, why don't we get started? Be nice to have a horse to ride, don't ya think?"

"Uh, yeah," Tina looked confused.

"I think that means you should get Candy out of the trailer, girl," Tom teased.

"Oh, uh, oh sure!" Tina went to the ramp of the trailer to get her horse out.

"I'd like to watch how that horse comes out of the trailer, if you don't mind, Tina," Gloria said as she followed the girl.

"Sure. My neighbor helped me get her settled in this morning."

Gloria watched the horse and girl, trying to get a sense of the two together. "Why don't you just lead her over to get a drink of water and let her get familiar with the field for a while? There ain't no other horses in this field and she can't go too far in this small field."

"Mrs. Anderson, got a few minutes?" Tom thought it might be a good idea to explain a little about the physical and psychological effects of her cerebral palsy. He and Janet had hoped that in some ways, her horse might provide an outlet or perhaps a distraction. He talked about her academic abilities, social problems both real and sometimes imagined, and the limp in her walk that was probably not as big in reality as in Tina's mind. Nevertheless, it was a part of her life.

Gloria's response was unqualified, "It doesn't have to be a problem. It's all in their communication. I can teach that. And girls are better in some ways with communication than boys are. A boy thinks he can muscle his horse around. I might be thinking in stereotypes here, but girls are just better at talkin' and listenin', if they're not too scared. The first thing I have to work on is how she walks up to Candy, so let's get a start." She called for Tina to come closer.

"Now, Tina, we gotta figure out a way to walk up to that horse so she knows you're there because you want to be and you're not afraid of her. We can't do anything about the way you walk...."

At that, Tina looked at her dad, horrified and angry and looking as if she was about to cry. Tom pretended to be absorbed by something in another field, but his heart ached.

Gloria charged ahead. "But. We can make her think the way we want her to think. Your horse may see that as lack of confidence. These animals can sense a rider's mood, you know. So, you gotta go up to her, at an angle, towards her shoulder, making sure you have eye contact, talking to her. Just direct and steady...not too fast, not loud, but talkin', sayin' her name. Just slow and easy...not like you're afraid. But just a sure, steady approach. Put your hand on her neck, pat her and rub her a little."

"They pick up things that surprise me all the time, after all these years. I'm still learnin'. Once I was gettin' ready to saddle up a horse of mine, walkin' up to him, and I was about four feet away when some yahoo yelled at me. I turned around to answer, and that old horse…I'd been ridin' him for years… stretched out his neck and liked to take a bite out of my butt! Damn critter! So, what do I do? Beat him? What good would that do? I walked away, waited a minute, and started the whole process over without the interruption. There were no treats that day! Now let me see you walk up to Candy."

Tina did as instructed, self-consciously, but as best she could under the circumstances of her embarrassment.

"That's not so bad, girl, not so bad at all. You're gonna have to remember, and practice these little things until that horse trusts you. That little 'hitch in your-get-along' is just that, a little 'hitch' and nothing more. If you let it become a big thing, Candy will sense it and the two of you will be just two separate beings. I want to make her kinda become part of you, so she responds to the littlest commands, slight pressure with your knee or tiny movements of the reins, things that most people won't even see."

This went on for fifteen minutes or more, Gloria just talking and explaining horse and human psychology, while Tina brushed the horse and got her ready for riding. Tina seemed to get over her initial shock, but Tom knew it might be a cool, silent drive home. *Maybe this is a good thing. Come back once every few weeks, more often November through March?*

Gloria explained to Tina the verbal commands for the horse to change its gait, the "kissing" and "clicking" sounds that riders use. She told her about how a horse's natural response to avoid pressure is the key to directional control, the rider using a knee and the reins together to turn the animal. She watched Tina circle the field, practicing the commands to change from a walk to a jog to a lope. Gloria called out for

Tina to turn to the center of the ring and stop. Then she tried to teach backing up, but soon decided that was for another day.

After the session was over Gloria said, "Tina, why don't you unhook your lead from her halter. Then let her roam around the field on her own for a while." Tina was glad to get out of the spotlight for a while.

Gloria walked over to Tom, who was leaning on the fence. "I'd just like to watch how they get along. See if the horse comes when called for. That sort of thing. That's a good kid you got there, Mr. Lawton. Hope I didn't hurt her. I know I surprised her, but we talked a little psychology, and if I didn't, I wouldn't be a good shrink, would I? Shoot, we hardly got started on ridin' lessons. That horse has been rode, but I've got my own way of teachin' that. Next time, maybe we'll make more progress."

"Mrs. Anderson, maybe a neutral party can do more than Mom and Dad sometimes. I appreciate what you did today. Hope to continue."

"Sure enough, Tom. Just give me a call and we'll set up lessons that are a bit more engaging than we had today. You know, I drive up your way once in a while, to shows. I could stop at your place and just talk to Tina and watch her work with Candy on her own turf. Horses act much different at home. And by the way, just call me Gloria."

"Sounds good, Mrs. Anderson."

"Didn't I tell you to call me Gloria? Do you men ever learn to communicate?" she teased.

"Guess I should practice what you preach, huh?" Tom smiled and showed he got the point.

"Well, I want to watch how that horse responds when Tina calls, see how well she minds her. Why don't you get ready to load up, okay?"

It was a quiet drive home, but not as cool as it could have

been. "Thanks, Dad," was about all Tina had to say about her "lesson." Tom tried to steer the conversation to small talk—weather, school, movies—until the conversation just sort of faded out for the last twenty miles. Tom knew that Janet would get her version of the story from Tina, and that's when he would learn how well it really went.

Chapter 4

Chuck called Tom on Monday at the station. Tom was leaning on his workbench, sipping coffee and enjoying a rare treat, a donut that Janet picked up for him on her way to work.

"Tom, Billy says he's ready to go next Sunday."

"I figured as much. Counting weeks, days, and hours. Eager to go, even if it makes sense to wait another week or two," Tom said, resigned.

"Here's what I'm thinkin'. I'll get the car ready for him. He's hot to race, you know. But, how about you go along with me? Just in case he's not up for it, arm hurting too much, and you can get in the car then? I know what you're thinkin'. You could get in someone else's car, I know. But right now there aren't any good cars open, and the junk you'd have to drive wouldn't help your reputation or bank account any. So…I'll pay you to ease your pain a little anyway."

"Don't need to pay me, Chuck. Who knows what might happen? Maybe Smitty'll have such a hangover that he won't see straight, and I can get in Olsen's car!"

They both laughed at the likelihood of the hangover and the improbability of that outcome. Nothing ever kept Smitty out of a race car. That was the way the Sunday plan was left. Billy back in the race car, Tom going along for backup.

. . . . .

James got to the station around nine o'clock, his usual starting time, plus or minus fifteen minutes. His summer hours freed Tom's time for chasing repair parts, dropping by Bennie's for "second breakfast," stopping by the farm store to talk to Janet, or even going home to check on Tina. Tom told James he'd be back in about an hour, that he needed to go to another shop and get a few parts.

"See you in a little bit, James. Gotta get a belt for old man Heaston. That old Dodge of his is squealing like a pig. I ain't got that one in stock so I'm goin' to Wally's. Hold down the fort!"

"When you get back can I get some advice 'bout that car I got an eye on, Mr. Lawton?" James asked.

"You are determined to join the world of automobile and financial insanity, aren't you?"

"Yes, sir! Can't wait! So, can we talk?"

"If I must be your confessor, okay," Tom joked as he walked out the door and headed for his truck.

After getting his parts at the Wally's shop, Tom drove out to the farm store. Janet was stocking shelves with a co-worker.

"Well, look what the cat dragged in, Missy," Janet teased.

"Why, Ah do declare, if it ain't Mr. Lawton," said Missy Wilkins, in her corny attempt at a Southern drawl.

"Ma'am, may I interrupt your leisurely morning to speak with the lovely Mrs. Lawton?"

"Sure, what's up?" asked Janet.

"Well, it's about this weekend. Chuck's putting Billy back in the car and wants me to go along for back-up. You know, in case Billy can't drive all day. So, I thought, I can do that. Might help in the long run. Who knows how long Billy will stay at this level? But, anyway, you interested in goin' along?"

Janet thought for a little while, debating quickly with herself. She knew it would probably be a stress-free day for her, without Tom driving.

"I guess that would…"

Tom interrupted, "How bout I talk to Chuck and see if you and Ernie could ride together? Now I will tell you this: there ain't no good, grassy infield at this new place. *Eldora* they call it. Depending on the weather, the infield is either a dust bowl, or mud hole. So, you'll probably want to sit in the stands."

"Oh, for the love of God! Hard wooden seats and drunks!"

"Yeah, I know, but we'll stop on the way home and get a good meal!"

"Well, I know what that means. A racer's treat: greasy burgers and cold fries. You know how to win a girl over, don't you, Tom Lawton?" she teased.

"How 'bout Tina. Think she'd want to go, too?"

"Your guess is as good as mine. She's moody. We'll ask her and let her do what she wants. She's not a little girl anymore, wants her time to do…whatever…or…nothing. We'll just see," mused Janet.

*   *   *   *   *

Wednesday evening, after the regular day ended and the shop was closed, Chuck and Donny were in the back of the shop working on the race car. If they had just finished a race on a dirt track, the first job would be clean-up. That wasn't a problem after the Winchester race. Pavement doesn't leave a lot of dust and mud on a car. Chuck liked a clean and neat car, so the most Donny would have to do would be to wipe off the body, and while he was doing that, look over the frame tubes and running gear for cracks. Occasionally, Chuck would say, "Donny, get out that little paint brush and the touch-up paint. Look over the car and fill in those little stone chips. It can't be a show-piece all season, but it don't have to look like a tractor either."

They had three days to change the car from a pavement set-up to a dirt set-up. They were preparing for a track that had

a number of unknowns for them. Chuck had run a modified
at Eldora, but never a sprint car. He had that advantage on
some other mechanics who had never raced there. They had
to rely on advice from others. And that was not always good
advice. Some mechanics figured, "Why give away my secrets?
They'll use 'em to beat me." Some had to try to transfer their
experience from similar tracks to this new one. So, take what
worked other places and combine that with a best guess about
how to solve this new track. But Chuck did have the advantage
of experience at Eldora.

Some mechanics thought that the half-mile dirt track
at New Bremen, Ohio, may have been a track that offered
some clues. It and Eldora had long, sweeping turns and short
straight-a-ways. They were both banked, although Eldora
had much steeper banked turns. And it was faster because
of those banks. Both tracks had a tendency to dry out and
turn hard and slick for a daytime race. If the clay at Eldora

held moisture well, it provided a tacky surface that gave the cars excellent traction. When conditions were right, it was a wickedly fast dirt track, perhaps the fastest half-mile dirt track in the country. Night races most often provided those conditions, but this was a day race.

"Donny, I want you to look on the top shelf over there by the drill press. See that box that I wrote 'HQC' on? Bring that down and get out a smaller box that says 'Set 11', okay?"

"HQC, don't tell me. That probably means 'high quality crap', huh, Chuck?" Donny thought it might be fun to rattle Chuck's cage.

"Clown! That means 'Halibrand Quick Change.' Them's the gears we gotta use to make this thing run right Sunday! Next, I want you to get those two rear wheels outta the back of the shop. Sixteen inch wheels, OK? Then I'll tell you what we're doing and why. And while you're up there get set number eight, nineteen, three, and thirteen. Then we'll have some others to work with if that set eleven ain't right."

Chuck took his brass hammer and gave the knock-off wingnuts on each rear wheel a whack to loosen them. Each wheel nut had three large tabs. A well-aimed hammer would break the nut loose on the axle, and then it would easily spin off, allowing the wheel to be removed.

After he broke the nuts loose, Chuck used his floor jack to raise the back of the car up. He placed two jack stands under the axle and let the car down to rest on the stands. Many years ago his father drilled into his head, "Never work under a car that's on a jack." Now, he could work under the rear of the car safely while Donny changed the rear wheels.

"I'm gonna change these gears back here. We ran set number twenty-six at Winchester with fifteen-inch wheels. Set number twenty-six gave us a 4.41. And I wanted to drop the whole car down a little that's why we ran fifteen-inch wheels, not sixteen. Get it? A fifteen-inch wheel drops the car down a bit lower than a sixteen-inch wheel, not much—a half inch or so. Pavement is smoother, theoretically, than dirt, so there's not as much need for suspension movement. So, we settle the car a little lower on the track, lower the center of gravity, see? Handles the turns better."

"Okay," Donny was following Chuck's reasoning.

"But, Eldora—dirt. Gotta make room for that car to ride the bumps. So, we gain just a little by going up to sixteen-inch wheels. That's your job now. Take off those fifteen-inch wheels and slicks and put on those sixteen-inch wheels with Firestone diamond treads. Brand new tires, so Billy should get a good bite on that Eldora clay."

Chuck continued, "But we can't run that same 4.41 rear end gear with sixteen-inch wheels. Well, we could, but we might be slow and we'd just be watchin' everybody else race while we loaded up to go home. So, you change the wheels while I get down here and change these rear end gears to what I *think* might work, set number eleven. That gives us a final drive ratio of 5.04."

Donny said, "So, that's it? After tonight we're ready to go?"

"No. I want you to take off them front wheels and put them ribbed tires on. The ones that look like you put on the front of a tractor. They're good for steering on dirt. Then later, maybe tomorrow night, I gotta take off that 'half wrap' I put on the right front spring. We're not gonna be leadin' quite as much with that right front as we did at Winchester. Billy should be drivin' off that right rear if we got it right and he's got his mojo back!"

"You want me back then tomorrow night, Chuck?" Donny asked.

"Maybe. But Friday, no. Ernie and I are goin' to Richmond to see her sister. And Saturday I just like to tinker around with the car. I'll let you know."

"Okay, Boss, see you tomorrow morning!" Donny left Chuck alone with the race car.

. . . . .

Ernie drove as far as the Lawton home, and then Janet drove the rest of the way in the family sedan on the Sunday morning of the Eldora race. If one drew an eight-inch circle on a map of this part of Ohio and Indiana, perhaps five or six race tracks would fall within that circle. A two-hour drive would find most of them. This drive today would take an hour and a half or so. Enough time for Janet and Ernie to cover many topics, some to explore more deeply than others. Small talk inevitably leads to "shop talk," in other words, their husbands, kids, other drivers and their wives or girlfriends, who's driving what car, what happened at the last race, and on and on.

Ernie was a bit sour this day. "Once in a while, there are a few things that make this less enjoyable, Janet. Especially when I have to sit in the stands. I like to be more connected with what's going on. I don't do much, but at least if I'm inside the track, I feel more a part of it all."

"Yeah, and it really looks worse from the stands sometimes. Even more dangerous," Janet offered, more of a worried wife's perspective.

"Where you want to sit at this joint? I was here just once with Chuck when he had that old modified."

Janet said, "That's up to you."

"Let's get away from the center of the stands. There's a grassy hill outside turn four where people set up lawn chairs. Bit more roomy and we can get some 'insulation' around us, if you know what I mean," Ernie said.

"Sounds good to me," agreed Janet. "Some fans…well, just a few, once in a while."

Then Janet brought up the last race at Winchester and

Smitty's rough treatment of Tom. "What's with that Smitty guy anyway? This is not some go-kart racing at twenty-five miles an hour!"

"You're right. There's always one like that, it seems. Smitty's smart enough not to do that at every race. He likes to make that statement every once in a while, hoping to intimidate one or two drivers. Then maybe it'll pay off for him in a race. Might make a guy think twice about how close to race him. Make that other guy back off, and…Smitty wins."

"Don't seem right, or fair! Can't the officials do something about it?" Janet asked.

"Well, they do pussy-foot around, I know. But this stuff is not for the lily-livered, and usually the drivers handle it themselves, one way or another," said Ernie.

"What about the car owner. Smitty always drives that yellow car. Don't the owner care about gettin' his car banged up?"

"Olsen? He loves Smitty! Those guys understand each other. They're cut from the same cloth! A few bumps, occasional bent race cars, angry drivers or officials…small price to pay for winning," Ernie explained. "That's the way he runs his business, too, rough."

"Well, my husband drives these things…."

"I know what you're saying, Janet, I know. Chuck don't drive, but I know."

And that's where the conversation ended, just as they were arriving at the race track. Janet turned off the highway and into the gravel parking lot of the dancehall/speedway. This owner kept his options open. If the race track didn't make a profit, there were always the teen dances on Friday night to bring in some cash, or wedding receptions on Saturdays when there were no races scheduled.

The facility was fairly primitive. The ticket window was part of the back wall of the concession stand. Two women sold tickets. General admission got you a less than choice grandstand seat, probably way left or right of the center section, near the start/finish line. Or you could go to the infield, which was mostly dirt with some scrubby grass or weeds. Photographers and some fans went there, but not like many other tracks that had nice grassy infields that accommodated picnickers. This place was a little more primitive, if you can imagine that. It was set up for night racing, but this first visit by the sanctioning body was scheduled for a Sunday afternoon race. Officials wanted to see this place in the light of day.

Janet and Ernie got their tickets, walked through the gate and onto the wide concrete area behind the top row of seats. The stands were mostly all covered, except out to the sides. The burgers were already sizzling and sending up a cloud of beef grease from the concession stand. Some early arrivals were lined up for lunch. On the left were the vendor's tables of cheap plastic cars, mini checkered flags and crash helmets, patches to sew on fan's jackets, photo books, programs, and assorted trinkets.

The two women turned left and stopped just long enough for Ernie to pick up a program to record the usual: times, race lineups, results, and other pertinent notes. They headed out past the seating area to the sloping hill beyond the seats where there was a grassy area that followed the contour of the track. A few fans had already placed their lawn chairs or blankets and were talking quietly. This is the place that Ernie had talked about in the car, the place where she appreciated the "insulation" that it afforded. In the stands, some fans might not be as tolerable at four o'clock as they were at noon. Not as many fans chose to sit here, and that increased the likelihood of a more pleasant day.

They set their lawn chairs up and settled in for a long afternoon. Ernie began writing in her program while Janet looked through the Sunday newspaper that she brought from home. Most of the cars had been unloaded from their trailers, and mechanics were going about their usual routines. For some reason, Chuck had been forced to set up in a different spot. He usually preferred to be in the center or closer to turn one. He was nearly in front of Janet and Ernie, although perhaps two hundred yards away from their place on the hill outside the track.

Janet could see Chuck, Tom, Donny, and Billy all milling around the race car. Donny was busy with something on the front axle and the other three men seemed to be talking easily and intermittently. Billy was in his driving uniform (the word "uniform" stretches that word—more like a workman's coveralls) for the first time in six weeks. He was cleaning his goggles and the flip-up face shield on his helmet. The first warm-up session would start in about fifteen minutes. The field of thirty-two cars had been divided into three groups of about ten cars each. Chuck had drawn the first warm-up session and the third qualifying spot for Billy. Not bad. That would give Billy a little seat time and a good opportunity to qualify well. The track should still be in good shape for him.

Two young girls, barely into their twenties, put a blanket on the slope about five feet in front of Janet and Ernie. This did not present a problem, but it raised some questions in Janet's mind. These girls have dates? Where are they? What will their guys be like? Or are they alone? Why would two pretty young girls come to a dusty race track?

The girls were nicely dressed, in white shorts (at a dirt track race, Janet mused), pretty, flowered blouses and white (again!) Keds. They seemed to have a well-developed, close friendship. Their conversation was easy and confidential. Janet didn't listen for details but just observed the general tenor of their relationship. Long-time friends from school, co-workers with a close friendship, cousins? They knew each other well and liked each other. They enjoyed each other's company, smiling and talking, not looking straight ahead, but intimately engaging face to face. Nice to watch. *Must have a lot in common*, Janet thought.

"Wake up there, Janet! Bout time for Billy to saddle up for the first time in many, many weeks. He's strappin' hisself into Chuck's car!" Ernie broke into Janet's thoughts.

Janet looked down to the pit area and could see that Billy was in the car, helmet and goggles on and testing his belts and harness by slightly leaning forward, straining against the belts and then swaying left and right. Chuck stood to his left, and Tom and Donny stood behind the car, hands on the roll bar, ready to push the car up to the edge of the track . About a dozen cars were in this first hot lap session, and a few were idling slowly around the track as others joined them. Clods of dirt flew off the rear tires, straight up about six or seven feet. Each newly started engine added to the lazy growl of the pack of cars. The starter was waiting until all the cars in this session were started and all push trucks cleared of the track. Billy got his start and joined the other cars on the track.

When the green flag flew, instantly all the cars seemed to jump from forty miles per hour to eighty. The rear tires clawed at the dirt and flung clods over the guardrails, sometimes even reaching the first row of seats. The track was damp and sticky from a Saturday night rainstorm. This, together with the relatively high banks, gave the cars great traction. This place on a day like this could be extremely fast for a dirt track. Many dirt tracks have little banking so half mile lap times are usually around twenty-three to twenty-five seconds. But on these banks eighteen second laps were the norm, very similar to paved high-banked tracks like Winchester.

Most of the drivers stayed in the middle of the track. A few ran low towards the inside, but none ventured up toward the guard rails. When a cushion developed later, that would attract some, but not just yet.

Billy got up to speed quickly, but after four laps several cars had passed him. Ernie and Janet could not make themselves understood above the engine noise, but glanced at each other and shrugged a "Huh?" when Billy suddenly pulled toward the inside of the track on the backstretch and slowed down. He coasted toward Chuck's pit, engine off.

Janet said, "What's that about? Four laps and he shut off?"

"I'd love to be down there to hear that conversation. I got no idea. Engine problem?" Ernie was just guessing.

As soon as Billy pulled in, Chuck, Tom, and Donny surrounded the car. Billy was talking animatedly, moving his hands the way drivers do, trying to explain something about the car. Chuck and Tom walked to the trailer where Chuck kept his spare tires, talking all the way.

"Must be handling. When a guy starts that hand-stuff, the car doesn't feel right to him," said Ernie. From this distance, Janet and Ernie could only guess what was going on.

Then Billy unbuckled, took off his helmet, and stepped out of the car. The two ladies then saw Chuck walk toward the officials. The starter put out the red flag to bring the first warm up session to an end. Quiet gradually returned as the cars coasted in, some with engines off, others with drivers punching the throttles to keep the engines running. Ernie, using her binoculars, watched her husband as he talked with an official. Both men nodded, turned, and walked away. Janet could see that Tom was standing near the trailer and Chuck's pick-up truck. Donny had the hood up on the race car and had a jack out and positioned at the back of the car. Billy was sitting on the back of the trailer. Then Chuck and Tom went and stood beside the pick-up truck, exchanging a few quick comments.

"What is going on?" Janet wondered out loud.

She got a partial answer to her question when she saw that Tom was walking toward the race car, helmet in hand, now wearing some kind of jacket with a number and an oil company name on the back.

"Oh, crap! Tom's getting in the car. He told me this would be a piece-of-cake day, he wouldn't drive today!"

Ernie cautioned, "Well, let's just see, Janet. Maybe Tom's just…Well, just wait."

Chuck had leaned on the officials to let Tom feel the car out for Billy. Tom ran the whole second hot lap session of twelve laps. He passed two cars and looked smooth. The track was a little torn up, especially in turn one where a rut appeared in the middle of the track. A little cushion began to build up about six or seven feet away from the guardrail. When Tom drove into the pit area, Billy, Donny, and Chuck gathered around as he sat in the car and took off his helmet. After a little talk and more hand motions, Chuck leaned closely to Tom and said something. Tom got out of the car, walked back to the trailer, and picked out a new wheel. Donny began to jack up the right rear of the car, and proceeded to change that tire. Billy again got ready for the last hot lap session.

Billy looked a little better in the last session. He didn't pass any other cars, but he didn't get passed either. Tom's role must have been as either counselor or test pilot. That was about all Janet and Ernie could guess from experience and long-distance observation. It must have done some good. Billy's time trial draw was third to go out. The track was still good although the slight breeze and sun had begun to dry it out. Billy ran a 19.71, which might put him in the third heat, a so-so time.

Janet relaxed knowing that Tom would most likely not be driving today. She could look around and be more of a spectator and not participant. She again let her attention turn to the young girls in front of her. She began to get the impression from their discussion that they were more than just casual fans. One of the girls said, "Will is in that same car he drove here last year. They just took the cage off so they could run it here today."

"That's kind of okay, ya know. At least he knows what he's got. Kenny somehow hooked up with that car owner out of Dayton. He's got that old car, must be going on fifteen years old, that used to be really good, but now, well…it's old. But at least it's a real race car, not some old jalopy," her friend said. "Oh, look, Kenny's going out to qualify."

Both girls had full attention on the track now, following the car for the driver's warm-up lap and two laps against the clock. They sat more upright and attentive. In about a minute or so, Kenny's turn was over. He ended with fast lap of 21.8. The girls clapped like they were at a high school baseball game, and a cute boy just got a hit that put him on first. Kenny's friend kind of bounced with excitement and wrote his time on something.

"Not bad for a forty-hour-a-week welder, don't ya think?"

"Let's hope Will does good, too. Don't want a cranky boyfriend."

As it turned out, he didn't do "good" as she hoped. Will timed too slow to be assigned to a heat race, and his only hope was that he could reach the feature race through the consolation race. It could happen, but not likely.

Neither Ernie or Janet knew the girls or drivers. They must have been local guys, and these girls were too young to know what Janet and Ernie had learned. This isn't high school sports, and they may have to find that out the hard way. Nevertheless, Janet enjoyed watching them and their youthful innocence.

Billy would start fourth in the third heat. To transfer to the feature, he just had to hold his place in the seven-car field.

Seemed like a sure thing. But things didn't work out that way. He got a poor start, never recovered, and had to run the consolation race, in which he would start eighth. The top four cars in that field of sixteen would then start in the thirty-lap feature.

The consolation race was made up of those cars that did not finish higher than fourth in their heat races. Four slow racers who didn't qualify for the heat races were added to make a field of sixteen. This was a "last chance" to get into the "money" race. This at times made for desperate racing. The race was set for twelve laps, and the first six places at least would get a crack at the feature race.

Janet and Ernie watched as Billy drove a steady, unspectacular race to finish fifth. He got some lucky breaks when one car didn't answer the "Roll 'em out!" order from the starter. This moved him up to seventh starting position. On the third lap of the race, a yellow and white car spun and stopped in the third turn, and Billy took advantage of the situation when the car directly in front of him, the "Will" of the young girl, had to slow and take evasive action to miss the spinning car. Billy passed him before they completed the lap and claimed fifth place. The race resumed after two caution laps, and Billy held that position to the checkered flag. That gave Billy fifth place and that translated to starting seventeenth in the eighteen-car field, inside row nine. Not the same Billy Wallace as six weeks ago, but at least he had a challenge ahead of him in the feature race. The driver sharing the last row with him was the "Kenny" boyfriend.

There was usually a fifteen or twenty-minute period of down time after the last preliminary race and before the start of the feature, time that allowed crews to finish any last-minute car preparation. Fans would make restroom visits, get another hot dog, beer, popcorn, soda for the kids. The PA announcer, often a local TV sports reporter, would chat with a driver or two who agreed to come up from the track to the announcers' booth. Kids would work their way down to the fence separating the track from the stands. Some would take pictures, others would just hang their hands on the fence and gaze at the cars. Many hoped that when the cars were pushed to their assigned places on the grid, that they could beg an autograph. That almost never happened. One autograph would attract a horde of kids and create more of a distraction. Most crews and drivers were focused on the task at hand: getting mechanically and mentally prepared for thirty laps of racing. A few drivers were standing near turn one, probably trying to predict track conditions after five, ten, fifteen, twenty-five laps.

Janet just sat and relaxed as a wife whose husband was not racing could. She had seen this many times, knew many drivers and their wives and families, knew what could happen, knew that she had to accept that, or just move on. Janet and Ernie had become part of this life and to them it was just that, a part of life—natural and normal, at least to them. Outsiders could not understand this: how can you accept that a roster of perhaps thirty to forty men in April might be fatally reduced by one, or sometimes more, come season's end?

As she looked at the two young girls in front of her, she wondered if they really understood. They looked to be perhaps six or seven years older than her daughter. "Babes" she thought to herself (meaning "so young" not "so sexy"), they can't know yet. Might as well be school girls.

"Wake up, Janet! You dozing? Ain't said much," Ernie broke in on Janet's musing. "Chuck and Donny are pushin' the car up. They'll be about in front of us here. Billy startin' way in the back ain't a bad thing the way I see it. Probably irks him a bunch, but he's not been in a car for a long time. Give him a chance to sort of ease back into it. And put some challenges in front of him. Them cars at the back may be easy pickin's for him."

"I doubt he sees it that way," Janet replied. "We'll see how good that arm is. Billy won't let on a thing about it, but I think Tom will know." She and Tom exchanged long-distance waves when they made eye-contact. Then Janet settled in to watch the crazy spectacle that so held her husband's attention.

The white convertible pace car pulled away and the first few rows of cars followed, engines coughing to life after a few yards of pushing. One of the cars did not start, reducing the field to seventeen. During several formation laps, eager drivers punched the throttle and swerved right and left trying to get a feel for the track. Then the field made a last preliminary parade lap, and the drivers waved to the crowd, and the fans waved back and remained standing for the start.

The pace car pulled off the track and the field was ready

for the start. As the cars rounded the north turn, they began to accelerate and the engine roar grew. When they left turn four and entered the straightaway, the starter unfurled the green flag and the roar rose to outright thunder. The noise abated slightly as seventeen four-hundred horsepower cars were thrown into turn one.

Connors started inside row one and used that position to his advantage, driving high in the first turn. C.J. in the blue number five fell in line behind Connors, parking his right rear Firestone diamond tread tire on the ridge of clay that marked the cushion. Smitty, starting third, and James Warren in the black number twenty held their places, side by side, as they went through turns one and two. Bud Brown, a midwestern "fair circuit" champion, got an excellent start from eighth, passing two cars, and took fifth place coming out of turn two. Walt Bowers in number six followed Brown. West Coast racer Roger Castle followed in seventh. Johnny Miller was in eighth. As the leaders started their second lap, a local driver named Nixon was struggling with inexperience or an ill-handling car. He entered turn one very low and drifted up from the bottom of the track, nearly clipping the outside wall as he exited turn two. Billy Wallace took a high line on lap two, passing two cars that started in front of him. The "Kenny" of the girls trailed the field.

Many racers drove high on the track, but some experimented with different lines through the turns, using the middle of the track. One tried a low groove with some success. Connors, C.J., and Smitty held their places in nose-to-tail order, just a few feet from each other. Brown passed Warren, diving low in turn three and drifting in front of the black number twenty as they exited turn four, gaining fourth place. Castle passed Bowers on the back stretch.

At the beginning of lap three, Billy passed two cars that

bounced off each other and slowed. That put him in thirteenth place. *Best to make progress early in the race, field's not all strung out. And this arm ain't a hundred percent,* Billy thought.

The field began to stretch out in laps four through eight. The first six or seven drivers used much the same line, aiming for the middle of the track entering turns one and three and letting their cars drift high on the cushion, exiting two and four. Connors and C.J. held their spots, but Brown passed Smitty for third place. Castle took advantage of Warren who caught a rut in turn one, his car lurching over on its right-side wheels. Warren regained control, but slewed up into the loose dirt above the cushion. His black car wallowed in the deep dirt, scrubbing off speed. Castle dove low on the banking and under the struggling Warren to take fifth place. Billy found a higher groove to his liking, passed another car, and took twelfth place.

Janet was always awed by a race like this. She didn't know where to look because it seemed as if there were action and drama everyplace on the track. One pair of eyes could not take it all in, at least now when all drivers seemed to be risking so much. A haze of brown dust rose up over the entire track, hovering in the air, swirling in clouds as the cars passed under. Her eyes began to itch and burn from the dust and fumes.

On lap nine, the blue number twenty-four that started in front of Kenny spun in turn three. Kenny in the old red number thirty-three steered high and slightly grazed the wall with his right front wheel. His girlfriend stood up and clutched at her friend's arm. Seeing that he was alright, she sat down, relieved. Perhaps she learned a small lesson.

Several laps were run under caution, all cars slowing and maintaining position. The blue car was retrieved by the wrecker and retired to the pits.

When the green flag came out to start lap thirteen,

C.J. timed his restart slightly better and passed Connors in turn one. Connors tucked in close behind. C.J., took a different line entering turn three, staying high on the banking. Perhaps the track there held a bit of moisture and so better grip. He started to pull out a little lead on Connors. Castle passed Smitty on the backstretch. When they passed her, Janet could hear that Smitty's engine did not sound quite right. On lap fifteen, Billy passed a car in turn four, moving him into eleventh place. Janet thought, *Not bad, Billy not bad.*

During the next five laps, most remained in position, although the leaders began to lap the tail-enders, making for fan confusion and moving obstacles to be passed. Kenny was becoming one of those obstacles. The starter waved the "move-over" flag, meaning he should drive to the inside and allow faster cars to pass. His inexperience showed as he struggled to get out of the way. Drivers often could make use of slower cars, using them to improve position. That was how Brown moved up on C.J. and Connors, who were stuck behind the erratic Kenny. By lap twenty, those three cars were just yards apart, driving high on the track, their right rear wheels just a few feet from the guardrail. As the cars began lap twenty-one, Brown drove lower in turn one to pass. Just as he did that, the track lights all flashed red.

Nixon, the local driver in car ninety-seven, was being lapped by Bowers in the black and white number six exiting turn four. Bowers went to pass on the inside, just as Nixon veered sharply left. Nixon grazed Bowers car, bounced off to the right, and hit the wall. Nixon's car did several quick snap rolls. Bowers' steering was damaged by the contact, his car angled toward the inside of the track, and stopped near the inside of turn one. Bowers unstrapped his belts and climbed out. The rest of the field slowed and stopped near the exit of turn four, close to where Janet and Ernie sat.

Janet saw men run to the car lying on its side, the driver motionless, still held by his belts, his arms and head lying on the dirt. She saw Tom running to the car. The two young girls stood with their hands over their mouths.

"That was not good, Janet. Those were quick, high speed rolls," Ernie said matter-of-factly.

All Janet could say was, "Uh huh."

They could talk now that it was quiet, but did not have a lot to say. It is always surprising how quickly a race track gets quiet when this happens. The sudden absence of engine noise combined with the concerned quiet of the four or five thousand fans contrasted strangely with the previous noisy chaos.

Emergency crews arrived quickly and tended to Nixon, placed him on a gurney and put him in the ambulance. The crowd of officials, mechanics, and wrecker crew tended to the clean-up. A crowd of kids hung on the fence. Janet hated to see that—kids at an accident scene.

The accident clean-up and restart took about thirty minutes. Janet saw Tom walking back to Chuck, Donny, and Billy, all gathered around the race car. The announcer called out for the push-trucks to restart the racers. Some drivers stepped back to their cars, strapped in, pulled on helmets and gloves and prepared for the last laps of the race. Some had never gotten out. This could be like shuffling a deck of cards: engines cool down and may not run as they did just thirty minutes ago; tires lose their heat and harden, changing grip; drivers may lose the rhythm that they had developed. Usually, accidents don't bother drivers. This is a profession, and they have a job to do.

When the race restarted, Brown continued to experiment with the lower groove, but did not move up close enough to threaten to pass Connors and C.J. Laps twenty-two through twenty-seven saw the remaining cars all maintaining position.

All except for Smitty. His engine continued to worsen and he lost two positions, dropping him to seventh.

On lap twenty-eight, Brown made his move, passing Connors in the middle of the track as they entered turn one. Connors stayed in the high groove, using the little bit of cushion that remained. On the next lap, C.J. moved to the middle to protect his lead after Brown showed the nose of his car in turn three. As the two cars passed the flagman, the white flag indicated that they were on their last lap. C.J. moved to the middle of the track to block Brown, but Brown went back to the top of the track, found just enough traction and took the lead. That was the way they finished: Brown, C.J., Connors followed by Castle, Warren, Miller, Smitty, and Billy—in eighth—who had picked off one more car in those last three laps.

Brown slowed and pulled his car up sideways on the front stretch for the honors: trophy, interview, pretty girl, autographs, and handshakes. The other drivers stood by their cars in the pits, wiping dirt and sweat from their faces with shop rags and taking cotton plugs out of their ears. Most lit a cigarette and sipped a can of beer to restore some calm.

Chuck and Tom congratulated Billy on his race when he pulled into his pit. Donny slapped him on the back and gave him a cold beer. Billy said, "I guess that was okay." He released his belts, got out of the car, and walked to the trailer.

"Okay you say? You started way back there, passed, what five or six cars, finished eighth?" Chuck tried to make his point. "You ain't raced in six weeks! Not bad, son, not bad! I'm happy!"

Billy sat slumping on a stack of tires, head down. He rubbed his arm. "Yeah. I heal fast so it can only get better."

"I think you did a good job today, Billy. Can you sign this for me?" said a young woman, holding out a program for an autograph.

Billy sat up a little straighter and smiled. "How do you want me to sign this, like 'To'? Uh, what now what would be your name, miss?"

"Here's a little piece of paper that has my name on it. You can see, Roxanna there, but most people call me Roxie. Just write 'To Roxie' and whatever you like. Oh, and just keep the card. It's got my phone number on it, you see?"

Tom, Chuck, and Donny just smiled. Janet and Ernie walked up and offered their congratulations to Billy. "Nice job, Hotshot," said Ernie in her usual brash manner. Janet smiled at Billy. Then Billy turned back to Roxie and several other fans, not all quite as promising as she seemed to be. But Billy was professional, signed autographs, chatted and thanked all his fans. "He's learning," Janet said to Ernie.

* * * * *

Thirty minutes later, the crowd thinned out and the guys began to load the car and equipment on the trailer. Ernie rode home with Chuck and Donny. Tom and Janet drove away in the family car. Janet was the first to speak as they got on the highway. "You had me goin' there for a while when you took over the car. What was that about?"

"Oh, Billy thought the car wasn't right. So, I was the 'test driver' for Chuck."

"And?" asked Janet.

"And…I found it was just fine, handled great. Billy must have got a little 'shorter' over the last few weeks. His 'short-man syndrome' needed some stoking," Tom said, half smiling.

"Must have been more than that. I saw Chuck changed the right rear tire."

"It was a different tire, yes, but it was exactly the same tire: diameter, diamond tread Firestone, same width, same hardness. Brand new tire just like the one we took off! But…I told Billy that he was right, that maybe another tire would help.

I did not lie, you see," Tom laughed.

"So that was just a little 'head tinkering', in other words," said Janet.

"Yeah, Chuck's been around a lot of drivers and knows how to adjust more than cars," Tom said.

"Spose he ever tinkered with your head, Tom?"

"Now that's a good one, Janet, that's a good one. No body messes with my head!"

"Think so, Tom? You really think so?" Janet looked sideways at Tom and smirked.

"Tell you what, Janet, I think in the future, I'll let professionals handle accident aftermath, if at all possible. That guy will be okay, I think. Seein' a man on the gurney is not a pretty sight! I hope to never see that again."

Both sensing a change of subject was in order, they began small talk—the coming week, Tina's plans for the rest of summer, the service station business, Janet's job. They rode along quietly until they turned up the lane to their home.

Chapter 5

Tom looked over scattered papers and receipts on his desk. James had left a few notes. One said he would be a little late, but did not explain. Another was about a customer who wanted a new muffler and tail pipe put on his car. That was old man Carson out in Twin Creeks. Twin Creeks, two miles away, was even smaller than Barton. It had been by-passed by the railroad back in the late 1800's. Barton got the railroad, Twin Creeks didn't. And as everyone joked, that's what made Barton so successful, allowing it to grow to its amazing population of two thousand one hundred twenty-three. And little Twin Creeks ended up with the derogatory nickname "Twinkies."

Old man Carson lived in Twin Creeks and wanted his exhaust system fixed. Carson ran up a bill that he tried to make payments on. Tom didn't make a big deal about it. He knew Carson didn't have a lot of money. People said he had a disability pension from the army in World War I. Tom remembered his mom saying once, in a hushed and confidential tone, that he had "shell shock." Tom didn't know what that meant until he was a senior in high school. His government teacher was one of those teachers whom students loved to lure off topic. It was one of those days that some kid asked the perfect question to avoid the boring lesson that they all knew was coming. That was when Tom learned about shell shock, and that many people thought it indicated cowardice. When Tom was much younger, he was fishing in one of the creeks that Twin Creeks is named for. Old man Carson was walking along the creek bank and passed Tom. The old man and ten-year old Tom looked at each other. Carson's eyes were all watery and red looking and downright spooky. *Is that the look of shell shock some forty-plus years after the war?* he wondered.

Later he learned that perhaps Carson handled shell shock with alcohol. That explained the red, watery eyes. Some people said that Carson was a ditch digger, and that's all he was good for. Tom remembered that his dad said he once hired him for just that kind of work. He wanted to dig a ditch to drain a field into a stream. He said after about thirty minutes of digging, he was ready to quit for the day, but old Carson just kept going, steady and even for another hour and a half, finishing three-fourths of the ditch by himself. Tom often thought about that teacher's lesson about shell shock, World War I and the trenches. *Trenches, the war, shell shock, and Carson's a good ditch digger now, Gotta wonder.*

Carson's car was an old '31 Model A Ford, two-door sedan. He seldom drove it. Probably wasn't sober enough to drive it very often, though that didn't seem to stop him. James' note said that he could drive Carson home after the old man dropped his car off. *Well, James,* he wondered, *why not let the old man hang around here (which would not be the most comfortable situation—Carson is weird and has an unsettling effect on people with that watery, red-eyed stare of his) or, more likely, let him walk down to Bennies for a few hours?*

As promised, James arrived about thirty minutes late, and Tom then understood much more about his eagerness to drive Carson home, or to drive anyone, anytime, anywhere when he got the opportunity. James waved, honked his car horn, parked in the side gravel lot, and stepped out of a car, an old black '46 Ford coupe. The only thing brighter than the white-sidewall tires was the smile on his face.

Tom said, "I tried to tell you James, but you wouldn't listen to me would you?"

"No, sir. Ain't she a beaut?" James could not stop smiling.

"Well, at least, I can count on you now," Tom said.

"What do you mean?"

"Your dad gonna give you gas money, pay the insurance, fix it when it breaks? The way I see it, those things are all up to you. I know your dad fairly well," Tom explained, "and he'll let you take care of it all. You've got to earn that money yourself, right?"

"I don't care, Tom. I can do it. And I know a place where I can work on it!"

"Oh, really? And where would that be?" Tom just smiled.

· · · · ·

About eleven o'clock Monday morning, Chuck Williams called. "Tom, how you doin' today? Busy over there, serving the public and rakin' in all the rewards of private enterprise?"

"Just like you, Chuck, 'cept I don't have to drive noisy kids to school, then fix buses so I can drive them to school again the next day," Tom joked back.

Tom was thinking to himself, *What's this about. Billy's his driver, that's understood by all of us. I don't relish the thought of going along as paid help. Maybe he's got a line on another car for me.*

Then Chuck spelled out his plan. "This coming weekend, I'm takin' the car out to Langhorne for the Twin Fifties. Now, you know that track…."

Tom interrupted, "Not well. Only drove there twice and…."

Chuck continued, "So you know enough about that place. It is downright brutal! Some guys are hanging half way out of their cars after just forty laps. Tremendous speed. Dusty and all rutted up! You see Billy rubbin' that arm after the race yesterday?

"Yeah, I noticed that," Tom replied.

"I don't think there's any way in hell he can drive a hundred laps, even if they do split it into two fifties. So, here's what I want to do. Mind you, I'm not gonna mention any of this to Billy. And, again I know I'm askin' a lot, Tom. How 'bout you go along, as back-up? Then after that first fifty, you get in and finish the second half? Billy don't have to know all of this. He'll probably be as mad as hell, but I'll deal with that."

"Langhorne is one hell of a long haul from here. We'd have to leave Saturday. That's two days away from the station for me."

"You got that kid, right? He can pump gas, right?" Chuck asked.

"But a kid in charge for two days? He needs money now, but I'm not sure how I feel about him bein' all alone there for a weekend. Course, Janet will probably stay home. She'd be there in case of a problem," Tom knew this opportunity could help him, too.

"Motel, meals, whatever, I'll take care of it. And here's the rest of my offer. Billy, like most other drivers, gets forty percent of winnings. I'll give you half of my sixty percent for his finish in the first fifty," Chuck offered. "I want to make this work. You drive that second fifty, and I'll give you fifty percent of winnings. Course, Billy don't know I'm takin him out, so we gotta play that cool, ya see."

"All right, Chuck. I'm gonna have to sell this plan to Janet and James. Janet knows all about the 'Horne' and the repu-tation that place has. I had made some 'sort-of 'promises to my daughter, so that won't go well. And James, he just got a car and you know what that means to a young pup. He won't be too fired up about working the whole weekend. But, this is my deal, and I'm in. We'll talk again, how 'bout Thursday?"

"You're on, Tom. I'm gonna start on the car tonight."

· · · · ·

James and Tom settled in for a Monday of routine work at the station. Old Mrs. Faulkner came in around eight and said she wanted her car washed. She had a car that James thought was just the oddest thing he had ever seen, but Tom knew it had more character than the boy could understand.

"Just what in the heck is a Graham?" James asked Tom once.

"You talkin' about Mrs. Faulkner's car? I tell you what, that is a rare one. That was her husband's car. He was a salesman and drove that thing all over when he worked for Thompson Products. He was their rep in this part of the Midwest," Tom explained. "That is a 1936 Graham Businessman's Coupe. Supercharged six cylinder. Made about a hundred and ten horsepower, which was pretty darn good for that time. A Ford about that same time had maybe ninety horsepower."

Mr. Faulkner had died just after the war and she just kept his old car, driving it around town—church, grocery, and so forth. She probably put on a few thousand miles in fifteen years all within a three-mile radius. Tom thought that car could probably find its own way around the town, like the milkman's horse.

"Well, she wants it washed and the oil changed, and she don't want to wait, so I'll drive her home. I'll take her in my car!" James offered.

"Keep her comfortable. Drive her in her own car. She would prefer it that way, I think. Anyway, that's a good way to warm up the oil. Just treat that car with kid gloves, OK, hot rod?" Tom advised.

James returned in fifteen minutes with the old Graham. "Something's wrong, Tom. That engine has a funny sound, sort of a whir or low whine. Funny sound," James said.

"That's the supercharger, son. That's what I told you about before. So now you know. Even your old Ford doesn't have that. Treat that car with respect. Its days are numbered. If I had the resources, I'd buy it. But do you see me makin' a lot of money here? I can't be a collector. Hey, why don't you change the oil in the pit first, then wash it. I got to use the lift to put that muffler on Carson's car," Tom said.

"Aw, Tom, the pit?" complained James. "I hate that old hole! Can't I use the lift?"

"Do it the way I said. If you wash the car first, you'll be standing in the slop down there when you change the oil!"

James grumbled, but drove the car into the old service bay, while Tom got Carson's Model A out of the parking lot. The clutch grabbed and made the car lurch. The old, unmuffled engine sounded like a farm tractor. But Tom got the car up on the hydraulic lift, raised it up, and took a quick look at the job. He got out his half-inch drive socket wrench—he called it a "nut buster"—and proceeded to try to loosen up the rusty old clamps that held the exhaust pipe and muffler together. He was just about to give up and cut it all off with a hacksaw, when he decided perhaps one more twist of the wrench might do the job. The wrench slipped, Tom lurched and reached to steady himself. His left hand gripped a rusty, sharp piece of the metal, and ripped a deep gash in his left palm.

"Damn, damn, damn!" he shouted as blood immediately dripped to the floor. He knew that a band aid would not fix this. "James, got a problem here!"

James heard the cussing and tried to get out of the pit as soon as possible. When he got to the other service bay, Tom was wrapping his hand in a shop rag. "Crap, boss! That's bad!"

"Don't I know, James, don't I know. In so many ways," Tom just mused." You're in charge, Jimmy. I got to get this fixed. Doc's in today, if he's back from the hospital, I suppose."

Tom drove off, shop rag already soaking red. At least he didn't have far to drive and much traffic to deal with. Small towns can be convenient once in a while. Holding the steering wheel with his knee and shifting with his right hand, he got to Dr. Elsner's office in just a few minutes. Forty-five minutes and fifteen stitches later, Tom was back at the station. James had the oil change done on Mrs. Faulkner's car, but little else. He was gassing up Roger Hicks' car. Tom thought, *Great! That twerp gets wind of this and he won't let it go!* So, he drove right on by the station and out of town, killing time until Hicks would be on his way.

Ten minutes later, Tom parked in the station side lot and walked into the service bay. "James, get that hack saw off the bench. Come here. I want you to saw that damn pipe off right here. Put those gloves on and go to work. The wash job can wait a while. You're gonna be my mechanic for a little while."

The job really didn't take more than an hour. Cutting was simpler than trying to unbolt rusted, stubborn old clamps. "This is the way *you should* have done it, idiot!" Tom scolded himself.

This complicated the plans he had just made with Chuck, as if they weren't complicated enough already. He had to beg off the promise he had made to Tina. Their plan was to take the horse down to Gloria Anderson's place on Saturday, but that was out of the question now. He would have to leave for Langhorne on Saturday. Langhorne was close to Philadelphia, meaning a twelve-hour drive, plus or minus, who knows how long. So, Tina would not be happy, and who could blame her. Tom had "sort-of" promised her.

And Janet would not be happy. She wouldn't want to pull a horse trailer seventy some miles, and back. Furthermore, she would probably like to stay close to home, in case there would be a problem at the station. Then there was the reputation of Langhorne. If sprint car racing is dangerous, multiply that many times to comprehend the danger of that kind of car on the dirt mile of Langhorne.

Chuck would not be happy with another less than one hundred percent driver. There were only a few good things about Tom's injury: it was on his left hand and it was on the palm, if that could be called good. At least, by Saturday, maybe he could remove the wrapping from around his hand and replace it with some kind of pad or bandage on his palm. It might not look so bad that way. And he'd wear gloves. Tom knew that he could hide any discomfort, and maybe Chuck wouldn't pick up on anything. Once he was in the race car, he was in his world and in control. So, what if fifty laps later it was aching and bloody? Those fifty laps would only take about twenty-five or thirty minutes, anyway, and nobody ever bled to death from a cut hand. He would hold out a little on Janet, too. He would tell her that he was just riding out there with Chuck and Donny to lend some extra help. *That's really not a lie, right?* That was his plan.

Tom and James finished up Carson's old Ford, let the lift down, and backed it out of the service bay. James went back to Mrs. Faulkner's old Graham while Tom drove the Ford out to Twin Creeks to Carson's house. He would have to trust old Carson to be sober enough to drive him back to the station. He had not said a word to James about the weekend. No telling what James would do with that information. If he shot his mouth off about having to work all weekend, and if that got home to the girls before he got home, that would not help Tom's case. He'd have to talk to James about it soon, just to let the boy plan ahead. Maybe late Tuesday. But he'd have to deal with Janet and Tina tonight.

At the end of the day, Tom returned Mrs. Faulkner's car and James followed in his "new" Ford.

After they dropped off the Graham, Tom said, "James, let me drive your car, just to check it out." Tom drove deliberately, listening to the engine, transmission, and brakes, trying to feel the car out for potential problems. And he used the time to let James know that he needed his cooperation. "James, this injury—I've got reasons to keep it kind of secret. Can you help me with that?"

"Sure, it's between you and me," he paused. "Ya know, Mr. Lawton, for a race car driver, you drive kinda funny," James observed when they got back to the station.

"What do you mean?" Tom said, puzzled and amused.

"Well, you don't drive very fast. I figured you'd want to go everywhere fast, ya know?"

"On the race track I feel fairly safe. I know those other guys pretty well, what they'll do and so forth. But on the streets there's sixteen-year-old beginners, some drunks, some grandmas and grandpas that ought not be driving, people messin' with their radios, overloaded farm trucks…and what else do I have to put on my list? Do you get my point?"

"Yeah, but you race so fast…."

"Speed ain't always the biggest thing, James. Gotta have brains, too." They pulled in to the station and Tom got out of James' car. He stood beside the car, looking it over front to back. "James, this is really not such a bad first car for you. Just don't do crazy stuff. You need to keep that in mind. Stuff can happen. I lost a friend once when I was a kid, so…, "his voice trailed off.

"Ah, Mr. Lawton. I know. I'll be careful. Say, uh, your daughter, Tina, she's gonna be a what, sophomore next year, right?"

"Yeah, why?" Tom asked.

"Oh, just wonderin', you know, tryin' to figure out her age and all and…uh…well…Goodnight, Mr. Lawton. I'll see you in the morning. Take care of that hand!"

Tom thought to himself, *Just what is that kid thinking? Perhaps I don't want to know.* He closed the station and drove himself home to deliver the news.

When Tom drove up the lane, he could see Tina out in the field with her horse. She waved to him in an eager way. Much can be expressed by such a "big" wave. And that wave meant that Tina was doing well today. That would make this task so much harder. He hated himself for what he knew he had to do soon. He parked his truck and walked up to the pasture fence.

"Dad, watch. Mrs. Anderson told me to do this for a few days, and Candy would quickly learn. I didn't believe it, but she was right. The first lesson was to just lead the horse by three or four feet. Make the horse respect that distance, don't let her crowd you. That's your space and she can't come in unless you want her to." Tina walked, the horse followed three feet behind. She stopped, the horse stopped three feet behind. The young girl was so proud of such a simple thing.

"That old hay-burner actually learned that?" Tom teased. "Or did the horse teach *you* that?"

"Dad, you old goat!"

"Them's strong words, little lady," Tom said in his corny John Wayne imitation.

"Hey, Dad, that old car went by here a couple times today," Tina said, pointing to a black coupe driving by the farm. "Who is that?"

"Not sure," Tom replied but he knew who it was. That would be James, showing off his pride and joy. "Your mom home yet?" He turned to walk away.

"No, she called. Said she'd be a little late. She has some things to get at the grocery," Tina turned back to her horse. "I'll be in later, Dad."

Tom smiled at his daughter and walked up to the house,

thinking about how and when to break the news to his two girls. Today or later this week? He went into the kitchen, opened the fridge, and got a beer. He walked through the front room, out onto the porch, sat down in the swing, and waited for Janet to get home.

*   *   *   *   *

Chuck Williams was in the race car part of his shop after he had put in his regular day. He drove his morning route and got back to the shop around nine o'clock. One bus, the oldest one that belonged to the school, needed a tune-up and routine maintenance. That took until around mid-afternoon, working right through, with lunch on the run. Donny handled the few gas customers that stopped. Most knew this was a repairs garage and not all that interested in selling gas, so they usually looked for cheaper gas. Chuck got called out in the afternoon for wrecker service. There was an accident on State Route 29 and the highway patrol called for him to tow the car in. He got back home around half past five. After a little "how was your day" chat with Ernie, Chuck was out in the shop, ready to start working on the race car.

Chuck had just ordered a "granny," a seat that had a tab on the right side a little less than shoulder high. Langhorne was nearly a circle. There were no real straight parts so the cars were in a constant turn. The centrifugal forces generated by those speeds exhausted drivers. That tab on the right side would support the driver and conserve some of his energy. Fifty miles at nearly a hundred miles an hour left many drivers leaning out the right side of the car. This would be Billy's first race at Langhorne and, considering he was still nursing that arm, he could use the extra comfort that this seat would provide. Chuck hoped it would be delivered in time, but he might have to just leave the old seat in the car.

The oiled dirt of Langhorne provided a number of

challenges for driver and mechanic alike. The oiled dirt would cling, especially causing a problem clogging up radiator vanes. Cooling was reduced and engines overheated. Chuck mounted an extra screen in front of the nose of the car to collect some of the dirt, although that was problematic; the screen could get clogged, allow less air to the radiator and still overheat the engine. But the screen would be easier to clean than the radiator.

He had to change the rear end gears. Chuck always ran a Halibrand rear end with a final drive ratio of 4.11, ring and pinion gear. That would not change. Chuck put an oil pan under the center section of the rear axle. Then he took the detachable plate off the center section, exposing the quick change gears. He ran the 5.04 gears at Eldora, but on a mile like Langhorne, he needed a higher gear so the engine would not hit peak RPM as quickly. After draining the oil, he put in "block out" gears that effectively matched the ratio of the rear end. This would be like driving a car in fourth gear instead of second. He wanted a "higher" gear, not a "lower" gear. Some called these "tall" gears, meant for longer tracks, like mile tracks. "Short" gears were meant for half mile tracks.

Years ago, when Donny was about fourteen, he was in the shop when Chuck was changing rear-end gears. He couldn't get through to the boy what he was doing.

"Donny, think of it like this. You got that ten speed bike out there. Do you start out in tenth gear?"

"Well, heck no. That's too hard. I usually start in third or something."

"That's right! You'd have to be Superman to start that bike in tenth gear," said Chuck.

"Yeah, but I can get going real fast, real quick, in second or third." Donny thought he made a great point.

"And tell me, Speedy, are your legs spinning like a fan blade?

How long you think you can keep that up?"

"So what? I can get a fast start!"

Chuck was determined to make his point. "OK, genius, let's try this. Take your bike, I'll take mine. We'll say the two gas pumps are the race track, and we go around them. You start out in second, I'll ride my plain old one-speed bike. We'll see what happens. Two laps!" At the ready-set-go command, Donny jumped out to a lead that Chuck could not overcome.

"OK, feelin' pretty good now aren't you? Now, this time we'll race all the way around the outside of the shop, two laps. You in second gear, me in plain old one-speed. No gear changing," Chuck said.

This time, Donny got a lead that he lost half way around the first lap, and Chuck won easily. "You see what I'm tellin' you? Pretend that first race was on a half mile track and the second one around the shop was on a mile track. That's why we change gears in the rear end. You need them high gears for long tracks, and low gears for half-miles."

"Well, why not just change gears like Dad does in his car? You know, push the clutch, move the gearshift?" asked Donny.

"We don't have transmissions in these cars. Look in here, kid," Chuck reached into the cockpit and pointed out the lever between where the driver's legs would be. "That's all you got. It's either in gear or out—no first, no second, no third. Just 'go' or 'no-go'. No transmission makes the car lighter and, just as important, there's one less thing to break."

"So why you tellin' me all that stuff about ten speed bikes?" Donny asked.

"Cause…well, come back here," Chuck led him to the back of the race car. "Get down on the floor here and look under the tail and between the rear wheels. See the rear axle and that lump right in the center? That's what some guys call the pumpkin. On the back of it is that shiny plate with the bolts on it. I take that plate off and there's two gears in there. I can put in a set of gears that will make the car run great on a half mile track, like around the gas pumps in our little race, or another set that is better for a mile track. Like our race around the shop."

That was a long time ago, and now Donny is his helper. He's twenty-one now, and thank God, has no desire to drive these things. His mother would blame Chuck for that, but Donny never said a word about driving. Maybe he's seen enough.

Chuck thought about slowing down the responsiveness of the steering. A half mile track requires quick and constant steering changes. Langhorne's big, constant turns were not as sharp as those of a half mile. He could change the location of the steering drag link on the Pitman arm, but thought that change could be made at the track on Sunday, depending on Billy's preference. That would be a very simple adjustment.

He looked at the tire rack and picked out two new eight-inch wide Firestone diamond treads. If he had to, he could swap them left to right after the first fifty lapper. The wheels were sixteen-inch Halibrands, front and rear. Chuck picked out a new six-inch ribbed tire for the right front and decided to leave the left front alone, and run it just as he had at Eldora. That tire seldom gets a lot of wear.

After a few hours, Chuck sat down in his lawn chair in the shop, wiped the grease off his hands with a shop towel, and glanced at the clock on the wall. "You work too late, old man," he said to himself. But he knew this wasn't work, this car was his toy, and just like a boy, time goes fast when you're having fun. Eleven o'clock wasn't far from five a.m., and he knew he had to rest. But he couldn't resist taking a shop rag to dust off the red car, just a little. Ernie would be fast asleep, so he'd have to take care not to wake her.

"Tomorrow night, I'll take a look at the engine. Change oil, plugs, and whatever. I only got five races on it, so it should be OK."

      • • • • •

As expected, Tom's weekend plans did not suit his wife well. It was not a cozy front porch swing that Monday night, and Tom ended up sitting by himself after a brief standoff. Most of what was said had already been said in one way or another many times over the last ten years. It had not been a high-volume confrontation, so Tina would not have gotten any idea about how the discussion impacted her. Tom would leave that for Janet to deal with on Tuesday. There would be two females unhappy with him. At least they could commiserate and be united in their frustration with him. He went into the house, opened a beer and sat down to watch whatever was on TV. Not many choices, but he really didn't care what was on.

      • • • • •

After the Eldora race, Billy rode back to Indianapolis with a mechanic and driver towing a race car. Billy sat in the back seat of the station wagon, opening beers and passing them up. Billy wasn't much of a drinker. One beer was his usual limit, or an occasional second one. He always liked to feel he was in control. It was a hundred-mile drive back to the garage area at the Speedway. Billy was still shacked up across Georgetown Road with some other drivers and their girlfriends and wives. By the time they got back and all unpacked, who knows what accommodations would be available. And despite his less than conventional upbringing, Billy did have some reservations about situations he might find himself in. *So, where do I go tonight?* he wondered.

The two front seat occupants got loosened up by the beers and the stories got longer and more convoluted, and slowly evolved into mostly fiction. The mechanic would start a story about something that happened in California, the driver would chime in with "Oh, yeah, and then...." They went on and on, talking, laughing, and calling, "Billy! Beer!" When they ran a red light, Billy volunteered to drive the rest of the way and the mechanic happily took over "cooler duty" in the back seat. The two got as far as the outskirts of Indy and passed out.

When they pulled up to the Speedway garage area, the mechanic and driver woke up and wandered off towards the gaggle of mobile homes and small houses on Georgetown Road. The mechanic muttered something to Billy about "Take care of stuff, see ya" and staggered away. Not sure of exactly what to do, Billy lay down in the back seat of the station wagon, and went to sleep.

· · · · ·

A little after nine o'clock on Monday morning, a nearly new red Pontiac Bonneville convertible drove into the Indianapolis Motor Speedway garage area. The radio was turned up, the top was down, and two men sat in the front seat. Billy, rousing himself in the back seat of the station wagon, recognized that the passenger was Eddie Spencer, but the driver was a stranger. It was the stranger who spoke up first. He had on a bright, Hawaiian shirt and a straw hat. His smile was about as wide as any Billy had ever seen. "Why, don't you think it's time to wake up, racer boy? And I do mean wake up, 'cause this man's been tellin me 'bout you."

Eddie Spencer spoke up. "Billy, this is Calvin Olsen. Goes by Cal. He's the owner of that yellow car that Smitty drives. I'm sure you've noticed that car around the Midwest."

"Yes, sir, Eddie. Great car and driver combination," said Billy, trying to wake up. "Smitty did real well in the "500" till he got in that scrape."

"Smitty's gonna be OK and the car will be ready for the

next big race at Milwaukee. My guys just about got it fixed. Now, Eddie and I go way back and I trust a lot of what he tells me. He's got a good eye for talent. Your name's been floating around out here for months now. And I saw you drive yesterday at Eldora. I spent the weekend in Dayton, catching up with old friends. Eddie said he'd come on over here with me this morning and see if we could catch up with you. Chuck told him you came back with those other two guys. I got a proposition for you, Billy." Cal was getting to the point.

"Sir?" Billy waited.

"Billy, I got two cars. There's that Watson roadster that Smitty wrecked in the "500" and it's just about ready to go again. And I got that Kuzma dirt car. Now, it's not the newest car on the lot, but it's a damn good dirt miler. Smitty ran second at Langhorne last year and won at Duquoin, and I think he had a fourth place somewhere. Anyway, here's my deal. I wanna run both at Milwaukee. Smitty'll be in the Watson, patched up and ready to go. And I wanna put you in the other car. I know, it's a dirt car and not as well suited to pavement, but if I run both cars, my chances go up one hundred percent, right?" Cal waited, another big smile on his face, "I seen dirt cars do real good at Milwaukee."

"I take this as an invitation to drive that car, right?" Billy asked, really without asking.

"That's the ticket, Billy! All the usuals apply, you know, forty percent of winnings, and I'll give you a hundred dollars travel money, up front. Whaddya think?"

"I'm in, Mr. Olsen." Billy and Cal shook hands.

"Oh, one thing more. I know you broke that arm, and I know you're going to Langhorne to drive Chuck Williams' car. Don't do nothing stupid there. It's a damn scary place, so just keep that in mind. I think this deal could go for more than just that Milwaukee race, OK? Those old upright dirt cars do well on Trenton's paved mile. I'd like to take both cars there, too."

"Let's race, Mr. Olsen. That's my job and I want to do it for a long time," Billy said.

Eddie Spencer stood off to the side and just smiled. When he got the opportunity, he pulled Billy aside and said, "This could be big, son. So, be smart."

"Thanks, Eddie. You been good to me," Billy rarely spoke like that.

Eddie nodded and smiled.

Billy walked to the station wagon, stopped, and started walking toward the Speedway gate. He was going to try to find the mechanic and driver he had ridden back with last night, but had no idea where they might be in the warren of mobile homes and two-bedroom bungalows. He walked back to the station wagon, took the keys out of his jeans pocket, and threw them onto the front seat. He also pulled out the note that said "Roxie, 317-4747."

"Well, Cal gave me a hundred dollars travelin' money and that should almost cover two for a weekend," Billy thought, smiling to himself.

Chapter 6

James was not happy about working the whole weekend, but Tom bought him off by promising an extra twenty-five cents an hour. He also told him that he could close early on Saturday, open at noon on Sunday, and close at six o'clock. That gave him Saturday night free for whatever he wanted to do with that old Ford he bought, and the added pleasure of sleeping in Sunday morning. Tom made an effort to establish peace at home, but it was more of a cease-fire. His wife and daughter did not speak much, although by Friday relations were slightly more cordial. There was not much more he could do. Perhaps he could patch things up somehow, sometime. Tina tended to be more forgiving, but he knew that Janet would not be. He couldn't blame her.

Chuck decided to drive to Langhorne with Ernie on Saturday after working most of the day. His plan was to have Donny trailer the race car early Saturday morning, allowing plenty of time to avoid rushing and any unfortunate circumstances that might result. The plan called for him to drive to Pendleton where Billy was still spending some time with his aunt and uncle, then pick up Tom on their way to Pennsylvania. It all amounted to about twelve hours driving time. Plenty of time for Tom and Billy to talk about the infamous dirt circle called Langhorne, if Tom could figure out how to get into the topic. There were things that had to be understood and appreciated, but Billy wasn't always willing to listen to advice.

The first part of the trip was on two-lane highways, no four-lane interstates. Donny drove through a lot of farm land, and even though farm equipment shouldn't be a problem in mid-summer, it was slow going for a few hours. His first stop was in Pendleton, east of Indianapolis. Billy said he'd be there, so Donny was not happy when his aunt said she didn't know where he was, and that he spent maybe three or four nights a week at her place. All Donny did was curse silently to himself. Chuck would be furious if he were here. Chuck would be furious with Donny if he didn't call within what he considered a reasonable arrival time at the motel near the race track. How could he find Billy? He had no idea where he could be and neither did the kindly old aunt. "Damn!" Donny cursed silently, went back out to the pick-up and race car on the trailer, and started to kill time, walking around it, dusting it off with a shop rag. He looked details over: hydraulic brake lines, brake rotors, axles, the tarp over the cockpit, anything that came quickly to mind and eye. A couple kids on bikes rode up and started asking questions: are you the driver, where you racin', anybody get killed in it, what kind of motor does it have, is it a dragster, and such "kid" questions. Donny answered with as much patience he could muster, considering the circumstances.

After another thirty or forty minutes, a blue Plymouth Fury pulled up and Billy hopped out of the driver's seat. The passenger, a twenty-something brunette, slid over to the wheel and said, "Hot rod, we still goin' to Milwaukee next weekend?"

"You betcha, Roxie. I'll call you when I get back from Langhorne," Billy leaned in and kissed the girl. Donny just stood there watching, wondering how that could all be so easy for guys like Billy.

"C'mon, Billy, we gotta move. Still gotta pick up Lawton!"
Billy was surprised. "What's he goin' along for?"

"Just like Eldora, I guess. Help out, maybe get a car to drive
there. You know a lot of guys don't like the Horne, so some
owners show up with driver-less cars. Maybe he'll luck into
a ride. If not, always nice to have more help," Donny didn't
really lie. He had guessed what the real plan might be.

"All right. I need to get some stuff packed and my helmet
bag, so give me a few minutes," Billy ran into the house and
came out in ten minutes, yelling goodbye and waving to his
aunt on the porch. He jumped into the pick-up. Donny was
revving the engine, impatient to go and make up lost time.
Pendleton to Tom's place in Barton was another hour and a
half of two-lane highways, fifty miles per hour speed limits.
Donny pushed the limit, driving sixty and sixty-five, watching
his mirror and looking ahead for hiding cops. The little towns
slowed him down to thirty-five or even twenty-five. That's
where he always looked for and found the local police, lurking
behind signs or overgrown bushes.

They picked up Tom around eleven o'clock. There was
still another hour of mostly two-lane highways to drive on
U.S. Route 127 before they got to U.S. Route 40 which had
many four-lane sections, the new unfinished Interstate 70,
and then the Pennsylvania Turnpike. Then they could make
good time. No lunch break—take out White Castle burgers
on the road. Seven, eight more hours of three men sitting in
the only seat of a pick-up truck. Not the most comfortable
way to travel.

Tom had thought ahead about how to hide his hand injury.
He would drive and put Billy by the window and Donny in
the middle, so to hide his injured left hand better. Neither
Billy nor Donny could see it as easily. In spite of that, Donny
noticed, "What's with your hand, Tom?"

"Aw, I just scraped it at the shop the other day. No big deal," Tom replied off-handedly.

Around two o'clock they finally got on the turnpike. That meant they had to cross the whole state of Pennsylvania yet, about six hours of driving. They'd be lucky to get into a motel by nine that evening.

Conversation covered many topics, usually all racing related: good cars, bad cars, lousy promoters, good promoters, drivers, mechanics, the whole range of roles and personalities. The three men were on solid ground talking about their mutual interest. When the conversation turned, they were less certain of other topics: politics, business, children—those were not things they related to. They were single-minded men. Even the topic of women fell flat. Tom was the "old married man" of the group. He was so far out of the dating world, he could not relate to Billy. And Donny was rather inept when it came to girls. The sooner they got back to race cars, the better, or it would be a long, quiet drive. And Tom wanted to talk to Billy about Langhorne, but he didn't want to just hit him over the head with it. So, he was relieved when Billy brought it up first, without prompting.

"Spencer told me to ask you about the 'Horne', Tom. He said you'd know about it," Billy said.

"I drove there just twice, so I don't have a lot of experience. I'll tell you what some guys told me, and a little I found out on my own," Tom said.

"Spencer said that place is spooky and spectacular at the same time. He never drove there, but he's seen both sides of the place," Billy tried to offer a starting point.

"He's right. Great things and awful things happen there. I think that's what he means. You have never driven anything like it. Let me start with the obvious: the place is a circle, a dirt circle. You might think, 'Big deal', but think about it like this. Let's say you take a car, passenger car, out in an empty parking lot, and there's nothing on the parking lot, no cars, nothing. Then you start going in a circle, going faster with each time around, you will reach a point, when the car just gets away from you if you try to go faster each lap. It'll slide away, spin, roll over, something. That's Langhorne. It's a damn dirt circle that lures you into going faster and faster. Pretty soon you're up there around a hundred, hundred and five and you're thinking, 'I got this place figured out', and that's when you need to back off. Some guys got to that point, didn't, and now they're gone. That's the spooky part," Tom didn't know how far to go with this. "But I tell you what, the place is downright thrilling! You're driving around there, kinda crossed up, the nose of the car is sorta pointed toward the infield a little, and the track is comin' at you sorta sideways at a hundred miles an hour! Not just two or three times a lap, like on a regular dirt track, but almost all the time! Remember, it's just one big turn, a circle. That Eldora place is kind of a big circle, half mile, but this is a flat mile. Now that is damn spectacular! You'll see."

"But you gotta know your own limits. And you gotta be in pretty good physical shape. It'll wear you down. The G-forces are tremendous, and your helmet seems to get heavier with each lap. I've seen guys finish a race with their head all tilted over to the right, hardly able to sit up straight in the car. It'll wear you down. Course, we got twin fifties—fifty laps, fifty miles—and then there's a break. You can recover for about thirty or forty minutes. So that will be a little easier on you. And that arm ain't a hundred percent yet, probably," Tom paused.

"I hate to get on my soapbox like this, Billy, but I want to warn you about the track," Tom looked over at Billy to see how he was reacting.

"You know, when I rode back to Indianapolis with those guys, that mechanic and his helper, they said them guys who prepare the track put oil on the surface! What the hell is that for?" Billy was honestly mystified.

"That place can be so dusty. They actually do put hundreds of gallons of used engine oil on it to settle the dust," Tom explained. "Especially along the front straightaway where the stands are. So the fans can see a little better. But you know, they get sprayed with oily dirt. When the race is over and they take their sunglasses off, their faces are black except where their glasses protected them. Two white circles!"

"I bet ladies really like that, dressed up and gettin' all dirty," observed Billy.

"And when you pull out of the pits early in the day for hot laps, be careful. That oil hasn't had time to soak in, and you can find yourself spinning, even at forty miles an hour. That's just plain embarrassing!" Tom laughed.

"And of course, there's the first turn, and after that, the famous Puke Hollow," Tom's voice slowed down and dropped a bit. "Puke Hollow, like the rest of the track is all oiled up, which is a challenge just by itself, but there are natural springs that run under the track, so it's always damp. It gets holes and ruts in it that can mess you up. You get up close to the fence to avoid them holes. Some guys say the fast way is right through them holes, but that's a chance you don't want to take. You can bust a shock, at the least, hittin' them holes, or…bust your head." Tom paused, self-conscious. He was not often so talkative, but this was easy. "You'll see tomorrow. Maybe if we get there early enough the silk shirts will let me drive you around the track in the truck. We'll be nice and crawl up to them on our knees!"

"You're just tryin' to scare me Tom," Billy joked.

"Not at all. Oh, and one more thing, the best thing about

Langhorne is that front straight. Of course, it's really a turn, and it's usually pretty smooth. It goes downhill a little! Now that's a ride! Goin by the stands at more than a hundred miles an hour, your back end drifting out a little, you're steering a little bit right into the slide, goin' downhill past all them people. You're giving the fans a close-up chance to see you at work. Now that is the greatest one thousand feet in American dirt track racing! I said it was a thrill, you'll see, Billy!"

Donny had not said a word during this whole interaction. He had seen a lot of racing, but had never had the opportunity to hear a driver describe his experience like that. He smiled and told himself to never forget what he had just heard. If he had any skill with words, he knew he should try to write it down, but he knew that was not likely to happen.

· · · · ·

Around nine o'clock that evening, the three men pulled off the turnpike and onto U.S. Route 1. It took them three stops until they found a motel with a vacancy. Donny and Billy went to a nearby tavern for burgers and beer while Tom stayed back at the motel to keep an eye on the car.

Tom called home to check in with Janet and let her know that they had arrived safely. The phone rang six or seven times until finally Janet picked up the phone. "Hello, Lawton residence." That was a nice voice to hear. Tom hoped that the feeling was mutual and the rough edges had worn off the icy relationship.

"Hi, Hon, just wanted to let you know we got here okay," Tom tried to be light.

"Wow, I was starting to worry a little. It's late. You have trouble?" Janet asked.

"Naw, Donny said that Billy held him up for about forty-five minutes. Late getting' home in the morning with his latest girlfriend."

"He's young, what do you expect? Can't be all serious at his age," Janet seemed to indulge the young man. "What'd you say Tina?" Janet tried to talk across a few rooms to her daughter and held the phone away from her face. "Well, it's late and we gotta go to Gloria's tomorrow. And James has to open the station. So just a few, make that ten minutes, and he'll have to go home."

"*What the hell?*" Tom thought. "*James?*"

"Janet! Is James there?"

"Yeah, he drove out here after he closed the station. Said he wanted to ask me about how much to charge for…something, I forget what. And he just *happened* to bring along his mom's apple pie, for a late snack while he asked his question," Janet said. Tom could hear amusement in her voice.

"So where is he now?" asked Tom.

"He and Tina are sitting on the front porch. He's going to leave in a few minutes."

"Huh! I wondered why he bought that car. And, you know, a few days ago, he asked me how old Tina is." Tom was not prepared for this. And he was five hundred miles away. *Did that kid plan this whole thing like this*, he wondered.

"Now settle down, old man. They're just talkin'," Janet was seemingly unconcerned.

"Yeah, but…I should be there," Tom weakly offered.

"Well, you're not! And I'm a big girl and I can take care of things just fine."

There was not much that Tom could say. He had made his choice, and Janet was dealing with it, just fine apparently. The best he could take away from this was that, yes, some of the ice had melted away but it still seemed chilly.

Donny and Billy got back to the motel a little before eleven that night. They brought a burger, fries, and a beer back for Tom. He ate about half of the food and had a few sips of beer.

It was too late and that was too much food. He turned on the
TV to catch the news but fell asleep after about ten minutes.
The last thing he was aware of was Donny and Billy playing
gin rummy.

· · · · ·

In the morning, the three men walked out for breakfast at
the diner across the road, and the first thing they noticed was
Chuck's car pulled up beside the truck and trailer. And there
was Chuck walking around his race car. "I thought about this
all night, Donny. I asked myself, 'Did you tell that boy to
chain everything together?' And you did, you did!"

"Hey, I listen, Chuck, yeah I do," Donny said.

Chuck defended his caution, "Stuff can happen! Race cars
been stolen off motel parking lots, you know. Well, anyway,
we're all here. I'll wake up Ernie so she can fix her hair and get
beautified a little. Let's go get some breakfast in that greasy
spoon over there. Good place…I been there a few times."

After breakfast, they drove just two or three miles down
U.S. 1 to the race track. This time, Billy rode with Chuck
and Ernie in the station wagon. Ernie sat in back so Chuck
and Billy could talk. Billy expected that this famous track
would look something like the Indianapolis speedway. All
the dramatic buildup he had gotten made it loom like an evil
giant in his imagination, a hulking monster visible miles away.
When Chuck turned off the highway, Billy was wondering
where the race track and grandstands were. "Here we are, Billy.
This is the famed Langhorne Speedway, the big left turn."

Billy almost said, "Where?" He was looking at the back of
bleachers, not a grandstand with a roof over it. Just wooden
stands, perhaps twenty-five, thirty feet tall at the back.
"Langhorne Speedway" was painted in white on the back of
the stands. It had become such a colossus in his imagination,
that this reality was puny in comparison. How could this be

"spooky and spectacular" at the same time? From this vantage point it was disappointing.

Driving into the track was not much different. It was all flat and indistinct. There were some scrubby trees ringing parts of the track, and there were roofs of homes visible in places. And when Billy stood on the front stretch, he looked at that "greatest one thousand feet in American dirt track racing" and he thought, *okay, I see the great arced front 'stretch' and the downhill run to turn one, and the stands lining it and… okay, I guess at a hundred miles an hour that would be pretty neat, but…I don't quite get it.*

Chuck interrupted Billy's thoughts, "I thought if we got here this early, we maybe could get in first, but there's Cal Olsen pitted about where I wanted to be. But this could be all right. Maybe Smitty'll be here early, too. He knows this place like his own back yard. Good guy to talk to, Billy." Just to save the space, Chuck pulled into the pit beside the yellow number seven that Smitty always drove. Olsen's car was new this season and borrowed a design feature common to Indianapolis cars, but new to sprint cars. Instead of a leaf spring front suspension, it had torsion bars, front and rear. Chuck's red car had torsion bar suspension on the rear axle, but a leaf spring mounted on the front axle, a rugged, reliable, and conventional suspension. Perhaps, Chuck thought, that suspension would be the way to go sometime, but not just yet.

Donny and Tom followed in a few minutes, and Ernie drove the station wagon out so they could back the trailer up and un-load the race car. Chuck unfastened the rear ramps on the trailer, folded them down, as Donny got ready to push the car off the trailer. Tom got in the seat to steer it out as Donny pushed the car down from the trailer. The three men set about routine tasks: unload spare wheels with tires mounted, tool boxes, fuel, oil, jack and other incidentals. Over the next thirty to forty-five minutes, most of the rest of the teams pulled in and unloaded their cars and equipment. A field of about thirty sprint cars assembled to compete for eighteen starting places in the two fifty lap feature races.

The usual chatter went on between and among the men. Good natured joking and macho talk, some just fun, some meant to psych out opposition. That was the kind of thing that Smitty was often prone to. Today though, when he arrived he seemed subdued, serious, and not his usual self. The cocky, light and confident attitude was more somber, more glum. Chuck saw Smitty walking across the front stretch and tried to get his attention, "How ya doin, Roughneck? Ready for this today?"

"Always ready," was Smitty's only reply.

"Any thoughts today, any words of wisdom from the master? I was hopin' to lean on you today," said Chuck. He was standing between the two cars, the brilliant, yellow seven, and his own red car. Donny was taking the rubber balls out of the injector horns while Tom was checking fuel level by pushing a stick down into the fuel tank.

"Lean on me? Now just what in the hell does that mean?" This was a different Smitty, and Chuck changed his approach.

Chuck backed off from his "banter mode" and went straight at it. "You know I got my rookie driver, just sort of a boy. He knows nothing about this place. And he can really be full of hisself sometimes. You know what I mean? Thinks he's got it all figured out."

"And, you want me to...educate this hotshot about...driving race cars?" Smitty said slowly as he polished his goggles, staring at the ground. "Tell him how to beat me?"

"Only a few pointers about this place. You know as much as anyone. Just give him a few ideas that might keep him out of trouble, okay? I talked to one of the 'yellow shirts' about maybe you and Billy' takin' the tow truck around once, you know, before you park it. But as you go around, say a few things about how to drive this place, okay?"

"Can't say that anybody ever did that for me, but what the hell, I'll do what I can. Can't do any harm, I suppose," and Smitty went on looking over his goggles, face shield, helmet, gloves.

By eleven o'clock, the stands were about half full and the pits were filled with cars, crews, officials, photographers, and a few hangers-on. The fence that separated the pits from the infield was lined with fans trying to absorb as much as they could. Tom and Billy talked quietly about the car, comparing notes. "You might want me to slow down that steering a bit, Billy. Just see how it feels to you after hot laps. This ain't Eldora and them dirt half miles where you gotta be quick with the wheel. See what it feels like. That's a quick and easy fix," Tom said.

"Yeah, I guess so," was Billy's only response. "You know, Chuck wants me to ride a lap in the truck with Smitty. Should I be ticked off or not? I'm a big boy, nobody needs to take me by the hand and show me how to do stuff!"

Tom said, "Smitty's not the type to say 'do this, don't do that'. I think he'll just be matter of fact about it. Tell you how he drives this place. What harm can that do? Anyway, I thought about doin' that myself, but Smitty's the master here, so you should take advantage, Billy."

Tom was right. Whatever differences they had, and there were a few, Tom understood the value of Smitty's experience. Smitty drove the truck and trailer just one lap with Billy riding along. It was textbook straight, a "here's what I know" trip around the mile circle.

Smitty's tutorial started, no surprise with his approach to turn one and Puke Hollow. "Comin off that front stretch into turn one, I try to get in there kinda high, up close to the fence. I try to make it as straight as I can. Get in there too low, slidin' sideways, and there's usually ruts and holes. You hit one of those wrong, and that's the end of your day. Don't need to tell you not to get *too* high, you'll hit the fence, and then you're off in the trees. But like I told you, do not go sideways between one and two. Them holes get deep in Puke and do evil things ."

"Yeah, but, somebody told me the fast way...." Billy started to say.

"I don't give a damn 'bout *somebody*! All I'm gonna say is how *I* drive this place!"

"I was going to say that turn two dries out and gets dusty a lot of times. But you can let it drift up high, then pinch down low and try to make that backstretch straighter. Rest a couple seconds that way. And you gotta know you can never see much in front of you, because of the big circle. You can't always see around a turn 'cause you're lookin' straight ahead. Somebody may be in trouble in front of you and you don't know it till you get on top of him. The dust makes it even worse. That dust can be so bad that you forget where you are...turn three, turn two? So I try to kind of 'check up' on the gas every once in a while, just to get an idea where I'm at."

"You go sorta uphill on the backstretch and turns three and four. I stay full on the gas about half or two-thirds of the time, and kind of 'feather' the throttle the rest of the time. You can go as fast as you want here, and you'll be steerin' with your foot as much as your hands. It can be a real ride, I'll tell you what, but it'll lure you into goin' faster and faster. You just gotta be ready all the time, ready to react."

"Ain't never drove no track like this before," said Billy.

"Well, *that's* for damn sure! If you remember that, it might help! Oh, and then there's the front straightaway. It ain't straight, but it's one heck of a ride. It's wide and just a little downhill, and there's all those people! Anyway, you can keep that drift going all the way out of turn four, past the stands, and like I said, head into turn one high, stay outta the pukey middle of Puke Hollow. Try to go in there as straight as you can. And that's a lap, at least my way. Oh, and watch this," Smitty punched the gas pedal on the truck, the tires immediately spinning, and the truck started to slew about with the trailer whipping a bit. "It'll take a few laps until that oil works its way in, so be careful. You can spin even going forty miles an hour. Feel like fool."

Smitty steered the truck and trailer to the infield, parked it, and said, "There you go, kid. Maybe you can follow me for a lap or two sometime. Good luck." He got out, slammed the door shut, and walked off. Lesson over.

When Billy got back to the pit, Donny and Tom were each sitting on a rear wheel. Chuck was leaning on the fence, talking to Ernie. Billy picked up his kitbag and went searching for a place to change from jeans into his uniform. It was just a glorified mechanic's coverall in some color between white and pale yellow. It had a red stripe down the outside of each arm and leg, and his name was sewn in cursive script on the left side of his chest. There was a decorative patch with crossed checkered flags on the right side. That's all: no sponsors, no tire manufacturers' name, no team name. The coveralls were supposed to be moderately fire inhibitive, but that was mostly in name only. They were dipped in some fire-retardant solution, but perspiration and repeated washing diluted most protection they could provide. Some of the young drivers, Billy among them, now wore light-weight, laced boots for driving. They had thinner soles and gave more sensitive feeling. They looked like a boxer's footwear.

Chuck said, "You talk to him, Tom, on the way over here?"

"Yeah, but you know, my experience here is limited. I

thought about that drive around, maybe I could do it, but Smitty's the guy to talk to. He won more than a few races here. I'm glad you leaned on him for that," Tom said.

"He was kind of, I don't know how to say it, odd, or something. Something botherin' him, maybe," mused Chuck. "But he done it, even if he wasn't in the best mood."

Tom just said, "Best teacher, though."

Chuck changed the subject. "We got second hot lap session. They got two groups, two sessions each. That'll be good for Billy. I asked the silk shirts to put us in the second, so he can stand around and watch. Why don't you two walk down to the end of the front straight and just watch 'em?"

"Okay, Boss," Tom smiled and started to look around for Billy. Donny was talking to a mechanic in the next pit, and Chuck went back to the fence to talk to Ernie and look at his book again. Push trucks and a few maintenance trucks were circling the track, trying to work the oil into the surface.

Most of the regulars from the Midwest were in the first session—C.J., Smitty, Connors, and men Billy had raced against already. There were a number of talented east coast drivers in the group also. Red Allen had earned several championships in his nearly fifteen-year career. He was driving his familiar blue number two. Charlie Pauling was in the red seventy-seven, and fan-favorite Bobby Wilson was driving the gold number one, last year's East Coast champion.

After the usual seven or eight minutes it took to get the first group of cars started and slowly circling, the starter signaled for green flag racing. Unlike the half miles where the cars were closer, on this mile there did not seem to be a sudden explosion of sound. It built up more slowly and came from farther away. Billy and Tom looked to their right, and just as Tom had said, that "front—not-a-straightaway" looked amazing. Smitty came out of turn four with Carl Connors on his left, maybe three feet behind. Both cars were spraying dirt into the stands and drifting out towards the outside retaining wall. They held the slide as they entered turn one. Just as he said, Smitty went high in turn one, up close to the fence. Connors went for the middle, right into Puke Hollow. That was just what Smitty and Tom warned about. It was a little damp there and Connors got a good bite with his right rear, launching clods of dirt to the outside where Smitty was. Connors could do that now, but if it rutted and tore up into holes, he'd be a fool to stay in that groove. Connors got a lead on Smitty and held it for two more circuits until Smitty passed him at the exit of turn four, still in his outside groove. That was the end of their race and Smitty's yellow car pulled away a little more each lap.

Billy studied each car going down that front stretch, watching to see how they entered turn one. Guys like Smitty went high on the track, shutting off power momentarily, then picking it up and keeping the engine speed up. Others drove low into the turn, probably trying to develop a groove under the dreaded ruts and holes that would likely develop. That made for a slightly sharper turn and bit of a slower route, but it was the shorter route and sometimes could pay off.

Connor's engine sounded as if it were running faster, than most other cars. It had a different, almost a straining, sound. Tom shouted into Billy's ear, "Gear don't sound right to me!" Billy just nodded.

Billy had seen and been told enough. It was his turn and he had to get ready to go. "Let's go, Tom! My turn! Gotta get ready."

Tom nodded and smiled.

. . . . .

Billy's first experience of the Horne went quite well. After his push-start, he circulated the dirt mile slowly with the other fourteen or fifteen cars, occasionally punching the throttle, and shaking the front end to break the back wheels loose a bit. He was anxious to get this hot lap session under way, to find out for himself about the famous dirt circle.

Puke Hollow was still fairly smooth and un-rutted. Much of the rest of the track was drying out and it looked like dust would be a problem. The front stretch was dark where the oil had soaked in, but the slickness had been worn away by this time.

Chuck's car ran smoothly and evenly, at least as smoothly and evenly as a 302 Chevy could. The heavy, stock flywheel on the engine is gone. Power is immediate and undampened, so only a steady foot keeps the car from lurching ahead.

Smitty had told Billy to "follow me," but he was not in this session. East coast hero Red Allen pushed out first, so Billy drove slowly hoping that his blue two would pass him. Allen had a lot of experience here and could serve as another tutor. Allen was nowhere to be seen so Billy thought to himself, "How hard could this place be? I'll figure it out."

About then the starter threw the green flag and all the instructions became academic. Billy was just entering turn three when the corner light went green. He pushed the pedal down, and the red car jumped. Billy steered through turns three and four and powered through the front stretch. He felt the familiar lightening of the rear end as it began to slide out to the right. In the middle of the straight, near the flagman's stand a blue number two passed him on the right, holding a long, steady arcing approach to turn one. That was Red Allen.

Allen steered close to the outside guardrail in turn one, as Smitty said was his usual approach. Billy was momentarily surprised when Allen passed him, but tried to follow. Billy aimed towards the middle of the track in turn one and the dreaded Puke Hollow. He saw Allen ahead of him by about six or seven car lengths, but still high on the track, near the outer retaining wall. The red car got a good bite on the dirt, in the usually soft and rutted middle, and Billy was able to keep the blue car in sight. Billy thought to himself, "Puke Hollow don't seem so deadly to me. Maybe I can use that part of the track and stay away from the rail."

Billy was up to racing speed by the time he cleared turn two and tried to aim for the inside of the backstretch. He wanted to "make it straight" even though it was just another part of the circle. That was a way to create a straight, allowing a short, few seconds of rest. But he really couldn't create much "straightness." It was all still that big circle with few places to rest.

He entered turn three at about ninety percent of what he thought was possible. Calling it turn three or whatever was all unnecessary. It was just a name for that quadrant of the circle. At this point he was, running at perhaps ninety-five miles per hour. The car was in a constant slide, with the rear wheels closer to the outside of the track. His arms seemed to be constantly in motion, sawing at the steering wheel, correcting the slide. His foot was mostly "on the gas." This is what they called "steering with your foot"; the amount of power his foot called for actually directed the car as much as the front wheels: more throttle resulted in a more pronounced slide; less and the car would start to take a straighter path with less slide. But, you can go faster sliding, as long as you can control it, and as long as the right rear tire holds up.

Billy worked his way through turns three and four and came to that front "straight." And suddenly there were the thousands of people in the stands on his right, a wide expanse of dark, oil-stained dirt in front of him, and the pits on his left. He stayed on the power, but it only seemed right to punch it even harder. The car held a long, steady slide all the way through the straight, the rear tires spitting up a shower of oily dirt. The track here seemed smooth, and made the transition to Puke Hollow even more startling. Billy tried to follow Smitty's advice. He tried to take the path Red Allen took through that turn: go high, up closer to the rail. Ruts and holes tear out in the middle of the track in turn one. But it didn't seem right to him, and again he went right through the middle. And it was okay now. But they had told him, two or three laps, even one lap, later it could be entirely different. If he got into one of those ruts sideways, he knew, he damned well better have that right rear wheel churning. He'd learned that the hard way, even at his tender age, on some of those western dust bowls. But this place was different. Here he was going a good ten or fifteen miles an hour faster. That's enough to get one in trouble fast. Tom and Smitty had said you have to be ready all the time. There's no letting up here.

Billy got another ten or twelve laps in before there was a spin in turn three. The starter threw the red flag signaling the end of this hot lap session. He slipped the gear lever to neutral as he passed the stalled car and kept the engine running as he coasted through turn four and into his pit. When he braked to a stop, Chuck drew his index finger across his neck, meaning "kill the engine" so he could get his "clean read" of the spark plugs. He wanted the electrodes to look sort of powdery grey. Light meant fuel mix too lean, dark meant too rich. Too lean means the engine could burn a piston. Dark means inefficient combustion and less power.

Tom and Donny gathered around Billy as he sat in the cockpit for a minute or so, collecting his thoughts. Tom said, "Billy, you looked good, damn good! Oh, and here. I forgot to tell you. You're going to need these today." Tom handed him some soft leather gloves. "You'll tear your hands to shreds without 'em."

"I had you at about a high thirty-five or low thirty-six, Billy," Donny was holding his stop watch. "Pretty fair first effort on the big dirt circle!"

Billy looked up, smiled, and lifted himself out of the car. His arms felt heavy and he exercised them in all different directions, just to loosen them up. He thought, *Not so bad, after all those big, bad warnings. But ten laps ain't fifty.*

Chuck asked, "So how was it, Billy? Want any changes? This is the way I had it set up last year, so I just started from my notes. I do want to change that right rear after you qualify. That one is a little softer. Might give you better bite, better time trial. But a new tire with a little bit harder rubber will last longer. What ya think?"

"Hey, you've been here before. I'll trust your judgment. Anyway, give me the car, I'll figure out how to make it go fast," Billy said and took a sip of Coke.

Smitty and Red Allen showed that they would be the class of the field this day. Each put on a masterful demonstration of car control and speed. The fans seemed awestruck by the display each put on, holding their cars in near constant slides, rear wheels spraying the outside fence. The crowd knew they were seeing masters of dirt track racing.

Billy's second session was uneventful, and his lap time improved to the low thirty-five seconds. He tried to keep up with Red Allen, but he knew his place here today.

When Chuck drew his qualification spot, his luck was so-so. At least it wasn't the last spot to take time trial, but getting out on the track sooner is usually better than later. As it was he drew sixteenth spot. Billy did quite well with what he was given, turning in a time of 34.7, good to start him in eighth place. That made his lap speed right around 104 m.p.h. Pretty good for a young rookie. Smitty ended up with fast time, 32.6, running the mile circle at 110 m.p.h. Between Smitty in

first and Billy in eighth starting spot there was a mix of east-
erners and Midwestern drivers: Red Allen in second, Bobby
Wilson, Carl Connors, and C.J. and a few Billy had never met.
Elite company in quality machines, no doubt.

Race time was two thirty, leaving the crew about thirty or
forty minutes for final preparations: fuel, tire change on the
right rear, oil and coolant check, radiator and nose screen clean
out, and a general "walk about" as Chuck called it. Chuck
would look at brake lines, shock mounts, visible frame rails,
even axles. Donny thought it was just endless fussing and
nitpicking, until Chuck explained why he was so paranoid
about such things. Chuck told about the time years ago, with
another car and another driver, when he wasn't always so
driven to be checking things. Just before he pushed the car
out for the feature race, a mechanic whose car was not in the
race looked over Chuck's car, frowned and said, "You know,
Chuck, does the right-side bend in that front axle look odd?"
Closer inspection revealed a crack which could have been
disastrous if not discovered. Chuck withdrew the car on the
spot, and that lesson was one he never forgot.

The track announcer called for all cars and teams to be
moved to the front stretch for introductions and push-off.
Most cars had already been put in their starting places and
just a few stragglers joined the field. Introductions produced
the usual crowd reactions: polite applause for most, vigorous
cheering for the favorites, and a few boos. Billy drew a very
enthusiastic response which surprised and flattered him; he
was a newcomer, and he was from the West Coast. These must
be informed fans he thought, fans who read their National
Speed Sport News.

Chuck stood to Billy's left, beside the left rear wheel.
"Usually I remind drivers, 'Thirty laps on a half mile track—
you got ten minutes' but here you're going fifty laps on a

mile. That'll work out to about twenty-nine or thirty minutes. And…just remember what these guys told you today, okay?" Then he slapped him on the back, motioned for the push-truck to come up, and walked to his pit area.

After four laps of slow circling and sorting, the field settled into the proper line-up, and as they passed the starter, he signaled for one more lap. Drivers took this last chance to adjust goggles and face shields and tug at their gloves. As they rounded the third and fourth turns, Smitty steadily increased his speed. The green flag waved when Smitty was about forty feet away from the starter. The car on the inside of the second row darted forward and left, hoping to get to the inside of Smitty in turn one. He forced Smitty to the middle of Puke Hollow, which was not rutted yet, but not really the line he preferred into that turn. The car to the right of Smitty stayed right beside him, making three cars race into that turn side by side. The first four or five cars raised a cloud of dust that the rest of the field drove through, mostly by following the car ahead.

Smitty got a good bite in the middle of Puke and pulled out a lead on the second-place car, the blue and white car of C.J., who made a bold move, passing three cars. Billy dropped back to ninth place at the start as a black car got by both him and Carl Connors in the white number two. Billy went high in turn one, partly because he was taking the advice he had been given, and partly because he really had no other place to go. And while he was up there another car slipped by, putting him back one more place to tenth.

As the field worked their way through turn two and onto the "backstretch," they began to string out. Billy reminded himself that he was going fifty laps and this was a learning experience, but the racer in him spoke louder. He found himself still high on the track, near the guardrail, and as he entered turn three, his momentum carried him too high. He backed off the throttle slightly and tried to move toward the inside of the turn, but another car held that spot. He exited turn four alongside that car and found his line to the front stretch and turn one to be 'not bad', at least. A good run through the front stretch gave him a better approach to turn one. This is the line that Smitty talked about. He got out of turn one in good shape and put one car behind him to regain ninth place. Then Billy worked on developing some sort of steady approach to the track. *Go as fast as possible, but "check-up" once in a while. Try to remember that,* Billy thought.

Five laps quickly went by, Billy running smooth and consistent laps around thirty-five seconds. The leaders were circling faster and steadily pulling away from the rest of the field. Being lapped was inevitable, perhaps within twenty laps or so. Billy tried to "race the track" here today, making the challenge of the big circle his adversary, instead of other cars. He tried to develop the rhythm that drivers fall into, each track seeming to have its own. On the power hard in the straightaway, back off for the turn, steadily increase power through the turn, then back hard on the power for the next straightaway. Repeat. Repeat. Repeat, each lap. Each track had its own variant. But Langhorne was different: no straightaways. Billy found out what they told him was true: you can go as fast as you want to. You don't have to slow down or back off for a turn because you're always turning. So, he concentrated more on the track than his rivals.

That total concentration and the constant steering to correct and control the sliding car began to wear on him. It wasn't until there was a yellow flag around lap thirty and the field slowed for three laps that Billy realized how hard he had been working. The necessary slow-down allowed him to relax for the first time in maybe twenty minutes. His arms ached, especially his still-healing left arm. It throbbed deep inside the bone. His uniform was wet from perspiration and his hair felt sticky inside his helmet, all things that he had not been aware of just minutes ago.

By his calculation, he had gotten back one position when a car ahead of him spun out, causing a yellow flag. So he was back to where he started, eighth place. There were two cars within striking distance in front of him. If he got a good start when the green flag came out, he had a shot at moving up a bit more.

As the lights went green, the blue car in front of his stuttered when the driver hit the throttle. That momentary lapse gave Billy the opportunity to pass as they went by the stands. He held that position for the next two laps until he heard an engine behind him. Moving low in turn four on lap thirty-nine, Billy expected to be lapped by Smitty. He was surprised when Red Allen blew by on the outside as they passed the crowd, followed immediately by Smitty's yellow car. As they entered Puke Hollow, Billy tried to follow the two leaders, but he was unable to maneuver to the outside of the turn. The middle was deeply rutted, the route better avoided. So, Billy could only watch as the two masters slid high on the track, up near the guardrail and began to draw away. Billy concentrated on the white car in front of him, Carl Connors, who had made the banzai charge at the start.

As they raced through the front stretch on lap forty, Billy thought he saw a chance to pass Connors in turn one. Connors drove low into the turn as Billy aimed his car higher, above the ruts and holes in Puke. But Connors, slipped out of the low groove and into the middle of the turn, right into the holes. Billy and the red number eleven were even with Connors' right rear wheel. Connors launched clods of dirt and rocks that rattled like bullets off the red car and clear windscreen. Billy was showered with dirt and stone projectiles. He was stunned when a large object, dirt clod or stone, hit the left eyepiece of his goggles. The lens shattered and there was sudden stabbing pain in his left eye. Billy got off the gas momentarily, trying to regain his senses, and drove as best he could.

Passing the pits at the end of lap forty, he could see Chuck holding up a chalkboard that had the lap count written on it. He held his position in seventh for several more laps, following Connors as closely as he could, his vision now reduced fifty percent. He knew he had a better car than Connors and just waited for a chance to pass, in spite of his handicap. That opportunity presented itself on lap forty-eighty as the two negotiated turn three. Billy sailed around on the outside of Connors and held sixth position until the checkered flag brought the first fifty lap race to an end. Billy took the checkered flag, slumped down in exhaustion and pain as he coasted to his pit. The crew surrounded the car to congratulate him, but knew immediately that there was a problem.

"Damn, Billy! Your eye!" Donny was the first to speak. Tom and Chuck helped get Billy out of the car. They removed what was left of his shattered goggles, loosened the chin strap of his helmet, removed it, and sat him down in a lawn chair.

"How in the hell did you finish the race like this?" Chuck asked. "You could pull off, you know."

"I had a shot at passing Connors. Give up 'cause of this?" It all seemed so obvious to Billy. "Now I got a better starting spot for the second fifty."

"Won't be no second fifty today, kid. You got glass in that eye and no thirty-minute break ain't gonna be enough to heal that," Chuck let Billy know his day was over. "Ernie, why don't you take Billy over to the medical tent and get them doctors to look at this eye." The young man tried to resist, but Ernie had no trouble with stubborn young men. She escorted him to the infield emergency tent and talked him out of his indignation.

"Well, saddle up, cowboy! Your turn!" Chuck said to Tom and turned to get the car ready for the second fifty miler.

Tom changed into driving clothes as Chuck and Donny got the car ready for the second fifty. They refueled, changed the rear tires, opting for the same rubber compound on the right rear, but putting a softer rubber on the left rear. They cleaned the oily dirt out of the wire nose screen and radiator to prevent overheating. Chuck did another "walk about," checking the usual details, finding no problems. He went to the officials at the starting line and explained the situation, that Tom was replacing Billy in the second half.

"That's fine, but you know where he'll have to start, right?" said the supervisor.

"Yeah, I know," Chuck said and returned to his pit. He had about ten minutes left before the race resumed. "We didn't get a chance to ask Billy about the car or anything. You know. Handling, engine, that stuff."

"Must have been alright, the way he moved up. Just watching and listening, it seemed okay. What did he say to you before? 'Give me the car, I'll figure out a way to make it go fast.'

Not a bad attitude. If he can do that, so can I. And starting at the tail end of the field gives me quite a challenge," Tom joked as he pulled on his helmet and helped push the car out to the apron. His leather gloves hid anything that Chuck might see and Donny didn't say a word. His right hand would do the hard work today.

Starting last gave Tom the challenge of working his way past slower cars. Fourteen cars took the green flag for the second fifty lap race, four fewer than the first race but that didn't make anything easier. The track was still dusty, and turn one was torn into holes and ruts where some drivers momentarily hit the brakes, tearing holes in the dirt. Some looked as if they were five or six inches deep. Hitting those would at least shake the living crap out of a man; next, they could break things—shock absorbers, torsion bars, springs, fuel tanks, frames; the worst they could do is launch a car into the air. So, turn one, lap one would be interesting, to put it mildly. And lap two, three, and so forth would not be much different. At least Tom would not be in the middle of the field at the start. Starting last gave him a much different perspective. "I'll get through those first four or five laps, let everybody get sorted out, then see if I can make some progress. I can pick my path instead of getting forced someplace."

And that's the way it played out. Turn one and Puke Hollow were a dusty, bumpy mess, but all fourteen cars got through without incident. Red Allen got a good start and pulled ahead and up high in turn one. Smitty followed, and the two resumed their battle. Tom, starting outside row seven, was naturally higher as they approached turn one so he was able to easily settle into that higher groove. As the field passed the stands to end lap one, Tom was up two places to twelfth. The car was, as always, solid, responsive, and easy to drive. At the end of six laps, he had picked off one more car.

Then another car, an eastern car and driver that he did not recognize, dropped out, moving him up to tenth. So, the way he figured, there were cars that he would never catch. Some were probably a half lap ahead of him now. The leaders—Allen, Smitty, C.J., Connors, that other local guy Bobby Wilson, and others—would lap him in another maybe another ten laps. He thought, *Winning ain't goin' to happen today, even third, fourth, fifth—all out of the question.* So, Tom was surprised when he passed C.J.'s blue number five parked inside the backstretch on lap twenty. *Well, ninth. That was easy,* he thought. Soon after that the leaders lapped him.

By half way, he settled into the big dirt circle—the outright speed of the place could become just routine. Like he had learned in his two races here, a guy must not get complacent. *Gotta remind yourself all the time where you are on the circle, "check-up" once in a while, don't keep the hammer down all the time, don't let yourself think you can go faster than the lap before. There is a limit at this place. But damn, this is one hell of a ride! Sliding sideways at one hundred plus for thirty minutes!*

Tom began to feel the fatigue build up in his arms and stabs of pain in his left hand. The constant steering, correcting, redirecting, all in a state of hyper-attention and awareness combined with the centrifugal force on his body that tried to fling him to the right, out of the car—all wore at his physical and mental reserves. And he didn't have a straight-a-way to look at his hand, but it felt sticky inside his left glove. Sweat or blood made no difference, he wouldn't stop. To make matters worse, there was the pounding a body gets from the holes. *Piss red tomorrow?* Tom wondered. It had happened to him once a few years ago after a particularly brutal race on a track that might as well been a plowed field. It pounded his kidneys like a hammer. No wonder some drivers have to be lifted out of their cars after a hundred-mile race here.

But they all had to drive the same track, so the other drivers were experiencing the same thing. Tom began to creep up on the red and white number thirty-three of Bud Brown. Brown was running about the same groove as Tom, except he usually drove low in turn one to avoid the ruts. Tom was just a little faster, not much, so passing would not be simple. And Brown took the low route—thus, shorter and faster—through turn one. Tom stayed high, Brown low, lap after lap. Each time as they exited turn one, Brown would drift up to the high groove in front of Tom and they would run nose to tail until they got to the front stretch, where Brown would begin a lower approach to turn one, and Tom would stay high to get above the ruts. The fans were not unaware of this and some began to watch this battle. Finally, on lap thirty-five, Tom got a good run through turn one and pulled ahead of Brown. He then began to stretch his lead a little each lap, closing in on a car five or six car lengths ahead. *Not a lot of time left, so eighth place—that might be it for today, unless somebody's engine goes up in smoke.*

Then on lap thirty-eight, Bobby Wilson in the gold car, made a desperate attempt to pass Tom, and drove right through the middle of Puke Hollow. His right rear wheel dug into a rut and Wilson's car was launched into a series of flips that seemed to take the car higher and higher. Wilson's arms were out-stretched and flailing as the car's trajectory took it right over Tom. He could actually see the shadow of the car over him, in the air, as it launched itself out of the track. It seemed as if it might land on top of him. But just as quickly, Tom drove ahead and Wilson's car flew over the guardrail and into the scrubby trees outside the track.

All the corner lights flashed red and the field slowed and stopped on the front stretch. Chuck, Donny, and Billy all gathered around the car, not saying a word. Tom said very little, except for, "That looked bad." Donny and Billy just nodded. Chuck said, "Yeah. You were lucky."

All the activity was outside the track. Some fans and crewmen stood at the guardrail, watching the emergency crews. The crowd of thousands was absolutely silent for five minutes or so, but slowly returned to a subdued murmur. They had seen this many times and understood what it might mean. After about twenty minutes, those sitting highest in the stands could see the ambulance pulling away. No siren—could mean a few things: they wanted to wait and not make the situation seem worse to the crowd; or, it *was* "worse," and Wilson was beyond help; or, there was no need to rush because his injuries were not fatal. At any rate, fifteen minutes later the race resumed.

The field was pushed off for the single-file restart and took two laps to get sorted out. On the restart, Tom pulled even with the seventh-place car as they entered turn one, as that car held a low line through turn one and two. They stayed even all through the back stretch and turns three and four. Tom moved even closer to the outer guardrail, searching for any traction left in the dirt as they entered the front stretch. The other car dropped back and Tom was clear in seventh place as he sailed into Puke Hollow. The rest of the race was subdued, if anything can be at Langhorne. Red Allen re-established his lead and Smitty settled for second place. One car whose mechanic had opted for a softer tire compound, threw the blistered tread and retired on lap forty-seven. After that there were no position changes. So as a result of the usual variables—mechanical issues, accidents, driver skill, luck—Tom finished in sixth place. A so-so day as far as he was concerned. But when Tom crossed the finish line, Chuck stood out near the edge of the track, hand raised. He must have been pleased. *Last to sixth, guess that's not bad,* Tom thought.

For Wilson, it could have been a lot worse. The unofficial word from the ambulance crew was that he had a broken arm and some fractured ribs. Those were quick estimates from a number of volunteers who served as emergency staff, not judgments from doctors. But at least, he survived what appeared to be a typically gruesome Langhorne wreck. Wilson was a lucky man.

Chuck and Ernie waited in the station wagon while Tom went to the infield first aid tent. He had told them that he had a bad case of blisters that needed attention. A nurse cut off his glove, washed and put a disinfectant on his injured hand, and told him to wait until the doctor finished up a case of sunburn.

"What the hell? You drove with a stitched hand? You guys are a mystery to me sometimes," was all the doctor had to say. Tom just shrugged and did not say a word. Some things can't be explained so why even try.

"Thanks, doc," Tom got off the exam table and walked out.

Donny and Billy towed the race car home. Tom walked into his house at three on Monday morning after Chuck dropped him off. Janet never woke up when he crawled into bed. He slept late, until seven, and figured anyone needing gas can easily find it a mile or two away at Barton's other two stations. By the time he got up, Janet had already left the house and Tina was still sleeping. When he left the house at a quarter past seven, she was still sleeping.

Chapter 7

Janet often had breakfast with a small group of women from the Methodist church that she attended. On this Monday she had invited Missy Wilkins, her co-worker at the farm store, to go with her. Missy was twelve years younger than Janet, but they maintained an easy friendship despite the age difference. She had lived at home since graduating from high school and was satisfied with her life thus far, dating a few boys casually, but seeming to just drift along, for now, as she sometimes said. Her parents were older than most farm couples when she was born, in their late thirties. She was their only child and they had indulged her. She was their princess. Missy was happy, mature for her age, and sometimes distant with others, but not Janet. She and Janet had a younger sister/older sister bond, without sibling rivalry.

Janet drove up the quarter mile long gravel lane to the Wilkins farm, turned around in the big gravel area between the white farm-house and barns, and waited for Missy to come out on the porch and get in the car. Janet waved to Missy's dad Paul, standing just inside the big, open barn doors. He gave a friendly smile and waved back. Janet had known Paul and Ruth Wilkins "forever," she always said. She could remember when Missy was born and how the neighbors were so excited for Paul and Ruth. Janet was twelve at the time, and it wasn't long before she was baby-sitting little Missy on Saturday nights when the neighbors got together to play cards.

Missy came out a side door, walked past the water pump handle, petted the dog good-bye, and got in Janet's car. "Mornin', Mrs. Lawton. And how are you today?"

"Peachy," Janet smiled, put the car in drive, and drove down the lane. "How was your weekend? Go out Saturday night?"

"Sorta. Went to the drive-in movie with Ray. Saw some cowboy show."

"You sound really impressed with the entertainment."

"It was okay, I guess. How about you, your weekend?" Missy asked.

"Well Tom went out to Langhorne with Chuck and the race car," Janet answered as if to say "not great."

"Where's Langhorne, in Indiana?" asked Missy.

"No, it's way over the east side of Pennsylvania, real close to Philadelphia. One *long* drive, so I stayed home. Maybe your cowboy show woulda been fun for me!"

"Not a bad idea, Jan. Ray is a bit too serious sometimes. You and I coulda had a great time makin' fun of those cowboys! Oh, listen to me, Janet! He's a good guy and I shouldn't talk like that. I'm sorry."

Janet said, "Well, at least you know a little about what you want in a guy, so…no problem bein' honest with yourself, and me!"

Their conversation turned to guys and personalities for a few minutes, and soon they were at the Grove Café, better suited to the Methodist Women's Breakfast Club than Bennie's tavern. Three of the usual ladies were there, a group that numbered from four to seven depending on schedules and circumstances. Janet introduced Missy as a guest and she was welcomed to the group. After a few "good mornin's," "nice to see you's," and other such greetings, the women proceeded to order coffee and look over the menu, an unnecessary routine because it hadn't changed in years.

Janet noticed Suzy Hicks with her mother at a near-by table. They waved and smiled to each other. The tensions of the high school triangle of Tom-Suzy-Janet had eased considerably after fifteen years, but not disappeared. The two women were cordial now. But Janet was surprised when Suzy got up and came to her table.

"Janet, you must think you are one lucky woman this morning," Suzy said with sincere concern.

"Why...I don't know what you mean, Suzy."

"You didn't see this morning's paper?"

"No, why? What did I miss?" Janet was puzzled.

Suzy went back to her table, got the morning newspaper, brought it to Janet, and folded it back to the first page of the sports section. There was a picture of a car high in the air directly over a car number eleven.

Janet looked and said, "Lord, that Billy Wallace is one lucky guy! That's him in Chuck's car at Langhorne yesterday."

"No, Hon, if you read under the picture it says 'Tom Lawton slips under Bobby Wilson'."

Janet was speechless. Missy and the others looked at their coffee or menus. "I...I didn't think he was going to drive... no...uh...I didn't even talk to Tom this morning. He got in real late and was sleeping when I left. Guess I'll find out more this afternoon. Thanks, Suzy."

"Sure, Janet. Tell Tom we always have him in our prayers."

"Thank you, Suzy. Thank you," was all Janet could say. And she could say very little for the remainder of breakfast. The ladies and Missy searched awkwardly for a topic for several minutes and finally settled on the usual: children, county fair plans, vacations, weddings, until it was time for all to go to

work or back home. Janet had little to say as they walked out
and to the car.

Missy brought the subject up as they were walking, "I'm
on the outside of that whole auto racing thing, Janet, so…"

Janet interrupted, "I don't know what to do, think, feel
sometimes! What choices do I have, really? Sometimes I go
along with him and that's somehow better than staying home!
Can you imagine that? But I can't leave everything here—our
daughter, the station, you know. And some weekend work."

"It must be…." Missy started.

"From April to October, or even November if he goes out
west! So, what's that, eight months and how many events,
twenty-five or thirty? I guess I just need to accept it for what
it is. Isn't that what soldiers' wives do? Here's the keys, Missy.
Can you drive?" Janet got in the passenger's seat and turned
toward the open car window beside her, fighting back anger,
embarrassment, and tears. Missy made an attempt to console
her friend, but decided that silence might be better.

Janet's mind went back two years to when the officials had
scheduled a series of races in the east over the Fourth of July
holiday. Tom had convinced Janet to go along…it could be
like a vacation, he had said. They could take a day to drive
there and a day to drive back…no rushing. He would hire
someone to just pump gas, nothing else, no repairs.

Janet hardly saw race tracks as a vacation, but they had not
gone anywhere alone since their "honeymoon." And that was
more of a weekend in a cabin at a state park. Glamorous it was
not, but love can overlook some things, at least at the time.
They loved each other then, and still did, but Tina arrived seven
months later; they quickly became adults, when they were still
young, with all that implied. They did not have a hard life,
just one that was not filled with abundance. So, after thirteen years of marriage, even a "racing" vacation sounded good.

Missy would be the live-in babysitter for twelve-year-old Tina while they were gone.

This "eastern swing" meant that perhaps fourteen or fifteen of the teams from the Midwest would take part in three races over four days in Pennsylvania. The first was a night race at Williams Grove speedway on a Saturday night; the second was a daytime event on Sunday. Monday was a day off and the last race was on Tuesday, the Fourth, at Allentown. The Midwestern cars would be challenged by some of the best local talent. That summer Tom was competitive, never failing to finish and winning one race. He was contending for second place in the point standings and driving the best car he'd had in his career.

They found a motel on Friday about ten miles from the track and spent a few hours resting before dinner at a nearby restaurant. It had been a day-long drive so they were grateful for their air-conditioned room. And the motel was located close enough to the track that they would not have a long drive for the Saturday race, but not close enough for many of the teams. That way they could avoid the usual racer rowdiness and hi-jinks.

One other team stayed at the same motel. The two mechanics and driver were young, perhaps in their mid-twenties. They traveled in a station wagon, pulling their race car on an old, beat-up trailer. There were no female companions. At breakfast, Tom noticed the car in the parking lot and told Janet that he thought the car looked familiar but he wasn't sure. As they were leaving, they met three young men who had that "racer" look about them. There were introductions and jokes and "good lucks," and as an afterthought Tom said, "Hey, guys, we're in no hurry and we're gonna swim. Want to join us?"

"Might just do that," said the youngest, a boy hardly into his twenties.

So that is just what the five of them did, for perhaps an hour. Janet could never forget the sight of that young boy… so trim, muscular, and such a graceful swimmer. Still to this day she could see him swimming laps in the pool, even doing flip-turns. His name was Eldon Knowles.

That night at Williams Grove. Tom and Eldon raced side-by-side, trading positions as they fought for second place in the thirty-lap feature. On lap twenty-one, Eldon darted to the inside of Tom as they entered turn one. The boy got by but had too much momentum and too little traction. His car slid sideways in front of Tom. Tom's left front wheel penetrated the cockpit and hit the boy squarely in the chest. Tom's car then flipped end-over-end three, maybe four times. Janet had never forgotten that sight, just as she could still recall the ride to the hospital in the ambulance with Tom, the attendant saying, "He just woke up ma'am. He'll be okay. Just got a little concussion, probably. I got that in high school football once. But them eyes are gonna be red. All that spinning busted veins in his eyeballs. But that'll go away. He' gonna be okay, ma'am. He's lucky!"

Eldon Knowles was not lucky.

Janet drove home after Tom was released from the hospital on Monday.

The "discussion" three days later ended in a stormy cease-fire that was never resolved.

· · · · ·

Missy pulled into the parking lot of the farm store. Janet said, "There will be some tension at the Lawton home tonight. Or maybe I should just grow up a little more and let it go, huh? Really, nothing will change."

Missy didn't say anything, but took Janet's hand and walked into the store with her.

"For heaven's sake, I used to be the baby-sitter! Now look

at us!" Janet said and smiled at her friend, drying her cheeks.

Tom got into the service station a little after eight o'clock. James had already opened up. He had enough presence of mind to go ahead and set up for the day, not that there was really that much to do. At least the boy was tending to the customers who came through: a few men on their way to work, a high school kid with his lawnmower in the back of his dad's pick-up truck heading out for his round of yard mowing, and one farmer asking if Tom could put two new tires on his farm wagon. Tom had slept until seven. He knew as soon as he got up that sometime this day he'd have to deal with a number of issues: there would be a trip to Dr. Elsner, there would be a chat with James and his "visit" on Saturday evening, and he had to explain to Janet why he drove the race car Sunday.

The last issue was not to be a debate with his wife. There was no question in his mind about that. Janet was not a great fan of his chosen profession, if you could call it that. Or was it a hobby? That description was demeaning, in Tom's mind. The gas station was the hobby that helped keep his real vocation somewhat afloat. And it was the "somewhat," he had to admit, that was the issue. Janet had to work to keep the three of them going. This last was the issue that simmered often at the Lawton home.

"Mr. Lawton, good to see you!" James called out when Tom walked by the gas pumps. James was washing the windshield of a customer car. Tom didn't say a word, but smiled to his young helper as he walked into the station, looked at the "jobs" calendar on the wall behind his desk, and sat down at his desk. He looked at the note for Monday about the farmer's wagon tires. James at least wrote a question mark behind the job. He'd just have to ask the farmer to pull the wagon in to the station and park it in the side lot. He knew that the man wouldn't need it for a few weeks, until corn picking. He'd have to leave it for a day or so. He could get the tires at the farm store at near dealer cost since that was better than going through his supplier. For some reason, the area rep had not been "price cooperative" lately, and Tom could get a tire at nearly the same price at the farm store more quickly than the rep could deliver. He sat at his desk, looking out the window at James as he finished checking the oil, closing the hood, and getting the cash from the customer. "That's fifteen gallons at twenty-four cents a gallon. Makes it three dollars and sixty cents," James told the lady, Mrs. Bolton, the bank president's wife.

She handed him four dollars, "Keep the change, Sweetie," started the big Buick, and turned on to Main Street for a day of, who knows what.

"Nice lady, Mr. Lawton. She gave me four dollars for a three-dollar sixty cent bill."

"Put the money in the register, James, and take forty cents for your pocket."

"But, that's money for the station, Tom."

"Naw, you can use it sometime. That's a burger sometime, right? 'Bout the same price, huh?"

"Thanks Mr. Lawton," James said.

"James, I started to put some things together in my head, you know," Tom started. "Us old guys, you know, are not stupid. A little slow on the uptake sometimes, but we get things figured out eventually."

James stopped and looked at Tom, "Huh?"

"Well, you bought a car. Then you drove by our place a number of times. And it wasn't but a few days later you *just happened* to ask how old my daughter is. And then on Saturday night, you were out at my place, with an apple pie, and a few questions about the station."

"Those are some fairly obvious clues, I guess, aren't they?" James admitted. "I think Tina is a pretty nice girl, Mr. Lawton.

"James, you've worked for me, what now, almost two years?"

"Two years in October, Mr. Lawton."

"I think I know you pretty well now. You can come out to visit, but Tina will have to go through 'channels', you know. She'll have to ask her mom if it's okay. That's a good way to go about this, James."

"Sure, Mr. Lawton, sure!"

"Okay, James, let's get Monday started. You call that farmer and see if he can spare that wagon today. If he says yes, take the truck out to get the wagon. Then stop at the farm store and get the right size tires. Put them on my tab and bring everything back here. As you can see," (he held up his left hand) "I'll need help again. I'll get you started then see if Doc has a spot for me to fix this."

Doctor Elsner looked at Tom's hand and said, "I won't ask how this happened. It really doesn't make any difference. But this will take longer to heal now. You'll have to keep it clean, somehow. That's not easy for a man who works on cars, is it? At least it's your left hand, so you can baby it some. You tore the stitches loose, but we'll leave them in and just let it heal from the bottom up, as they taught us in med school. That's about all we can do. You'll have to change the dressing several times a day and keep looking for infection. Could you wear a loose-fitting glove over the bandage to keep dirt out? And, by the way, it would be a good idea to stay out of a race car for a month or so."

"Doc, I got nothing going in respect to race cars for two weeks. But I cannot make any promises beyond that."

"You *heard* me, but I know you well enough to know you may not *listen*. Do what you must, but I told you what's best, Tom."

Tom thanked the doctor, then drove to the farm store to get some extra-large work gloves. Missy was at the register when he walked in and Janet was nowhere in sight.

"Mr. Lawton, it's a surprise to see you here this time of day," Missy said.

"Hi, there, Little Missy," Tom said using his pet name for the girl he had known since she was a baby. "Where's Janet?"

"Back in the stock room," Missy dropped her voice to a confidential tone. "You know, this might help you. Give you a 'heads up' sorta thing before you talk to her. We had breakfast at the Grove this morning, and Suzy Hicks came over with a newspaper picture of you yesterday at Langhorne. Janet was shocked. She didn't know you were going to drive."

"I didn't plan it that way. The regular guy, Billy Wallace, he got…"

"I don't think that will help much. She was just caught flat-footed…oh, she's coming up this way," Missy tried to change the subject gracefully. "What can I do for you, Tom?"

Tom said, "Gloves, work gloves."

Just then Janet walked up and said, "Well, last time I saw you, you were out cold, sawin' logs. But now you need gloves, huh? Follow me, mister."

Janet led Tom to a rack of work gloves. "As you can see, we have a lovely selection of many styles. What exactly did you have in mind, sir? Elegant silk dinner gloves, some soft leather polo gloves? We got' em all, sir," she said, coolly. "Seriously, though you know what you need."

"Doc says I gotta keep this hand clean, so maybe a glove over the bandage will help."

"You *drove* yesterday with that hand!"

"That was *not* the plan. Chuck wanted me to go as kind of a coach for Billy, that's what the plan was, but he got hit in the eye with a rock."

"He could have just called it a day," Janet said.

"After a five-hundred-mile haul? Load up and go home

when the car was perfectly good, and there was another guy who could drive? Not likely."

"At breakfast this morning, Suzy Hicks showed me a picture of you and another car flyin' over you. Jesus, Tom!"

"Well, it all worked out okay. I really made some good money. Chuck made a promise to me and he kept it. Good money!"

"Tom, money doesn't help right now. See you at dinner tonight." Janet walked back to the stock room.

· · · · ·

On Tuesday evening, Chuck was in the back of his shop where he kept his race car. It was after dinner and the station lights out front were turned off to discourage any late business. Earlier he had asked Donny if he had any plans for later in the evening. Donny seldom had plans and this evening was no different. "Why, Chuck? What's up? Trouble?"

"Nah, nothing like that. I just want to show you something and see if you have any interest in it. That's all. Come on around to the back door of the shop. I'll be there. Seven thirty or so be okay?"

"Sure enough, Chuck. See ya then."

• • • • •

When Donny got to the shop, he walked past the large window on the side of the building. He could see Chuck, sitting in the race car. Now, that was a sight. An old man smoking a cigarette, sitting in a race car. He seemed too small for the car, and the cigarette somehow made it funnier. Donny tapped on the window and said, "Need a push start?"

"Take a hell of a lot more than that to make me drive this thing!" Chuck joked. "Come on in, boy!"

When Donny walked in, Chuck climbed out of the car and tossed his cigarette out an open window. The other, non-race car, parts of the shop and station may have been disorderly and messy, the floor strewn with parts and tools. But not where Chuck kept the car. It was well-lit, orderly and neat, the floor was clean, the work bench tidy, and all seemed to be in place. Along the big window wall was a Bridgeport vertical mill, an old Monarch lathe, drill press, welder, and power hack saw. There was more than enough extra space here.

"I'll get right to the point, Donny," Chuck said. "See that engine stand there? That's an old 283 engine that I salvaged out of a wrecked 58 Chevy Impala. That is, basically, the engine I got in my race car."

"Yeah, same but not the same, right?"

"Right. Same like that fullback in high school is the same as Jim Brown," Chuck said. "Now, here's my thought. Mind you, say 'no' if you want—no harm, no foul. And I want you to know, that I can't pay you to do this exactly. But I will make it worth your while someday, somehow. You know I can't cheat family."

Donny stretched out "o-k-a-y" in a suspicious manner.

"Here's the deal. One evening after work, maybe every other week, but more often in the winter months, I want you to tear that engine down, piece by piece, replace lot of stock parts with good racin' stuff. You know good pistons, rods, rings. We'll keeps some stock stuff, I'll show you. Then you reassemble it, and make it run again. First, of course, we'll take it to Dell's in Muncie to degrease it, line bore it, and deck the block. I could bore it out here, but maybe I'll have Dell do that, too. Then I'll have another extra engine, just in case I need it. Course it's my second extra, and it would still need to be made race-ready. And the way I figure it, I'll be right here workin' on my car so I can see what you're doing and give you help. You can learn a lot that way. I watched my dad work on cars a lot, got wrenches for him, held the flashlight. Came in handy for me."

"Sounds neat, Chuck. Maybe work, what, seven to nine in the evening?" Donny asked.

"Thereabouts. Little later once in a while. Depends on what we got goin' on," answered Chuck. "And what you got goin' on, too. You're single yet and maybe datin' some girl, so we can make time for that."

"The datin' thing is kinda slow now, so that won't be a problem. So, sign me up! You want to start tonight?"

"No, hell no. But I do want to show you that you got to keep it all organized and neat. Look at this place. Pretty clean, right. Well, we'll have parts here and there, but they'll be in boxes, labeled too."

"Hey, I know how you can pay me, Chuck! Let me drive the race car sometime!"

"That is *not* gonna happen, boy! You cannot believe what that is like. It's like…Well, what if there was a tiger sleepin' on the shop floor. And you jump off that workbench and land on his back, to ride him like a horse. Can you imagine what that would be like? That's what one of my drivers told me once. And I thought, 'Crap, can't be that bad.' So, I own the car, right? I can do what I want, right? I took the car and a few friends out to the new four-lane highway when they were still buildin' it, on a Sunday evening when no workers or cops were around. I had them push-start me. That thing slammed me back in the seat, and I swear it pushed my eyeballs back in my head! No speedometer in it, but it seemed like in a few seconds I was goin' ninety miles an hour! I pulled it out of gear, shut it off, and coasted to a stop. They had to bring the truck and trailer to me! You think I want to explain to your mom why I let you drive that thing? No way!"

"Yeah, you're probably right, but I can always dream," Donny said.

"That was some lesson for me. You saw me sittin' in the car when you got here. That was just fantasy-time. When I do that, I almost hear voices sayin' 'Who in the *hell* do you think you are, *boy?*'" Chuck mused.

By Wednesday, the Lawton house had settled down to something close to normal. There was a chill in the air, but normal homes are not perpetually sunny and warm. It was at dinner that evening that Janet was able to talk about her weekend. Tom saw that as a hopeful sign.

"Tom, I just could not bring myself to take Tina and the horse down to Gloria's place, so I called her and backed out of it. Tina wasn't happy."

"Oh, Mom, it's not such a big deal anymore, with what Gloria said and all," Tina protested.

"That's not what you said Saturday, Tina," Janet reminded her.

"Yeah, I know, but Gloria said she could stop up here sometime, maybe in a few weeks, and that would even be better, you know, to see my horse at home," Tina said. "And, as it turned out, Saturday was kinda fun, wasn't it?"

"How often does a part-time gas pump jockey just happen to show up with *important* questions for the owner's wife

AND have an extra apple pie on Saturday night? An apple pie that looked a lot like his mother's work! You know I've known James' mother for a long time, girl," Janet teased.

"Well, it was kinda fun, like I said," Tina knew that unexpected visit took some of the tension out of the house. And, just as important, Janet knew it, too. Tom saw that it was probably a good thing.

· · · · ·

At the station, Tom nursed his injured hand as much as he could. He changed the dressing several times each day and often wore a ladies' rubber glove over the bandage to keep it as clean as possible. He leaned on James to loosen any stubborn or rusted bolts. Tom thought that he could "baby" that hand back to something close to healthy this way. The second race for Indianapolis cars was on Sunday at Milwaukee. Billy was scheduled to drive the team car to Smitty, Olsen's mile dirt-track car. The Sunday following that, Billy would be back in Chuck's car for the Dayton race. At least that's what Tom assumed, and he had no reason to think otherwise even though he had not heard from Chuck. Tom figured that in ten days his hand would be ready to go, in his judgment, if not the doctor's. Perhaps he could get a ride in another car. He'd settle for less than perfect, now at this stage in the season. The number of races would soon be winding down.

· · · · ·

That same Wednesday, the local auto race fan club in Dayton held their monthly meeting. Eddie Spencer drove to the Linden Tavern on the east side of town where the meetings were held. These were actual club meetings with call to order, reading of minutes, old and new business, and the usual activities of any club. The actual participants in that part of the meeting were few. Most of the club members hung around at the bar, drinking, smoking, and reviewing the latest news in the world of racing. They came for the association of like-minded fans, a night out, an occasionally interesting speaker, and the racing films. Often those were a fan's eight-millimeter films. Once in a while, an oil company or auto parts supplier would secure the use of a professional race film. Firestone filmed the Indianapolis "500" and reduced the hours of practice, time trials, and race footage to a watchable thirty to forty-minute film. Once the business meeting was over, the movie started and attention slowly went from the bar to the movie screen set up on the band stage. With their attention then directed, the club members might then be entertained by a speaker after the movie. He could be a local driver, a sanctioning body official, a track owner or promoter, or a rare appearance by a nationally known racing celebrity. He might be a former Indianapolis winning driver, mechanic, or car-owner. That celebrity category always garnered immediate attention. It didn't matter what he said or how he said it. The fans hung on his every word, no matter how disconnected his thoughts.

During the film, an old 50's era Daytona Beach race (when they actually raced on the *beach*), Eddie stayed at the bar, working on his second whiskey, mostly sitting alone. A few old-timers who recognized him stopped to ask how he was doing and wished him well.

He didn't know many of the younger fans and didn't relate to their interest in "late-model" stock cars. In his mind, if it had sheet metal over the driver's head it was what he called a "taxi-cab." He even joked about some of the drivers and said they smoked cigarettes when they went "around the block tryin' to pick up customers"—Eddie's half-serious portrayal of stock car racing. He tried to keep his thoughts to himself so he didn't offend these fans, but it was obvious to anyone who knew him where his sympathies lay. Eddie knew what he thought was a real race car and real racing. What he had seen at Winchester and Indianapolis was in that category. But he would admit to himself, *Spencer, you're an old man now. Things change.*

Just as Eddie finished his drink, another "old-timer" came up from behind and put an arm over his shoulder. "Eddie 'Speed' Spencer. I ain't seen you since that race out in Phoenix in what, '52 or '53?"

Eddie looked to his left and studied the man for perhaps five seconds, searching for a younger face in this older one. Then he said, "Walt Morrow! I'll be damned! I ain't seen you in a coon's age! Last racing event we was both at was Arizona in, uh, '53 maybe. I was out there with that kid that Kinnison had in his car. Me and my wife drove out there, kind of a vacation combined with that old dust bowl race. I was supposed to haul the car out, and then Kinnison and the kid flew out later. Nice drive for us, really. And we got to see one of the kids. We hauled that wrecked race car back here, two thousand miles. Goin' was better than comin' back. You was just gettin' out of racing 'bout then, weren't you?"

"Yeah, never made no money owning race cars. Who makes any money in that game anyway? It's an expensive hobby for an owner and a poor-paying job for most mechanics and drivers," Walt complained. "Anyway, Eddie, how you doin'? I'm sorry about your wife."

"Well, you know, when half of your life is gone, that's a big empty spot. We were married thirty-two years so that's a lot that stays with you," Eddie said.

"Yeah, I'm sure. Alice and I been together thirty-six years now, so I guess I could imagine," Walt said. "Hey, can I buy you a drink? What ya drinkin'?"

"Barkeep, another Stroh's for me and whiskey on the rocks for my friend," Walt ordered and sat beside Eddie.

The meeting was over and the club-members had mostly gone.

The club president stopped at the bar on his way out. "Eddie, when am I gonna get you to talk about your board track days? Those would be some great stories to hear. I read about some of 'em."

"Aw, I don't think these guys could understand. Maybe some time, maybe," Eddie said.

The president walked away saying, "I'm not gonna take 'no' for an answer, Eddie. Keep thinking about it."

Walt took a sip of his beer and said, "Since I got out of racing, I've done real well. That race car was a money pit. And the money I used to throw down that hole, I been puttin' in my business. And I tell you, Eddie, we're doin' well."

"I drove by that place a few times and noticed that you added to it," said Eddie. "What do you call it now?"

"I call it Precision Tool and Machine. We built two additions over the last three years. And I could add again, but I'm going to wait, just to see how this next year goes."

"So, what brings you here? I ain't seen you around anything that has to do with racing for a long time," Eddie asked. "Can't stay away from cars with numbers, huh?"

"Well, sort of. I ain't never gonna own a car again, but I might like to see 'Precision Tool and Machine Special' on the side of some *good* car someday."

"Really. What are you saying, Walt?"

"I know you keep up with this stuff. Club president is a friend of mine and he told me you are usually here. I want to put a bug in your ear. Keep this in mind 'cause you see the cars, drivers, mechanics and most of these operations. Like I said, I don't want to own a car. But I would sponsor a *good* car. I would be very helpful to a quality operation that could advertise my business. Three-year commitment with an option after that time is up."

"You been thinking about this, haven't you Walt?" asked Eddie. The two men finished their drinks. "I got to go home. It's late and we both got to work tomorrow. I'll keep this all in mind, think about it, float the idea—won't mention your name though, it's all just supposin'. But a lot of the guys know me and trust me, okay?" The two men walked to their cars.

"Sounds good, Eddie. Glad I bumped into you tonight," Walt said.

"You didn't bump into me, now really, did you?" Eddie asked.

"No, I was pretty sure you'd be here, Eddie," Walt said and smiled.

Chapter 8

On Thursday afternoon, Billy Wallace picked up Roxanne Lytell a little after five o'clock. Roxie was a secretary at a factory in Muncie that made equipment for the steel industry. The company's customers were in the east: Youngstown, Pittsburgh, Bethlehem—smokestack America, in other words. Her job took her from the aisle of drafting tables to the factory floor-staffed with men who watched her every step, lasciviously—to the secretarial pool,where women watched her, enviously.

Roxie had driven to Pendleton Wednesday evening to pick up Billy at his aunt and uncle's place. They drove back to her apartment for the evening, so she could work the next day and just miss one day of work.

Billy had all the windows down on the '57 two-door hard-top Plymouth Fury when he got to the office. The office building was made of red brick, partly ivy-covered. The attached factory was also red brick. The roof looked serrated, with many parallel peaked ridges covered with glass to allow maximum natural lighting. It all looked quite nineteenth century. Neat and well maintained, but definitely not modern. A cast metal sign on the wall near the office door said "SECO." Billy parked near the front door in a place labeled "Visitor." He kept the engine running, the V8 engine burbling through the dual glass-pack mufflers. A few men in white shirts and narrow black ties looked down from the second floor engineering department, trying to figure out why some guy was in Roxie's car. Brother, garage mechanic?

Soon they had part of their answer. Roxie ran out the front door and got into the passenger seat with her mystery driver. She leaned over, kissed the man on his cheek, and then proceeded to protect her hair with a colorful bandanna. She had convinced her boss—using her considerable skills of persuasion—to let her leave fifteen minutes early, enough time to change into shorts, sandals, and a summer blouse. Billy pushed "Drive" on the push-button gear selector on the left side of the dashboard, and they drove off with a roar and tires scratching up stones. A spectacular departure, just what Roxie enjoyed—that and an equally spectacular arrival. That explained much about Roxie.

Muncie to Milwaukee was around three hundred and fifty miles, and Billy figured that to be a six-and-a-half-hour drive, plus or minus, depending on traffic. Much of the drive would be on two-lane highways, except when they got on U.S. route 30 which had a fair number of four-lane sections. Still, there were a lot of towns to go through. "So, I was thinking we'd go as far as some place about half way, I don't know. South Bend is kind of out of the way, but there should be plenty of motels on 30. What ya think?"

"Oh, South Bend. There's that college there, my sister wanted to go there, but Mom and Dad said it's too expensive, and anyway, it's a Catholic school. So, she went to Ball State. I don't care, Billy. Just don't book us into some fleabag joint! And let's find a nice restaurant, okay? My treat!"

"Hey, that Cal Olsen gave me a hundred bucks for the weekend. I can pay, you know. I ain't no freeloader bum," Billy protested halfheartedly, smiling.

"Well, Hot Rod, this is *our* weekend. I got an extra day out of that stuffy old office and a weekend, so forget about the money! We'll spend everything we got and have some fun! My boss gave me my check one day early, too!"

Billy just looked to his right and smiled. He had never known a girl quite like Roxie. He didn't ask, but he guessed her to be maybe three or four years older than him. That didn't bother him. He never thought of himself as sixteen or eighteen or his present age, twenty-two. He had many years of experience that had matured him far beyond his peers. So, in his mind, Roxie was an equal. Many of the girls he had dated still seemed like school girls, with school-girl interests— popularity, dance music, school sports. But Roxie seemed to be self-assured and ready to take care of herself.

They headed north out of Muncie on Indiana State Route 3. Billy's plan was to take that as far as Fort Wayne where they could get on U.S.30. The open windows provided plenty of air, although it was mid-summer Midwestern air, with all the humidity and natural farm smells. Roxie pinched her nose passing one hog farm, looked at Billy, but still mustered a smile. They drove without the radio on, chatting about any topic that seemed to last for a while. There was enough wind-noise that the radio would have been another distraction. And those dual exhausts never let you forget that they were there. Just a short distance north of Muncie they came to an intersection. The road sign said "Fairmount 14." Billy twisted his head back to his left, looking west as they passed the crossroad. "Fairmount, Indiana! Dang, Girl! You know about Fairmount don't you?"

"Oh, yeah, that actor, John Dean, was from that little town, wasn't he?" Roxie replied.

"*James* Dean, Girl! 'Rebel Without a Cause'! I saw that movie when I was too young to understand it all, but I got that attitude thing he had. I saw it when I was seventh or eighth grade!"

"I never saw that movie. My dad said he was a juvenile delinquent hood and I was not to be influenced by such trash! As you can see, I didn't have a lot of fun back then, Billy."

"Oh, he was so cool, just acting bored and smokin' cigarettes and sassin' the grown-ups all the time," Billy was enthusiastic, relating his take on the old film. "In spite of all that, I don't know why, even though I thought he was so cool, I never acted like that. Smoked a little, but I did believe what some of them teachers said about how it's not good for you. And the grown-ups I hung around with were really cool guys—race car guys."

"Hey, Billy, you know they have a special James Dean Day in Fairmount. I had some friends there and they said it was on the Sunday of the Homecoming weekend. Kinda for the older kids and they dress up in 50's style and they have a street dance. That might be fun to go see some time, don't you think, Billy?"

"Well, Sunday…might be a problem. But who knows? That would be fun though."

Roxie just looked straight ahead, smiling and thinking this was so much better than her high school life. After leaving the farm, she had one year of business school in Muncie, and then got a job at SECO. She rented an efficiency apartment near the university and forgot all about the farm and her first eighteen years. Then she bought this used Plymouth because it was just so sleek with those long fins, and she said it matched the color of her eyes, blue. She started a new life. She couldn't help do some quick calculations in her mind. *If Billy saw that movie in 1955 when he was in seventh grade, well, I am somewhat older than he is. I was a senior then and he was like, a child. But neither one of us is a child, not now.*

Billy and Roxie got as far as Valparaiso, Indiana, where they booked a room at a Holiday Inn. This was great luxury for them: air conditioned, color TV in the room, a nice heated pool, and there was a good restaurant attached to the motel. Billy ordered drinks after they were seated by the huge plate glass window in front. This was a first for Roxie. As far as she knew from her dating experience with high school boy friends, a "cocktail" was a Blatz beer before the burger and fries came. Billy ordered a single shot of Jack Daniels and a Miller beer. He asked Roxie what she'd like to have. She said, "Billy, nobody ever asked me such a question before! I don't know. You order, I trust you."

"Well, Hon, I think a screwdriver might be a good drink for you. Maybe go a little light on the vodka, for a first timer? A headache wouldn't mix well with three hundred hot Midwestern highway miles."

"I'm not a little girl who has to be chaperoned, Billy," Roxie stated. She looked at the waiter and said, "Just make it the way you'd make it for anyone, sir," and smiled for both men.

Billy looked at the waiter, smiled and said, "She's a woman fully growed. What can I say?"

The two looked over the menu and chatted about what looked good and what they might order. The waiter brought their drinks and asked if they needed more time. "Well, let's start with salads and we'll keep looking for a while," said Billy. "Roxie, a toast!" They clinked glasses, Roxie looked a little confused, wondering if a mini-speech was imminent. But Billy just said, "Thanks for comin' along, Girl. This is fun."

"You are so right," Roxie smiled and touched his hand.

· · · · ·

Race day, Sunday, promised to be a hot day. Temperatures were expected to be in the high eighties or low nineties. Add to that, Midwestern humidity, a large concrete and asphalt racing surface, and a two-hundred-mile race. That combination promised discomfort for many drivers, especially those older and not as physically fit as younger drivers like Billy.

His nearly healed arm should not be as much an issue here. The asphalt racing surface was smooth and even with few bumps, unlike the rutted dirt tracks that were the norm. Billy was assigned to drive the mile dirt track car, team car to Smitty.

Smitty had wrecked Olsen's A.J. Watson creation at Indianapolis. That was a car that was built for paved speedways. The engine, transmission, and rear end were offset to the left, and the driver sat to the right. That left-side weight bias worked well on paved tracks like Indianapolis, Milwaukee, and Trenton. But not as well on a dirt track. Olsen's Watson chassis was the one better suited to Milwaukee's pavement than the "dirt track" team car. But Olsen figured he didn't have much to lose by running two cars. He could give this new hot shot, Billy Wallace, a chance to show what he could do in the big time, even if it was not his best car for Milwaukee. Smitty had earned the better car and there was no chance that Olsen would take him out of that car.

A championship level dirt track car was built to the same specifications as an Indianapolis roadster, but engine, transmission, rear end, and driver were all on the center line of the car. There was no "offset" to the left as in Olsen's Watson race car. It was an old configuration, going back decades in car design, until the 1950's when the "roadster" with its left-side, offset design became the norm. It could be competitive on a paved track, but that was much less likely now. These "dirt track cars" actually were the norm at Indianapolis until about ten years ago. Billy knew this was an opportunity to demonstrate his skill to many car owners, even if the car performed better on a dirt track.

The yellow number twenty-seven (Cal Olsen had a thing for yellow and the number seven—his sprint car was number seven, his Indy roadster was number seventeen, and all were painted a bright yellow) that Billy would drive looked like the sprint cars he drove, except it was roughly a foot longer and had a larger tail to cover a larger fuel tank. One hundred or two hundred miles, as in Sunday's race, required much more fuel than the fifteen or twenty miles that sprinters usually raced. Engines were much the same size, but often the cars were more robust and heavier that a sprint car. They carried more weight and were subjected to longer races and more constant pounding so it stands to reason that a heavier car with the same horsepower as a lighter car (sprint car, in other words), would respond differently. Billy learned that quickly during his first practice session. The first issue was the engine, a 255 cubic inch Offy, an engine that Billy had little experience with. It required a different approach. He ran with a quarter of the fuel he would race with just to get a feel for the car. The car was geared up for longer straights and did not "jump" like Chuck's car when he put the power down. And he learned he'd have to use the brakes here, but judiciously, so they would last two hundred miles. Billy also got his first experience with a really good Offy. That engine vibrated so much, Billy knew that two hundred miles would not be a cake-walk.

Billy was able to qualify his car for the race with an outstanding lap of 35.67, an excellent performance for his less than optimum equipment. That put him near the middle of the twenty-six car field. The fast time was 34.72, set by the winner of last year's Indianapolis 500. Cal Olsen was pleased with both of his drivers in the two hundred-mile grind. Smitty was able to finish a close second after leading twice, once for thirty-seven laps late in the race. But the air temperature and demands he made on the car to maintain his lead caused the engine to overheat. He backed off to save his engine, but lost the lead and settled for runner-up. Not bad, but not what Smitty preferred.

Billy ran a steady race, getting as high as eighth place, but in much the same way as Smitty, he pressed a bit too hard and

had to make an extra pit stop to replace a right rear tire. That cost him a lap and ten positions, but that new tire allowed him to run hard for the last forty laps and squeeze out a respectable tenth place. In one way the old dirt car was really an advantage. Billy sat higher in the car, and was more exposed to cooling air than drivers in the more modern roadsters. The heat did not drain him as it did some of the other drivers.

Olsen was happy, Billy was pleased, and Smitty was, well, resigned. Most important, as far as Billy was concerned, a number of car-owners took notice of his performance.

After the race, the fans roamed the pits for the usual camera shots and autographs. The number of "good-job" comments, autograph requests, and photos with fans was encouraging for the young rookie. When the crowd thinned out, Billy relaxed, opened a beer, and looked around. Roxie was standing behind the car, holding her race program.

"Ma'am, you're next...for your autograph...I mean," a skinny, buck-toothed boy said.

"Oh, that's OK, Sweetie, I know Billy pretty well. I already got his autograph. You go ahead," said Roxie, smiling.

"Thanks, Ma'am," the boy said and then turned to Billy. "Congratulations, Mr. Wallace. You done a good job!" Then he stuck out his hand to shake with Billy.

"Thanks, son. Let me sign your program."

"Can I get my picture with you, Mr. Wallace?" the boy asked. "But I gotta get someone to use my camera. Hey, Mrs. uh…well, Ma'am…."

"Here, Sweetie, I know how to do that," Roxie took the camera from the boy, got the two of them lined up, said, "Smile, boys," and snapped the picture.

The boy said, "Thanks and good luck!" Billy Wallace had just made a fan for the rest of his career.

Roxie waited for Billy to change roles—from racer, to hero, to friend. She guessed that was what Billy and she were— friends. She pretended to have had her vanity greatly insulted. "That boy called me ma'am three times, Billy! Why I never! He must think I look like his mother!"

"Well, Babe, you don't look like a mother to me! Kids think anyone out of high school is a geezer!"

"I know, I'm just teasing. He was so cute though, so shy," Roxie said and smiled.

"How'd you get along with Cal's wife today?" Billy joked. "You know that is Andrea, pronounced 'ahn-dree-uh', right?"

"Oh, yeah. That's how she introduced herself to me. She wanted to call me Roxanne, but I told her I've always been Roxie, except when my dad got mad at me. Then I was Roxanne, and that seemed like all the time. I don't want to be Roxanne anymore. Andrea didn't know how to take that, so I told her I was joking. But plain Roxie is fine with me."

She went on, "She is another story. Those people do have some money. They had a big tent behind the fence. I never saw a woman dress like that at a race track! Heels and gold jewelry! And the food! I'm used to hot dogs, burgers, and beer at a race track. You know she actually had some restaurant *cater* food in! She was drinking martinis! I'm not complaining, Billy, but that is another world that I never knew about. She was good to me, though," Roxie's amazement was evident.

"This has been quite a weekend, Girl. And we got a long drive home. I suppose you have to work tomorrow, don't you?"

"Yeah, if I don't show up Monday, after leaving early on Thursday and taking off Friday, I might not have a job to go back to," Roxie sighed.

"We got probably seven or more hours ahead of us, so we get back to Muncie around, what, midnight if we're lucky. You can sleep on the way back. I could put up in a motel tonight. Olsen gave me forty percent of just over a thousand bucks! I made four hundred and change today so I can afford it. Or maybe I could stay at your place, huh? That be OK with you?"

"Sure, Billy."

"I'll figure out some way to get back to Pendleton on Monday. Heck, I could hitchhike!"

"Nah, you don't have to do that. Just hang out at my place, and I'll drive you back after work," Roxie offered.

"Well, there's another issue, sort of related, I want to talk about with you," Billy began to carefully open a new topic.

"This doesn't sound good, Billy. I think I've heard this before."

"No, no, it's not that, not at all. I think I need to be in Indianapolis, full time, to be there at the center of it all. Most of those teams work out of Indy for the racing season, and I'd be in contact with all the teams, drivers, mechanics. Be good for my career. I can't afford no apartment, but some guys rent houses on Georgetown Road. I think I could sleep on someone's floor or couch. They do a lot of that, even have their girlfriends stay, too. I want to tell my aunt and uncle that I'm movin' out. So what do you think?"

"Billy, you have to do what's good for your career."

"Roxie, I don't want you to think I don't want to see you. You could come over and stay with me when I get in with somebody," Billy tried to put a good spin on his proposition. "Think that will work out?"

"That sounds kinda odd to me, puttin' up with total strangers. That might work for a bunch of guys, but I don't think that's for me. Billy, I've got enough money. If I come over there for a few days, can't we get a motel room?"

"Really? You'd do that?" Billy was mildly amazed.

"Sure. Why are you so surprised?"

"Well, that's different. Girls usually aren't so nice to me."

"Billy, it goes both ways, you know," Roxie said and smiled.

Chapter 9

On the same Thursday that Billy and Roxie left for Milwaukee, Chuck Williams and Donny were in the shop. Chuck had the rear axle of his red car up on jack stands with the cover off the rear axle center section, the "pumpkin," and an oil pan underneath was catching the heavy gear oil as it drained out. The next race was at the big half-mile at Dayton, a paved high-banked track that was somewhere between a half and five-eighths of a mile. It called for a higher gear set and Chuck was trying to decide what would be best.

Donny was in the first stages of his engine tear down project. Chuck had said at the outset,"Let's pretend that this engine is still in the car and you got the hood up, and you're lookin' at the engine, standin' at the front of the car, lookin' toward the back of car. You say the left side of the engine from where you're standin', but that left side is really the right side of the engine, 'cause we figure left and right from where the driver sees it. So, you gotta reverse it, okay?"

"First lesson, is to reverse left for right? I used to keep that stuff straight when I talked to customers by askin' them 'You mean driver side or passenger side 'cause that avoided the whole issue of left and right, 'cause it depends where you're lookin' from," Donny offered his solution.

"Ain't no passenger in a race car, so we look at it from the driver's perspective, sittin' in the car, Son. And that's for the rest of the car then too, you know. Right front tire is from the driver's perspective," explained Chuck. "Anyway, let's get this started, okay? I got some cardboard boxes and wood shipping boxes from the barn. That's what you're gonna use to put parts in as you take 'em off the engine. When you take a part off, and the bolts for it, put all that stuff in the box and label the box with a black marker. You know, like 'water pump' and so forth. Heavy parts go in the wood boxes. That cardboard will get oiled-soaked and those boxes will fall apart when you pick them up. And keep in mind, what I said about right and left. Start there at the front of the engine. Take off the water pump, pulley, vibration damper. I gotta figure on that gear for Dayton, Donny, but I'll be right over here."

"I'm on it, Boss."

"Oh, and before you leave tonight, help me get those fifteen-inch wheels with slicks down from the rack up there. I might wanna run those at Dayton. Helps drop the car a little lower on the track."

"Sure thing," replied Donny just as the shop phone rang.

"Now what's that? Ernie never calls. She just walks over from the house. No buses running yet. Could be a wrecker call, I guess." Tom picked up the phone. It was Jack Dowty, the owner of the white number two that Carl Connors had been driving.

"Chuck you old so-and-so! You told me you never worked this late on your car! Said that car just kind took care of itself! The truth will out!" Dowty, Chuck's long-time friendly rival, joked with his old friend.

"Ah, Jack, I'm just putting a muffler on one of these school buses here, you know the red number eleven bus."

"Just as I thought. Bet that's a fast bus!"

"What can I do for you, Jack? Nice to hear from you, but

this has to be more than a social call," Chuck wanted to get to the point.

"Well, I don't have a driver for that Dayton race. Connors' dad is really sick and it looks like he's not going to pull through this time. He lives out in L.A., so Carl's flyin' out tomorrow and says I can't count on him for Dayton. If the old man doesn't make it…well, you know the service and arrangements and all, the time it takes, the lawyers, and people who will want to see Carl. He doesn't want to keep me hangin' so he said just get someone else to drive. Is Lawton drivin' for you?"

"He just filled in when Billy was hurt. Tom could get a ride, but he'd rather wait for a good car. Not too many of those open right now. He needs to stay in the game, but a back-of-the-pack car won't help his reputation. He knows all that. You want to give him a shot?"

Dowty replied, "I wanted to check with you, what you think of him, and all."

"Tom will not tear up your car. He's not a crasher. Sometimes I wish he'd run just a little harder, but he's good. Better than a lot of people give him credit for," Chuck was pleased to help out his "sometimes" driver and satisfied that he did not have to stretch the truth to do it. He hung up the phone, turned to Donny, and said, "Looks like our man Tom may have another car to drive. This is just between you and me. Don't say nothin' to Lawton about this. That was Dowty, owns that car that Connors drives. He's gonna ask Tom to fill in at Dayton. Connors will be out west on family matters."

"Hell ya say! We'll be racin' against him!" a surprised Donny said and smiled.

．　．　．　．　．　．

On the Saturday of the Milwaukee race weekend, Tom had been at his station trying to stay busy with anything to kill time. In the morning he finished the last of the jobs he had scheduled for the week, two new tires for Mrs. Fortner. Then he busied himself with fussy jobs: he cleaned all his wrenches with a rag soaked in kerosene and hung them on the pegboard; he then used the same rag to wipe off the tracks of the hydraulic lift; he wiped the pneumatic greaser and hoses; swept and mopped the floor of the shop. He even gave some thought to cleaning the big glass over-head doors, but didn't want to work that much.

James was in the washing bay, cleaning his old Ford for what seemed like the third time this week. "So, James, you got plans for a big night tonight? Movie, dance? What's up?" Tom asked

"I got no plan. Sometimes we go out to Ronnie's house and play cards. Poker, all kinds of poker games. Games I never heard of before I went out to his place: acey-deucey, night poker, liar's poker. His mom and dad are real cool people. They live out there on the state highway. Sometimes their driveway is filled with all our cars, and some guys even park in the side ditch. Then the older guys leave about ten or eleven and go to some taverns. Us young guys go to the Dari Queen, if it's still open. Or we go over to Conway to the burger joint and hang out."

"Wild place, out there at Ronnie's?" Tom asked.

"Nah, not at all. Just guys playin' cards and…." The phone rang, and Tom answered, expecting a problem that he didn't want late on a Saturday.

"Hello, Tom, Pine Street Station."

"Hey, Tom, this is Jack Dowty. You know me, right? Probably know my driver, Carl Connors, better."

"Sure, I know you, Mr. Dowty. And I know the back end of that car of yours pretty well, too," Tom joked. "Connors and that white number two have thrown a few clods of dirt at me over the years! What can I do for you?"

"Connors can't drive for me at Dayton next weekend. His dad ain't well out in California and he told me he can't commit for that next race. You wanna drive for me? I seen what you can do, and I think you can handle my car. Okay?"

This was an unforeseen opportunity that Tom did not see coming. That car was equal to, if not even better than, Chuck's car. There was no hesitation in Tom's thinking. He didn't even want to discuss money. "Yes, indeed, Jack. I would be happy to drive that machine."

"The usual forty percent, and add this: just like I tell Connors, you win, I'll give you fifty percent of the purse," Dowty was a motivator, but Tom didn't need incentives.

"See you Sunday in Dayton, Jack," Tom said and hung up the phone.

"James, I got a car to drive at Dayton next week! Hot Damn! Not just any old box, but it's the car that Carl Connors drives. Good car!"

"Cool, Tom! I hope you do well! I never been to but one car race. Dad took me to some place out in Iowa when we were visiting his old army buddies. Dirt track at some fair," James said.

"Lucky guy. You may have seen some unsung heroes out there. Hey, you ought to come to Dayton next Sunday. That is a spectacular race track. High banked asphalt. Cars get some serious speed at that joint. Think about it, James," Tom suggested.

"That's a good idea, Tom. But drivin' in the city will be a new experience for me. Probably need some written directions."

"You could ride with Janet and me," Tom offered.

"Tina goin' along, too?" James asked.

"Well, she's got a mind of her own, James. I don't know," Tom replied and suppressed a smirk. "Hey, I'm goin home. Close up early, seven, seven-thirty, if you want."

* * * * *

When Tom turned up the lane, he saw an unfamiliar pick-up truck parked in the gravel lot close to the barn. He saw that Tina was out in the field with her horse, and Janet and another woman were leaning on the fence. He parked beside the pick-up, read the side of the truck, and understood that Gloria Anderson was the visitor. "Anderson Stables, Eaton, Ohio" was neatly painted in red cursive letters on the door.

"Gloria Anderson, good to see you! What brings you up north here?" Tom asked.

"The county fair board up in Paulding County wanted me to talk to the junior fair kids. So, I was on my way home, had some extra time, and decided I'd make a 'horse call' here. This is a nice set-up you have here, Tom. Plenty of room for you folks and Tina's horse. Nice lookin' farm house and barn.

"Thanks, Gloria. We like it out here. It's nice and quiet.

Close to town too," Janet said. "Tom, this lady has forgotten more about horses than you and I put together know. I never realized."

"Make that you, me, Tina, our neighbors, and extended families, Janet," Tom said as he gestured around to suggest the whole area.

Janet said, "I think we just got lucky when we bought that horse. We didn't have a clue. Gloria's got so much common sense that could have helped us. Here's where we got lucky. Gloria says, 'Buy a horse you like, but don't buy a horse just because you like it.'" She says you've got to think about how your personality, and the horse's personality mix. Never gave that a thought, but Tina and that horse seem to communicate pretty well. That's what I mean by us getting lucky."

Tom said to Janet, "When Tina and I were at Gloria's place, she talked a lot about little things that communicate to a horse. News to me."

"She was trying to help Tina with what she called 'confident assertiveness'," Janet said.

"Yeah, Tina just about lost it when she talked about the 'hitch in her get-a-long', but Gloria's right about that. Those lessons can help with more than just riding a horse," Tom observed.

Gloria said, "Tina weighs, what a hundred and ten pounds? That horse weighs probably, eight hundred or eight hundred fifty pounds. Not a fair match is it. But Tina must be the dominant party, and she can be 'cause she can out-think and understand the horse. That horse may misbehave, just like a child, but she will respond correctly, 'cause, she really wants to. Small steps and small rewards. Look, they're coming over here now."

"I been watchin' the two of you, and Candy doesn't seem too cooperative, does she?"

"That's putting it mildly, Mrs. Anderson," Tina's frustration was obvious.

"I could be wrong, Tina, but that horse seems close to comin' into heat," Gloria ventured.

Tina blushed and said, "Well, that explains a lot, doesn't it?"

Tom and Janet looked at each other, smiled, and walked off a few paces while Gloria and Tina continued to talk. "Jack Dowty called late today. He offered his car to me next Sunday."

"Really! That's the white car, number two? Who drives that? What's up?" Janet asked.

"Carl Connors. He's won a couple races this year with that car. It's no dog. This is quite a break!"

"But did he fire Connors? Why are you driving if they're winning?" She still didn't have the full story.

"Connors dad lives out in L.A. and is really sick. Dowty said it looks like he won't pull through. Carl wants to be out there for the, well, the last days, instead of showing up just for a funeral. So, add it all up, and how long could that be, you know, before and after? Connors doesn't want to leave Dowty hangin', so he told him to get a fill in. That's me," Tom explained, trying to temper his enthusiasm with respect.

"That must be a good thing for you, Tom, considering that Connors has been winning, right?"

"I can't think of any downsides to this, Jan. I know that there's another guy's misfortune involved here, which is bad, so…you know what I'm saying, right?"

"Sure, can't celebrate, but it sure helps you," Janet mused.

"You know, Dayton has a pretty nice infield. Picnic suitable. You want to go?"

"I think I'd like that. Probably Ernie and a lot of wives will be there, huh? Think we could ride together again, like that Eldora race. It's always a lot more fun when they all kind of set up camp together like that."

"I was wonderin' if Tina would like to go along this time. She seemed to have a good time at Winchester, at least from what I could tell. This time maybe some other kids will come along with the wives," Tom offered his thoughts, tentatively.

"Not sure about her, you know teenagers are unpredictable," Janet replied.

"Now here's a thought, comin' out of left field, mind you. Just think about it, okay?" Tom ventured. "What if I asked James to ride along? He was here that night I was gone, and he seems to get along with you two pretty well? He might think it's a big deal, ridin' along with a driver. I could get him in the pits for a while as a helper. Just think about it."

"Tom Lawton," Janet said. "What you tryin' to do, anyway?"

"I just thought he'd like to see another side of Tom Lawton. And maybe Tina would have some company. That's all," Tom explained.

"Huh!" Janet said with a half smile. "You might want to ask your daughter, you know."

They walked back to Gloria and Tina. Gloria seemed to be wrapping up her discussion. "And I know this seems kind of super-careful, or something, but you should think about wearing gloves and some kind of boots, too. She could step on you in an instant, and there you have a broken foot."

"Okay, Mrs. Anderson," Tina accepted what she probably would have ignored from her parents.

. . . . .

Roxie Lytell drove Billy to Indianapolis on Monday after she left the office. She dropped him off on Georgetown Road, right behind the front straight-a-way grandstands. Immediately west of the road was an old housing development of two and three-bedroom bungalows and ranch homes. This is where many drivers rented, if they had enough money, or more likely, shared an apartment or home with a changing

assortment of individuals. That cast of characters may have
been drivers, wives, girlfriends, mechanics, wannabes, and
various hangers-on. A typical two-bedroom home might have
two individuals in each bedroom with perhaps another on
the bedroom floor. Another might sleep on the living room
couch, and two more on the floor. That might last for a week,
but depending on racing division schedules and travel plans,
some would find themselves supplanted by newcomers. Then
those who were replaced would find new accommodations,
which was not as difficult as one might assume. The racing
fraternity was welcoming and flexible so housing was not a
problem. It may not be optimum, but it was always available.
Money was scarce but company was not. Each "unit" took care
of itself and its own. A driver who won on Saturday or Sunday
bought the meat for the whole crew. The rest, non-winners
(can't call them losers) chipped in for the rest of the cookout.
It was a tightly knit group, not *always* happy with each other,
but *always* willing to take care of one another.

"Thanks a bunch, Roxie," Billy leaned in and kissed her.

"Thank *you*, Billy! That was such a fun weekend. I never
knew about this racing world, not in my quiet little life!"

"It *was* fun, well, it *is* fun. Want to go again?" Billy asked.

"Sure! Call me, okay?" Roxie drove away, waving as Billy
turned and walked up the first side-street he came to.

He knocked on the door and waited for an answer. He
could hear a television, but no one came to the door. *Maybe
sleeping or out in the backyard or garage,* Billy thought. He
walked around to the side gate, saw a big dog looking at him,
and hesitated. When the dog hopped up and put his paws on
the fence gate, wagged his tail and did not growl, Billy knew
it was safe to open the gate. He stepped in and the dog immediately was rubbing his right side on Billy's lower legs. This
was one of those dogs that loved physical contact, the kind of

dog that would rather lick an intruder rather than attack. Billy followed the narrow sidewalk to the garage, where he heard a radio playing country music. He knocked on the door frame and looked in. "Hey, how you doin?"

"Billy Wallace! What brings you here?" a man who appeared to be in his early to mid-forties looked up from the open engine compartment of a midget race car. "You don't know me, but I do recognize you. I'm one of the guys who pulled you out from under that blue car, when you broke your arm over at Kokomo. I'm Curly Clark. I'm a go-fer for any owner who wants an extra hand. But this is my car that I run whenever I can. There's a race over at Anderson on Thursday night and I'm tryin' to get it ready to go. What's up, Billy?"

Billy reached out to shake hands with Curly, who hesitated, saying, "Greasy hands, Billy. Sure you want to shake?"

"Little dirt don't hurt, does it?"

They shook. Curly said, "Well, these are better circumstances, compared to our first meeting, right?"

"Can't say I remember much of that. Those kinds of things stun you, and you're not your usual self. Plus, that arm hurt, I wanna tell you! Not thinking straight. Yes, this is much more pleasant, Curly.

I'll tell you why I'm here, if you haven't already figured that out. This is the place to be, seems to me. The center of racing. I been livin' with relatives in Pendleton who don't charge me a thing *and* feed me! But that's too far away from the action here. So, I'm lookin' for a floor to sleep on, or anything. Got any ideas?"

"I'm full up, or you could put up here. Just go on down the street. I can guarantee you that if someone has room, they'll let you in. But you gotta understand if you're gone for a few days, that could all change. Another guy might take your spot. That's the way it is, like a carousel, the riders keep changin',"

Curly said matter-of-factly.

"Okay, thanks, Curly. You runnin' at Anderson, Thursday night you say? If you ain't got a driver, here I am."

"Yeah, I got a kid, younger than you even, from Kentucky. But why don't you ride along? You might pick up a ride," Curly said.

"Now that's a great idea. I'll get back to you on that. First, I gotta find a place to stay, so I'll see if anybody has room."

"If you don't find nothin', come on back. You can sleep out here in the garage, with my car and Buck, that 'scary' dog you met out there," joked Curly.

Billy knocked on two more doors, getting friendly responses, but "we're full" answers to his question. It seemed like each call took about thirty minutes. There were "I know you's" and "Good to meet you's" and "Doin' good Billy's" and "Good Lucks," but no "Sure, we got room" until he came to the last house on the street. That house was actually *owned* by a driver, a real rarity here. Most of the residents had very little money and actual ownership was rare. He was an older driver, Charley Kirk, who lived here with his wife. Charley had raced before the war. In the spring of 1942 when he was eighteen, he drove in midget races, when that sport was popular. A driver could race several times a week and actually make fairly good money. Charley served in the army during the war, and when he came home, resumed his racing career, driving sprint cars and midgets in the Mid-west. But he had missed the prime years of his life, and a new crop of younger drivers dominated. He worked year-round at the Speedway on a maintenance crew, painting, fixing, whatever the boss had for him. That way he was free to drive weekends and still be at the center of American racing. Not a bad life as far as he was concerned, and his wife, Wilma, enjoyed the camaraderie of the fraternity. They had a fifteen year-old-son, Phil, born with absolutely no interest in auto racing, but gifted with a mind more suited to literary pursuits. Wilma nourished his talents as much as she could in this decidedly non-intellectual environment.

Wilma answered Billy's knock, "Hello, young man. What can I do for you?" She knew the likely answer she would get.

"My name is Billy Wallace and I'm a racer. I know a lot of the houses in this neighborhood rent rooms to drivers who need a place to stay during the season. Do you have an extra room I could rent?"

She called out, "Charley! There's a young man here. Says he needs a place to stay."

And that's how Billy found a place to stay for the rest of the racing season. The Kirks understood the instability of a driver's income and let him pay when he could, and didn't say a word to him when he couldn't. Really it was like living with his aunt and uncle in Pendleton, except the Kirks were able to better understand the itinerant racing life.

* * * * *

Billy called Roxie on Tuesday evening and told her he would be in Anderson Thursday for a night race. He said that he'd either be driving or just helping another guy with his car. Either way, he'd have very little opportunity to talk to her, but he just wanted to let her know, if she decided to come watch. "It's a night race, so things won't wind up until maybe eleven or so. By the time you get back to Muncie, that's gonna be a late night."

"I got nothin' goin' on, and so I miss a little sleep, so what?" Roxie was excited about a mid-week excursion. "How about I bring a friend along? That be OK?"

"Sure. I'll look for you and come up into the stands when I can. Warm-ups and stuff begin around six o'clock," Billy said.

* * * * *

As things worked out that night, Billy couldn't find a car that needed a driver, so he spent his time helping Curly and his young driver. When his help wasn't needed, he wandered the pits talking to drivers, owners, and mechanics. He wanted to make himself known to as many people in the sport as possible.

Curly's driver did not time well in qualifications and was forced to run the consolation race. He was unable to advance into the feature, so their evening ended sooner than expected.

"Curly, don't drive off without me. I'm goin' up in the stands to visit a girl. I'll stay up there for the feature race, alright? I'll see you after the race."

Billy found Roxie and her friend Diane in the top row near the first turn. The girls had questions about the cars: why are they so small, why do they sound different, are they easier to drive, are they as fast as the other cars you drive, why does this track look smaller? He answered all their questions as best he could, but when the race started most conversation ended. It was difficult to make oneself understood over the buzzing of the sixteen small cars. The forty lap race went off with no incidents or interruptions, allowing for a reasonable departure time .

"I'm glad we came over for this, Billy. Diane has never seen anything like this. It was fun for us, but I guess not so much for you, not driving and all," Roxie said.

"There'll be other times, I'm sure. Hey, I got a place to stay in Indy. A really nice older couple, racing people. I'm stayin' in their basement, not deluxe but it's clean."

"That's good…to have a nice place you can count on. I'd like to meet your neighbors there sometime, too. I'll drive over sometime. Well, we should be goin', Billy. Work tomorrow and all…so I'll see you…uh, when?"

"That's something I wanted to talk to you about. Sunday there's a race in Dayton, over in Ohio. There's a nice grassy infield, and a lot of wives and girlfriends kinda set up a picnic. You know...coolers, sandwiches, chips, soda, beer. It's a nice place to sit, enjoy the sun, chat with other racing people," Billy tried to make it sound pleasant.

"Oh, like Andrea Olsen's party in Milwaukee?" Roxie asked, teasing.

"Now, we have to lower our expectations a few notches, Roxie."

"Just joking, Billy. You're asking me to go along, right? I kind of interrupted your thoughts...it seemed to me that's where you were going. And I'm going to say, 'Yes, I'd like that.'"

I'll ride over from Indy with one of the race teams, so you don't have to pick me up. It's a long drive from Muncie, but it's longer still by way of Indy," Billy explained what seemed to him a reasonable plan.

"We'll see. But you will need a ride home, won't you?"

"I can ride back with the same..."

"Like I said, Billy, we'll see," Roxie smiled and kissed him on the cheek. "See you Sunday!"

Chapter 10

Roxie Lytell invited her friend Diane her to ride along to the race in Dayton. The August Sunday promised to be typical, hot Midwestern summer weather, but the morning air was cool. Partly closed car windows muffled wind and exhaust noise.

Diane said, "I don't get it, Roxie, those cars going round and round and all the noise. Do you enjoy that?"

"It's all new to me, so I'm still trying to understand it all and what it means to those guys. Billy, you know, thinks that's life, his life. Mostly it's what he's known since he was a kid and that's all he's interested in. He doesn't make much money, but doesn't seem to think about that."

"So, you interested in this guy much?"

"We're just havin' fun now. I've known him about, um, what three or four weeks? Just runnin' around and havin' some fun, that's all, Diane," Roxie said, to herself, and to her friend, wondering if it was the truth or if she was trying to convince herself.

The girls' conversation turned to their jobs, new movies, family issues, friends, mutual acquaintances and then circled back to auto racing. Diane asked, "You ever think much about things that could happen in a race? Accidents, you know what I mean."

"Billy has never said a thing about that, like it never enters his mind. I have not said a word about that. He knows what he's doing. He's a big boy and no one makes him get in those cars. Truth be told, I think he believes nothing bad will ever happen to him. He *never* says *anything* about that."

"Maybe that's what those guys have to think," Diane said.

"Yeah, maybe so," Roxie agreed. "Well, we're going to have fun today. You with me?"

"Always ready for that!" Diane said, patted her friend on the arm and smiled. "So how we going to get to this race track, anyway? You have a plan?"

"As a matter of fact, I do. I called Billy a few days ago. Really, he called me, just to let me know how to reach him. He found a place to stay across the street from the Indianapolis track. Stayin' with an old couple. The guy used to race before the war, but he retired after he got back. Works year round at the track now, helping on a maintenance crew, painting and whatever needs done. That whole racing family is a pretty tight bunch. They race against each other, doing whatever they can to beat the other guy, but they take care of each other. Just like that old racer, taking in Billy to stay. He was a complete stranger when he walked up and knocked on the door. They let him in, talked a little, and made a place for him. That's something, at least I think so," Roxie mused.

"Anyway, Billy said we just take U.S. Route 35 to Dayton… to Gettysburg Avenue, then to Germansburg Pike…that don't sound right. Here, Di, I wrote it all down. You read it and tell me the lefts and rights, okay?"

* * * * *

The half mile speedway on the southwest side of Dayton had started like many small race tracks, as a dirt track in 1934. Like its older Indiana counterpart, Winchester, owners and proprietors had over a number of years pushed dirt up to bank the turns, ostensibly for safety: cars would "stick" to banked turns better than flat turns—that was the theory. The dirt was oiled to control dust, but eventually asphalt pavement covered the entire track. However, banked turns allow for higher speeds and with no substantial railing at the top of the banking, the same banks served as a launching pad for an out-of-control car. Over the years, the Dayton Speedway had acquired a reputation for lurid, fatal accidents. Most of the men who sat in a race car there were acquainted with this part of the story.

The Dayton speedway was listed as a half mile, but in truth was about two hundred feet longer than most such tracks. For a number of years there was competition between the owners of the banked speedways in the Midwest—Winchester, Salem, Fort Wayne, and Dayton—for the fastest one lap qualifying speed. Dayton's length allowed cars to achieve higher speeds and for a time held claim to "World's Fastest Half Mile Speedway."

The track was located in southwest Dayton, on land that sloped east to the distant Miami River. The grandstands on the front stretch were located on the slope, affording fans a view of the track spread out before them on the flattened portion of the property. Beyond the back stretch, spectators saw a line of trees, TV and radio broadcast towers, and far off the eastern edge of the Miami River Valley rose up. Around the track there was a steel guardrail. The turns were banked at nearly thirty degrees. Looking off to the left from the front stands, one could see what was called the "workhouse," a correctional facility. A pedestrian bridge was built over the track at the exit of turn four. The front straight was a large expanse of asphalt pavement, including the racing surface and a very large paved apron, leading to the pit area. The track was notable for its wide racing surface. At one time, a quarter mile track had been paved inside the infield, but it fell into disuse in the mid 1950's. Most of the rest of the infield was grassy and allowed fans to enjoy room to set out lawn chairs and picnic on race day.

After turning off Soldiers' Home Road, Roxie parked her car and she and Diane walked to the ticket office. The girls carried lawn chairs, some soda and chips to add to the planned "ladies' picnic." They stopped and waited at the pedestrian bridge. Roxie hoped to see Billy or someone she had met at Milwaukee so they would not have to wander about in the infield.

Billy hitched a ride with the same team he rode with after the Eldora race. This morning trip was much different than that trip, although the return would probably be similar. Billy would drive back as the two men enjoyed plenty of liquid refreshment. Conversation centered on common topics: who's winning and who's not and why, who got fired or hired, plans for the off-season, plans for next year. Billy mostly listened, trying to learn as much as possible about the whole establishment he was now a part of. His listening—punctuated with "Oh yeah, Really, Didn't know that, I see"—and other such comments, was not judgmental. He was trying to see where he fit into this picture and how to make it work for him.

Billy was glad to finally get to the speedway and find Roxie. As he walked down the hill to the bridge, he heard his name called and saw Roxie and Diane waving.

"Good morning and welcome to the hills of Dayton, Ohio, girls." Billy hugged and kissed Roxie, and said, "I see you brought another race fan along."

After a bit of small talk, Billy said, "Chuck Williams is my car owner. His wife Ernie is the picnic organizer and general 'social facilitator' of this whole traveling circus. So, when they get here, she's the one I want you to meet. She'll welcome you and introduce you around to whoever comes. There will be wives, girlfriends, families. Let's just hang around here because the tow trucks have to go right by. We can't miss them here."

"Diane! When we went to Milwaukee, there was this lady, a car owner's wife, who had the most *amazing* party in the infield. Like fancy food and cocktails! At a race track!" Roxie was still in awe of that experience.

"Ain't gonna be like that, Roxie," Billy reminded her.

"Oh, I know, but a girl can dream, can't she?"

"Yeah, that was a step up, for both of us, wasn't it?" Billy shared in the recollection.

Just then Billy recognized Chuck's truck coming down the access road. He waved. Chuck stopped, stuck his head out the window and said, "How does a guy like you end up with such pretty company?"

"They call it 'magnetic personality', Chuck, but you wouldn't know about that," Billy always had an answer.

"Well, when you retire from all this (he gestured to the speedway grounds), you have a job selling snow to Eskimos and sand to Arabs! Billy, do you think your two young friends would like to join Ernie in a day-long picnic?"

"I was hoping for that," Billy answered.

Ernie leaned over, introduced herself, and said, "Meet us down there when we get into the track. Help me carry my coolers and picnic baskets, okay? We'll claim a good spot to watch."

Eddie Spencer had arrived at the speedway around eight o'clock Sunday morning. He knew the promoter well and helped any way he could. He would check with the ticket clerks, concession stand workers, security workers; asking if they needed anything. After he had made his rounds, he wandered the pits, chatting with owners, mechanics, and drivers. He was on home turf here and was known by most in the racing fraternity.

"Speed!" Someone called out Eddie's old nickname. It had to be someone who knew a little auto racing history, because that name was not applied often to Eddie now.

Eddie looked a few pits north and saw Walt Morrow smiling and waving. "Well, I thought you got this racin' bug out of your system, but like you said at that last fan club meeting, you been re-thinkin' it, huh?"

"Told you to keep me in mind for some deal," Walt said.

"I have done that, and I want to introduce you to a guy with a high-quality operation. And the kid he's got drivin' for him is the real deal. Young kid with talent to spare. Might need a little seasoning, but the kid's got the skills. He drove up at Milwaukee in that Champ Car race. Drove Olsen's dirt car and did a damn good job. That should tell you something. Olsen has good equipment and has an eye for winners. But the guy I've been thinking might fit your plan just got here. Let's go this way," Eddie said and directed his friend to follow.

Eddie and Walt Morrow walked toward turn four where Chuck and Donny were unloading the red number eleven in the infield. Donny had the ramps down and Chuck was in the car to guide it down as Donny pushed. As they approached, Chuck said, "Donny, get gear set number fifteen out of the box. I'm not sure about this, but I put those fifteen-inch wheels on to drop the car a little lower. And I'm not sure of that gear. I got set twenty-six in there now, the 4.41. But I want to be ready to change it fast if it don't sound right or if Billy has a problem with it. But just between you and me, I'll try to get Billy to see it my way.

"OK, Boss. Fuel?" asked Donny.

"I got that mixed in that blue can. It's the usual mix 90% methanol, 10% nitro. We'll see what that does for us, could bump that nitro up a bit. That motor is still strong. It could handle more juice." Chuck climbed out of the car and took the rubber balls out of the injector horns.

Eddie stepped forward, "Chuck, you may not know me. I'm Eddie Spencer...."

"We never met, but I know you from reputation, Eddie," Chuck offered his hand and the men shook. "Hey, Donny, get those two extra slicks down from the trailer. I got them pumped way up. I want you to lay them flat on the trailer, in the sun."

Eddie said, "Chuck, this is Walt Morrow. He was a champ car owner in the fifties. He lives here in Dayton and wanted to check out the state of racing these days." The two men shook and exchanged nice-to-meet-you greetings.

Walt looked over the car, trailer, and general appearance of Chuck and Donny. Chuck always insisted on race day that he, Donny, and any helpers wear clean jeans and a white oxford shirt. They might get dirty and greasy during the week, but on race day they showed up clean and neat to start the day. He insisted that presentation was an important part of his operation.

Chuck's mind was occupied with car preparation, and he turned his attention back to the tasks that still had to be attended to. "Donny, run that extension cord over to that post over there." He pointed to a wooden stump near the fence with several outlets. "Then plug the oil heater in. The tires? Yeah, just lay them down flat on the trailer. I want them to soak up some heat from the sun."

"You want them to get a tan?" Eddie joked.

"I'm not sure what gear I want to run here. It's a big half mile, so I put gears in that'll give me a 4.41. I'm running fifteen-inch wheels, but I'm not sure about how that gear and wheel are gonna work here. Got my options open. Might change to a little taller gear. Set number fifteen would give me a 4.32 rear end ratio," Chuck explained, seeming to almost be talking to himself. "Or, could put sixteens on. We'll just have to see how things work in hot laps."

"But the tires in the sun?" Eddie asked.

"Well, I pumped those way up, like seventy, seventy-five pounds. I let them warm up in the sun and they'll stretch a little, maybe add a quarter or half inch diameter. Then let some air off, down to normal pressure, and they'll hold some of that stretch. That tire would be a little bigger than what's on there now. Might be just the combination for one of those gear sets I'm running. Could use one to get a little stagger, too." Then Chuck turned back to his car, thought for a moment, and said, "I'm sorry, guys, I've got to get ready to go. Maybe we can talk a bit more, if you want to, after the race?"

"Oh, I know, Chuck, been there myself years ago. Good luck today," Walt said apologetically.

"Thanks, my new kid's got what it takes, I *think*," Chuck answered.

Eddie and Walt walked around the car, trying to stay out of the way. Eddie murmured to Walt, "This is the team I had in mind, Walt. You can see Chuck's attention to detail, in car preparation and his way of thinking. That and the right driver wins races

"You're right, Eddie. He seems to know what he's doing', that's for sure," Walt answered.

· · · · ·

The day before on Saturday, Tom had made a cardboard sign that read "Closed Sunday." Around mid-afternoon, he called home and asked Janet if Tina had made a decision about going along to Dayton on Sunday. He listened as his wife held the phone aside and called up to her daughter in her room. He could hear a distant "I don't know" then Janet said "Make up your mind. Dad wants to know." Then he heard an irritated "Do I have to tell you now, Mom?"

Tom said, "Tell her James is going along. They seem to get along don't they? You know better than I do."

"Just a minute. I can't yell that up to her. I'll go up and talk to her, okay?" Janet was aggravated.

Tom waited, thinking that he really did not get this all lined up properly. He had put the question to James , but did not have a definite answer. He just assumed he'd want to go. *This could all go wrong, he thought.*

Janet walked upstairs to Tina's room. There was a pause and then Tom heard her footsteps coming closer to the phone. "Well, Tom, are you, some kind of matchmaker now, too?" she asked. "She said she'd think about it."

"I just thought, get her out of the house and…."

"Sure, that's what you thought," Janet said. "That still bugs you when he came over that Saturday, when you were gone, doesn't it?"

"I'm not so sure about that. But now all I have to do is make sure James wants to go along," Tom said.

"Oh, for god's sake, Tom Lawton!" Janet angrily hung up the phone.

Tom walked into the service bay and said, "James, I think I'll close this joint tomorrow. You want to ride along to Dayton and watch a race? Janet and Tina are going along."

James smiled and said, "That would be cool, Mr. Lawton. But I could drive my car!"

"No, we'll have more fun all together. Pick you up at eight o'clock!"

* * * * *

Tom invited James to ride in the front seat with him. He thought that way he could explain to James what he was going to see. It could be a "guy talk" situation. Tom talked about the events of the day, the car he would drive, some of the other drivers, and who had won races so far in the season. James had never known Tom to talk so much. The topic was such a part of Tom that such a conversation seemed effortless. Tom also wanted James to be at ease, and this was his way of trying to do that. Sitting in the back seat of a car with a girl seemed to be too much like a supervised date, so this was Tom's way of setting a tone. He had invited his helper to ride along with his family, one of whom was the boy's school friend, who happened to be a girl; romance did not have to be a part of it.

They arrived at the track around nine forty-five, parked the car, and took the pedestrian bridge to the infield. "Look around from up here, James. You can get a good overall view of the place," Tom said.

"Well girls, time for me to get ready. I'll see you a little later." He kissed his wife and daughter and told James he could walk with him through the pits

Janet and Tina went to find the "ladies' picnic." Tom and James walked through the pits looking for Jack Dowty and the white number two race car. The car was parked not far from Chuck and his red number eleven. Tom stopped to chat with Chuck and Billy. Billy said, "Good luck today, Tom. I hope you finish second!"

Tom smiled and said, "Same to you, Billy, same to you." He picked up his helmet bag and walked off to the restroom to change into his uniform. When he came out, Smitty was standing with his car owner, near the snack stand, drinking coffee.

"Old man! What the hell you doin here today? Williams got Wallace back, right? So, what are you driving?"

"I'm in Dowty's car. Connors is gone for maybe two weeks or so, to California," Tom replied.

"Okay, I'll remember that in case I have to bang you out of my way. You're in the white car, okay, so I'll be lookin' for you," Smitty said and smiled. "Just kiddin', Tom. Just kiddin'."

"You know, Smitty. That crap can backfire on a guy. And you're smart enough to know it. I never done anything like

that on purpose and don't plan to start!" Tom turned and
began to walk away.

"I'm sure sorry for that. I'll never do it again!" Smitty said
and winked at his car owner, Cal Olsen.

"Come on, James. Let's go find my car," Tom said and the
two walked on down the row of cars. "You can stay with me
here, James, for a while if you want. Not much you can do,
really, but watch. Try to stay out of the way. After warm up
laps and time trials I might have some time. It all depends
on what number we draw. If I go out early, I can walk back
to the girls with you. Then you can hang out there or walk
around and watch the races. Maybe Tina would enjoy some
company close to her age, huh?"

"Whatever you think, Tom. This is all so cool. But that guy
back there was a real jerk, wasn't he?" James said.

"That's Smitty. Good driver with his own style. There is
always one like that, it seems. You have to learn how to deal
with 'em. I'm still workin' on that." They walked past a few
more cars and came to the white number two. "Here we are
James. This is the car I drive today."

Jack Dowty greeted Tom, "Hi, Tom. Ready to go here
today? Want to look over the car?" The two men walked
around the car as the mechanic worked on the engine, install-
ing new spark plugs. "You tell us what you think after hot laps.
You know, if we should put more weight on that left rear, and
see how that gear feels. We put a pretty high gear in it, you
know, kind of a longer track, so let us know."

"How did Connors like his car set up here?" Tom asked.
"Is this what he usually likes here?"

"Yeah, pretty much."

"Well, I can work with that. I'll try it, but you're probably
close if Connors drove it this way."

· · · · ·

In hot laps, Tom found the car ready to go, just as it was. In his second hot lap session, Dowty clocked Tom's best time in the high seventeen seconds bracket. That was a good, competitive time so Dowty and Tom were feeling good about their chances this day. When Dowty drew a late qualification number, twenty-eighth, they were not concerned. If the track were dirt, that would be a real problem. Thirty cars can wear away a lot of the traction on a dirt track, but a paved track stays much the same all day. A really hot, sunny day could make the track a little oozy and slick, but that was not the case this day.

In the down time before his time trial attempt, Tom walked with James over to the infield group of Ernie, Janet, Tina, Roxie and her friend, and a few other wives and assorted race track related friends. There were children, aged toddler to teenager, in the group. It would be a good place for James to spend his day.

"James, I'm gonna leave you in the company of these fans today. I'll be busy for a few hours," Tom said and walked over to Janet. "Hon, see you later." He gave Janet a hug and started to walk back to the pits.

"Good luck," Janet called to him and Tina chimed in soon after.

• • • • •

Tom had an exceptional time trial run. His first lap was a 17.70 and his second lap was even better at 17.43. That put him in the first heat race, and usual rules applied. Finish up front in your heat and you're assured a good starting position in the feature. Billy was slightly faster but would probably start near Tom. The usual front-runners all timed well: C.J., Smitty, James Warren, and even the eastern driver, Charlie Pauling, who almost never drove paved tracks, were all in the seventeen second bracket.

When all the preliminaries were over, the feature race lineup had C.J. on the pole and Billy right beside him. The second row had James Warren in third place and Tom in fourth. Smitty would start inside row three in fifth place, and Charlie Pauling was to the right of him in sixth place. The rest of the field contained Walt Bowers, Johnny Miller, eastern driver Red Allen, Bud Brown, Roger Castle, and even the beginner from the Eldora race, Ken Thomas, again driving the same red number thirty-one.

When the green flag dropped, Billy surged into the lead and Tom followed him into turn one. The cars on the inside of both, C.J. and Warren, dropped back as Smitty passed both on the back stretch to take third place. Billy, Tom, and Smitty raced through turns three and four nose-to-tail to complete lap one. Tom was just feet off the rear push bar of Billy, and Smitty followed Tom in the same way.

Tom watched the tail of Billy's car chattering over the rough spots in the pavement, the rear tires sipping slightly, then grabbing traction. He focused on the car ahead and forgot about Smitty behind him. *I'll drive my line and let him take care of his own.* This was not a time for defensive driving. Tom drove to the inside of Billy at the end of the backstretch, just showing the nose of his car to Billy's left. As they entered the third turn, he backed off and got into line behind the red number eleven. Tom felt like his car was faster but could not get the speed soon enough in the straight to pass. There was no way he could drive into those turns at that speed. Maybe they missed on that gear by so little.

Smitty trailed Tom, staying close enough to let him know he was there, hoping for a mistake or an opening. As fast as they were running, the trio would come up on slow cars in perhaps ten or twelve more laps, and that always presented opportunities to pass. Those first three cars ran in tight formation lap after lap. At these speeds, right front tires might be the factor that determined the winner. Smitty was running a more conservative race, watching for the tell-tale sign of smoke coming from the right front of Billy or Tom. Conservative was not like Smitty.

Lap after lap went by, all three cars seemingly glued to each other, until on lap fourteen, Tom stayed on the power just a split second longer on the front stretch, hoping to get by Billy as they entered turn one. He got his right front wheel parallel to the cockpit of the red eleven, but lost traction and began to slide into Billy. Tom backed off, lost momentum, and Smitty got by on the outside as Tom tried to get his speed back up. Tom fell in behind Smitty as they raced down the backstretch. It was the same nose-to-tail train, slightly shuffled, but with the same three nearly equal cars and determined men driving.

Fans stood and watched what may have been one of the greatest races on the storied old track. Ernie's infield picnic stood and watched every lap, turning in simultaneous circles to follow the spectacle, almost unconsciously holding their breath. By lap sixteen, the three leaders were catching up on the slower cars, preparing to lap them. It was the opportunity that Smitty was looking for. Billy hesitated to lap a slower car at the end of the back stretch on lap nineteen. He backed off, thinking he would pass as they came off turn four. That was the opening that Smitty was looking for as he drove low in turns three and four to pass both Billy and the slower car.

Lap twenty started with Smitty in first, Billy in second, and Tom in third. The race seemed to have resolved itself as Smitty began to pull a few yards away with each lap. But Billy and Tom resumed their own personal contest, neither one giving an inch. Tom nearly got by Billy on lap twenty-eight, but had to pull back into line. He knew his car was faster, but didn't have enough room, even on this "big" half mile, to take

advantage of it. Maybe with a lesser driver than Billy he could get by, but Billy was no "lesser" driver. Tom decided today he'd finish in third place. Still a pretty good day.

On lap twenty-nine, the trio saw the white flag as they went down the front stretch. They had started their last lap, and Smitty had a comfortable lead of about a hundred yards. As Billy entered turn one with Tom right behind, Smitty came up on two slower cars. Smitty stayed in his groove, high on the track, about three feet from the guardrail. The two slower cars were racing for position and had ignored the "layover" flag indicating a faster car approaching. They tangled and slid up to the guardrail. Smitty had no room or time left to maneuver out of the way. His car rode up over the right rear tire of one car, climbed the guardrail, and just seemed to drive right into the air, disappearing into brushy trees outside the track with Smitty just sitting upright, holding onto the steering wheel. It happened so quickly that anyone who was not looking missed it. Billy saw it and had to react quickly in order to avoid the two cars locked together. Tom took evasive action, just as Billy did, steering low to drive by the wrecked cars. The yellow caution lights flashed on, and Billy and Tom saw the checkered flag as they drove down the front straight-a-way to finish the race.

Chapter 11

In October, Chuck Williams called Tom Lawton late on a Friday. Tom answered the phone and soon knew who was calling. The caller had taken the phone away from his mouth, and was trying to make himself heard over the din of machinery and a loud radio—the unmistakable, hollow sounds of a large space.

"No, Donny! Take those old heads from that engine you been workin' on. Put 'em in the truck with the ones off the race car. Don't get 'em mixed up!" There was a muffled question from off in the shop that Tom couldn't understand. "No, from the red car! I ain't gonna work on the engine in the yellow car!"

"Jeezow, Chuck what you got goin' on there? You're probably gettin' ready for that long haul out to Ascot, huh?" Tom asked his sometime car owner.

"Tom, you got some free time that you could drive over here? I wanna show you something, and I wanna talk to you about something," Chuck was still shouting.

"Bring it down a notch or two, Chuck. I can hear you. Yeah, I can do that."

"How about Saturday afternoon, late. You could bring Janet along. We could cook out for dinner."

"You're on. I'll have to see if that works for Janet. Anyway, if you don't hear from me early tomorrow, we'll be there around five or so," Tom answered, wondering what this was about.

· · · · ·

The Midwest racing season had begun to wind down, and many of the participants had begun to settle in to the life that "normal" people lead. Tom had filled out the last part of the season with one more race in Jack Dowty's car, another second place at the dirt half mile at New Bremen, Ohio. His two second places earned him another two-race deal in a so-so car that had come from the eastern circuit. Those two finishes were, likewise, so-so mid-field places. That ended his racing season in late September. Since then he had just been working at the station, trying to pay the bills and get a little bit ahead. Tina continued to teach herself and her horse how to interact, but had changed her mind about entering any competitive events for the time being. Gloria had guided her to that conclusion, creating a sense in the young girl that she had arrived at that decision on her own. They both decided more experience was necessary. Janet was still working at the farm store. She was relieved that the racing season for her husband was over. She could look forward to the next five months, a less stressful time for her since Tom would not be racing.

Billy Wallace, as usual, was short on money. Charley Kirk got some odd-jobs for him at the Speedway, but that was still not enough to finance even the life of a single racer. He sometimes picked up jobs at some of the many shops near the speedway. He got a part-time job selling used cars in Indianapolis, a job that fit his personality well. And it kept him in the Speedway orbit with all the associated teams and owners. He hitched a ride out to the west coast with C.J. and his mechanic, hoping to get a ride for the Phoenix and Sacramento races. And he did get a car that managed just twenty laps before it threw a rod through the crankcase in the hundred-mile Phoenix race. The owner had no enthusiasm for an expensive end-of-season overhaul, so they all loaded up and returned to the Midwest, missing the Sacramento race. Roxie was not disappointed with Billy's reappearance in Indiana, and their friendship continued to grow. Billy had to think of career opportunities first, but even he had to admit that staying in the Midwest had its benefits.

Eddie Spencer still worked at his warehouse job, but had begun to think about retirement. Money should not be a problem. His mobile home was paid for, and his retirement income would easily cover his meager expenses. The problem for him would be "What can I do all day with no job to go to?" That was the sort of problem that might keep him working. His activities in the racing world were much more than just a way to kill time; they were like a hobby to him, a way to be connected to something dear to him. It was those contacts that led to the pairing of Walt Morrow and Chuck Williams, and all the implications that association would have for Tom Lawton and Billy Wallace.

* * * * *

When Tom drove up the lane Friday night, he saw Missy Wilkins' car parked near the house, close to the old water pump. But the car was parked somewhat out of the usual parking area, crooked-like, and he could see that she must have skidded to a stop. The tires had scrubbed a path in the gravel as they slid. *What the hell?* he thought. *A problem? Someone hurt? Couldn't be Tina. She was out in the field with her horse. She had waved at him and didn't seem to be concerned about anything amiss. So, the same thought, What the hell?* repeated itself.

Tom walked into the kitchen, and saw Janet and Missy sitting at the kitchen table, red in the face, apparently from laughing. There was a beer bottle in each woman's hand and four empties on the table. He heard Missy, "And then you know what he said? He said, 'I have never'…oops! There's Tom!"

"This looks like a fun pair of old buddies," Tom said as he walked in.

"Friday, Tom! We're not working this weekend, so…." Janet looked at Missy, they clicked bottles and started giggling.

"Girls, have a good time. But Missy, how about you let me drive you home when your party is over? And I'll be out in the field with Tina and her horse, so if you try to drive home, I'll see you. What's more, my truck will be in the middle of the lane."

"Oh, Tom, you old fuddy-duddy. I okay to drive," Missy protested.

"Yeah, you sure sound okay. I'm driving you home. You girls have fun, I'm going to see how those other two girls are doin' out there." There was some unintelligible chatter then more laughing as Tom walked outside. Tina brought her horse over close to the water trough and barn.

"Hi, Dad. What's up? Want to take a ride?" Tina teased.

"Why would I put my life in jeopardy on that old nag?"

"Do you want to stop and think about that question for a minute, Dad"

"That creature has a teeny little mind of its own! A race car does not have thoughts of doing harm to me…intentionally! I still don't see how you make that creature do what you want it to do."

"Gloria says you have to kind of listen to what the horse is telling you. Her snorts, nickers, neighs all have different meanings. Even her ears tell you things. The way she reacts when she first sees me says a lot. Race cars can't *talk* like that can they, Mr. Know-it-all?" Tom enjoyed this seldom-seen side of his daughter.

"Well, I could go on some time about how race cars 'talk'

to me," Tom paused as he watched his daughter's reaction. "Stop rollin' your eyes and give me a chance to explain. You know, sometimes I go into a turn, turn the wheel, and the car doesn't want to turn. Heads straight for the wall. That tells me something," Tom explained.

"Yeah, Dad. Maybe it's telling you to change careers!" Tina teased.

"Got some sass goin' here today, huh? What is this, crazy woman day? No, it's tellin' me that the back end needs to have a little less power over the front end. We'd say the rear end is too tight, so we'd take a little weight off the left rear. Might fix it that way. Could narrow down the rear track, too. Or could be that all of a sudden, I feel the back end of the car vibratin'. Might mean a tire is overheated and is throwin' tread. I'd have to back off to try to get that tire to last for the rest of the race. Anyway, that's enough of that. I guess we do have some things in common, don't we?" Tom smiled and patted Tina's arm. "Oh, by the way, your mom and Missy are in the middle of their TGIF celebration, so don't be surprised if you hear a lot of laughing if you go into the house."

"Think I'll stay out here. I knew something was goin' on. Missy drove up the lane like you in one of those races, Dad."

"I'm gonna hang around so I can see when Missy leaves. I'm drivin' her home." Tom said.

. . . . .

On Saturday, Tom left the station at two in the afternoon, giving James the keys and his instructions. "Sunday is your day, all day, James. I'll be here, so go have some fun. Or do your homework."

"Well, Mr. Lawton, I was wonderin' if I could come out to your place to see Tina someday?"

"Two other people you gotta ask. Tina and her mom. Maybe they don't want you out there. Ever think of that?

You got one 'okay' so far. See if you can get two more," Tom teased and winked at the boy.

· · · · ·

The drive to Chuck and Ernie's took a little over an hour. It was one of those Midwestern bright autumn days when everything outside looked gold and blue. The fields were tan in soybean stubble and unpicked corn. The sky was clear and brilliant blue and the air was cool and crisp—not cold, but still refreshing. Janet said little, not from any sense of irritation, but more from a sense of release.

They drove a long time with the radio turned low, not talking much, other than to make comments like "That is a nice lookin' farm" or "That is *some* house goin up there" or "That guy drives like a maniac!"

"How can two women so far apart in age have so much fun together?" Tom finally asked, referring to Friday afternoon. "You're like, sisters I guess."

"No, sisters have too many old grudges to have as much fun as we have. I don't know. I feel like she was my first baby-girl, the way I took care of her so much after she was born. And you know I was pretty young myself then, not really much more than a girl. We were girls together and then we kind of grew up together," Janet tried to explain what she herself didn't understand completely.

"That was nice to hear, you laughin' that way."

"Once in a while, it's good to do. Oh, and, thanks for driving Missy home. She was in no condition to be on the road. Just a little tipsy, not falling-down drunk, just a little too happy. Did her parents say anything?"

"They weren't home, so their angel is still on her pedestal," Tom joked. "If Paul or Ruth ask about her car, I'll say I had to check out a little problem on it. That's not a lie, is it?"

"You ought to be a lawyer or a politician, Tom Lawton.

Makes me wonder about what you tell me sometimes."

"Well, how lucky can I be? Here's Chuck's place! I don't have time to answer that question." Tom pulled off the highway and parked. Ernie came out to greet them.

"Ain't this different? A social visit that's some place other than a race track? Come on in, Janet. I've got to get a pie out of the oven. We can talk while I tidy up my kitchen. Tom, Chuck's out in the shop. He's waitin' for you," Ernie was her usual, friendly self.

* * * * *

When Tom walked into Chuck's shop, he saw the familiar red number eleven. But sitting perhaps fifteen feet away was the bent frame of a yellow race car, stripped of its engine, fuel tank, axles, radiator. It was a bare tubular steel frame, bent and twisted, still painted yellow. Another ten feet away were the body panels, yellow, bent and muddy, but clearly showing the number seven in black. It was the remains of Smitty's car, the car that was pulled out of the mud outside the second turn of the Dayton speedway. It was the car that carried Smitty to his death that day. The day that he had a win nearly wrapped up. But his split-second decision about where to pass the slower cars led to his violent catapult out of the track. It was the day Billy Wallace inherited the lead and his first ever major sprint car victory. It was the yellow car that Tom had seen so often. He just stared at it, and finally said, "That is one sad sight, Chuck. Why is it here? You buy it?"

"Olsen trailered it over here a few weeks ago. He asked me if I'd rebuild it for him. I looked it over and told him that I could get the frame back in shape. Rear axle's okay, but he'll need a front axle and…well, the details aren't that important. He told me to log in my time, keep track of materials and all, and he'll pay me. Make it well worth my while. I said, "I can do that, but I'll make you a counter-offer: I will reduce, by some factor still to be determined, your expenses if you'll let me copy that frame and suspension. That's a four-bar, cross torsion bar, front and back. Maybe that's why it worked so damned well all year. That's why that pile of 4130 chrome moly tubing is stacked up over there. I'm gonna build one just like it, for me. Just bought a high dollar tubing bender. And I'm gonna build me a new 302 out of the 327 block over in the corner. Try that instead of usin' a 283."

"That's one hell of an education. You fix one, and build another just like it. Good deal for you and Olsen, huh?" Tom said.

"How can I go wrong?" Chuck asked.

"And what, you sell number eleven?" Tom asked.

"Now here is where it gets even more interesting. You know that Eddie Spencer from Dayton? He introduced me to a guy who had cars back in the fifties, Walt Morrow. He wants to get back into racing, but as a sponsor. He made me a three-year offer, good money, if I put the name of his company on a car and in the winter come to some fan club meetings and talk. Maybe even bring a car along. The car will be called the 'Precision Tool and Machine Special' and he wants it painted pearl white, with red and blue trim. So, I told him to come on over. I wanted to tell him about my plan to copy that car, and just take a look at my operation here. Here's how we ended up. This 'Precision Tool' car will be the copy I build from Olsen's car. And I told Morrow that I've got just the driver for him: Billy Wallace."

Tom looked like he just got punched. He could see that next year would be more of the same, hopping from car to car. "And you sell number eleven, right?"

"Like I said, it gets more interesting. I'll keep number eleven, put you in it. It's your car, guaranteed all season. So, we run a two-car team. With the money that Morrow's putting up, we can do it. Morrow watched you and Billy running together at Dayton and something clicked. Says he wants to be part of all this again. He said he saw real quality there. For a while there I thought that Billy would jump ship, since Olsen's car is open now, with Smitty gone. But Olsen hired C.J. for next year. Billy knows that yellow car is a good one, and he knows that I keep a real good car. He knows my copy has to be as good as the original, maybe better. He's up for it. How about you, Tom?" Chuck laid his cards on the table.

"One question: who maintains number eleven? Can you keep two cars going?" Tom's skepticism was obvious.

Chuck answered, "Donny. He's been workin' with me since he was, what fifteen? He does what I tell him. It's to the point now, that he knows his way around a car really well. I tell him to put in such and such a gear, and he knows how to do it. He can set torsion bars and he knows about that spring front. Engine work, that's still mine, but I've been teaching him. And I'm thinkin' about farmin' out the engine work on the new car. I'll still call the shots. Everything on that car stays the same. It's yours for the season, if you want it."

Tom knew that he'd feel much more confident if Chuck was doing the work, but the guarantee of the car for the whole season was too good to ignore. "I'm in, as long as I know that we can still come to you. You are the boss."

Chuck lit a cigarette and sat down on a shop stool, "I ain't touched that car since we came back from that last race out there in Allentown, where Billy won. So here's what I want to do some weekend yet this fall, if you're willing, just for a sort of 'dry run'. Donny said he's okay with it. The car is set up for that dirt half-mile at Allentown. Like I said, I ain't touched it since. I'll give Donny my set-up book and tell him to get the car ready for the Kokomo quarter-mile. He can trailer it out there and you meet us, try the car out, and we'll see if you two can communicate enough to make it work. I'll just hang back, only speak when spoken to."

"Let me know when to meet you guys. But you know, Chuck, four men and two cars is a slim team. Seems we might need some help," Tom suggested.

"Yeah, I know. I think I can find another guy," Chuck answered.

"Maybe I can find another helper," Tom said.

After salads, baked potatoes, grilled steaks, drinks to toast the new partnership, and pie and coffee, the Lawtons drove home in the cool autumn darkness. Tom turned on a little heat to ward off the chill. Neither Tom nor Janet spoke for several miles, and when Janet broke the silence it was to comment on Ernie's cooking and hospitality. "That woman knows her way around a kitchen. I won't eat till Tuesday!" Tom managed an "Uh huh." He was wondering what Janet was really thinking, if he didn't already suspect what that might be.

Finally, he said, "So, what do you think of Chuck's deal anyway?"

"I know you and him already decided it, and, anyway, it's what you want to do. And you know what I think. But this is what makes you happy, and I see this as your best ever shot. So, I'm already past the wonderin' and holdin' back stage. Tom, you gotta take this opportunity," Janet said matter-of-factly, almost softly.

"Hon, it'll be alright. You know I drive more with…."

Janet laid her hand on his right arm, lowered her voice and said, "Just don't say that, Tom."

Tom squeezed her hand. They drove on toward home in the darkness of the car.

THE END

About the Author

Rich Gilberg was a teacher of history and language arts for forty years. He earned a bachelor's degree and master's degree from Wright State University. He taught in Graham Local Schools in Champaign County, Ohio. His long-time interest as a fan of open-wheel racing began in 1954 at age seven with a family trip to Winchester, Indiana, where he first saw the men who would become his heroes. Over many decades, he has seen nearly all the great men who chose to accept the risks and rewards of open-wheel racing. He is married to Beverly, his high school sweetheart, and lives in Piqua, Ohio. They have three children and nine grandchildren.

www.ingramcontent.com/pod-product-compliance
Lightning Source LLC
Chambersburg PA
CBHW070109030726
47506CB00002B/654